Arctic Protocol

Tyler Blackthorne

MT.HOOD PRESS

A Dylan Baker Thriller

Arctic Protocol
A Dylan Baker Thriller
by Tyler Blackthorne

Mt. Hood Press
Portland, Oregon

Published by Mt. Hood Press
Portland, Oregon
ISBN-13: 978-0-9772608-7-4
Manufactured in the United States of America.

Prologue

· · · · · · · · · ·

FOR THE LAST WEEK, it had been visible in the daytime sky, similar to a daytime moon. Unlike a moon, this daystar grew larger each day.

The asteroid was over twenty miles wide and moving at several thousand miles per second. In its wake were smaller asteroids keeping pace as the collection hurled toward an unsuspecting vibrant blue planet.

As the space-flung objects entered the atmosphere, they rapidly heated and edges began to vaporize. Nearly instantly, the softer elements burst into flame. Then the intense heat began to burn off various minerals and rocky parts. Gold, nickel, iron, palladium, platinum, magnesium—all changed to flaming gases under the intense heat.

There was one eerie component of the asteroid that seemed unaffected by the ever-rising temperatures—iridium. This otherworldly, super-dense mineral appeared unaltered by the thousands of degrees of heat destroying the rest of the asteroid.

At the point when the main asteroid struck the unsuspecting Earth near Central America, the atmosphere had managed to burn away over half of its mass, concentrating the iridium.

When the impact came, it released a colossal explosion over a billion times the energy of all the atomic bombs ever exploded, turning even the iridium into a vapor. An intense, hours-long heat pulse and a powerful compression wave destroyed living tissue on distant continents.

The impact also transformed thousands of tons of earth into a sulfuric vapor that would spread out over the entire planet and rain down as sulfuric acid for the next three years. The ash turned nearly all the sweet, breathable air on Earth to a toxic mix of harsh particulates and caustic gases.

The vaporized iridium and rock erupted into the atmosphere where it spread and changed into a dense cloud of ashy dust. The tiniest ash particles remained suspended in the air, turning day to night—nearly ending all photosynthesis for years. The iridium, heavier than the other particles, rapidly precipitated. The collision terminated the reign of dinosaurs, giant sea creatures and vast forests.

Today, at nearly any place on Earth, sediment located and dated at 66 million years ago, reveals a fine dusting of iridium to mark the change between the Cretaceous and Paleogene periods. Despite the many tons of iridium brought to Earth by the devastating collision, it remains one of the rarest minerals on Earth.

As that huge asteroid fell to Earth, some of the trailing, iridium-rich pieces struck Earth in present day South Africa, Russia, Canada and central Alaska. The smallish piece that landed in Alaska formed a deep crater that would be uplifted to over 5,000 feet above sea level. Later, massive continental tectonic plates folded the iridium-rich impact zone into an eerie mountain that the natives called Kila Ikpic and the whites called Shaman Mountain.

1

. . . .

RETTIEF SEME WAITED OUTSIDE the elegant doors of the Johannesburg corner office and planned how he would kill his white, African boss.

Nearly unconsciously, he scanned the waiting area looking for objects that could be improvised for defensive or offensive weapons.

A rolled up magazine could turn away a knife, one of the framed mineral samples on the wall could be thrown frisbee-style to unbalance an opponent, and a pen from a nearby secretary's desk could be thrust into the neck of the white executive.

He saw the black secretary look at a tablet screen and knew she would soon tell him to go on into the opulent office. Rettief could tell from her clan name, that she was Zulu, like his mother.

He wondered if his mother looked like her. Surely his mother would not have had the money for the stylish business attire and subdued make-up of the secretary.

His mother: black. His father: white. Himself: neither, and besides not belonging to any one culture, his existence was actually illegal during apartheid South Africa. When Rettief was a child, according to the state, he had no right to exist.

"Mr. Seme, Mr. Meijer will see you now," the secretary spoke to him in English, not Zulu. Maybe it was his Zulu last name, his Afrikaans first name, or perhaps his well-groomed and stylishly dressed appearance, but she appeared completely at ease with him. People who knew him well were not.

People told Rhett that he was so fine-featured and smooth-skinned, he appeared feminine, while his lean, well-muscled body spoke clearly of his masculine gender and high degree of physical fitness.

Anyone watching Rhett enter the office would not suspect he was ready for a fight. He moved with a relaxed confidence that reminded Pieter Meijer of a jungle cat. But Rettief Seme was always preparing for a fight. This constant state of preparation was involuntary and not specific to Mr. Meijer.

"Mr. Seme, I've got an important job for you." Pieter Meijer stood up from behind his desk. Rhett looked intensely at Meijer's facial muscles and posture. He determined that Meijer was not preparing an attack. Some wire-tight muscles inside Rhett relaxed a bit. He wondered why he always seemed ready to kill.

Meijer opened a drawer, Rhett tensed unconsciously as he watched Meijer's pupils dilate a fraction. He saw Meijer pull out a small, elegant box that looked like it contained a high-end men's wristwatch and handed it over. "Rhett, do you know what this is?"

Rhett noticed Mr. Meijer smelled like he had eaten Asian food for lunch as he opened the unusually heavy box. Judging by the weight, he expected to see a gold ingot. What he saw was a wickedly beautiful, silvery nugget vaguely in the shape of a melted transformer toy with a macadamia nut-sized chunk of quartz occluded in it.

Rhett knew this was a test as he hefted and examined the shiny metal. This white man was going to attempt to humiliate him. Rhett said nothing, but inwardly guessed it was a piece of raw platinum that had crystallized into an odd shape.

"Stumped? So was I. At first I thought it was platinum, but it's nearly pure iridium. Can you believe it?" Meijer took the nugget from Rhett.

Rhett was surprised. Meijer seemed to show no unease when his white hand touched Rhett's lighter, latte-colored skin. Rhett was certain that Meijer viewed dark-skinned people as something to be avoided, but hid his feelings remarkably well.

"I had the lab go over it. They'd never seen anything like it either, but it's the real thing. That piece of quartz has been shocked by heat and pressure. Can't fake shocked quartz. I think it's the biggest raw iridium nugget I've ever seen. Nearly a kilo."

Meijer held it up to a light and gazed at it. By the pulse in Meijer's neck Rhett noticed his boss's heart rate rose. The object fascinated him.

Rhett himself had never seen anything like Meijer's nugget. He'd been to Meijer's iridium mines. The most productive mine processed 100,000 tons of material to get one pound of iridium dust. A poppy seed-sized nugget would be a rare find.

"Mr. Meijer," Rhett switched the conversation from English to perfect Afrikaans, the Dutch-based language of the elite whites. "This is truly an amazing nugget. Did it come from your mines?"

If Meijer was surprised at Rhett's linguistic abilities, his pale blue eyes didn't show it. Few blacks used Afrikaans as fluently as Rhett.

"No. I'm not sure where it came from. That's why I called you. I need you to find the origin of this nugget, and do whatever is necessary to make sure no more of this comes onto the market." As he spoke, Mr. Meijer looked significantly at Rhett. The message was clear—"whatever is necessary".

2

. . . .

SLADE FELT COLD. He had folded his large, husky body into the small blind for more than four hours, and still no wolves.

Shivering behind the camouflaged netting, Slade wondered if his hairspray was tipping off the wildlife he was hunting. His last girlfriend teased him about looking like a 50s teen idol with his narrow face, strong jaw and extravagant pompadour hairstyle.

Now that perfectly groomed hair, which proved handy at getting dates, might be thwarting his mission. Slade pulled his down aviator hat lower over his ears as if to hide any hairspray odor. So what if it ruined his hair, he was deep in Central Alaska.

He could hear wolf howls in the clear, cold Alaska woods high on Shaman Mountain. The snow revealed the route the wolf pack had taken to the caribou carcass the day before. Bright yellow urine marks in the snow showed Slade the wolves considered the carcass theirs. Maybe they had eaten so much, they didn't want any more. Slade had spent considerable effort to kill a small caribou this high up the mountain. He did not want to go home empty-handed.

At a disturbance, Slade readied his rifle, but it was only the magpies and ravens fighting over the open rib cage. Earlier, several red foxes had visited the carcass and eaten their fill and left their obnoxious scent marks nearby. Now a lone vixen stood guard about ten feet away from the grinning face of the dead caribou, watching for anyone who might try to take over the hundreds of pounds of fresh meat.

Slade rubbed his eyes and again scanned the area. The red fox had vanished, and the ravens had flown up into some nearby tree branches. Silently, a smallish white wolf approached the carcass. Slade quietly reached over to a tripod and activated the silent Sony A7 rIII camera, which started shooting 4K UHD video. Any of the video frames could be processed as a high quality still. Nearby, Slade could see a mostly black wolf and two more white ones. He wanted a white one. They seemed to be different from any wolves he had read about or seen pictures of.

Silently gripping his rifle and holding the stock to his cheek, Slade sighted through the built-in iron sights on his Browning BLR 30.06. At 20 yards, he didn't need a scope.

The first rifle shot threw the small white wolf up into the air and down a snow bank. The other wolves vanished as if made of smoke. The ravens took to the air with harsh cries as snow, fine as flour, floated down from nearby trees. The bold magpies continued quarreling over the carcass undisturbed by the rifle blast.

Taking out a black Springfield .45 caliber pistol, Slade grabbed his pack, unfolded himself from the blind, and cautiously approached the place where he expected to find the dead wolf. Instead, he saw a blood trail leading to some bushes.

Pistol ready and on high alert, Slade approached the bushes where he could see the semi-conscious wolf panting heavily as it lay on its side. Once again, a gunshot disturbed the peace of the woods as Slade fired into the already bloody chest of the wolf.

One more headshot assured Slade the wolf was not faking its condition. For a moment, the shocking contrast of red blood on white snow made Slade pause. Then opening his pack, he took out two vials and filled them with the wolf's blood, labeled them, and shoved them back into his pack.

He was done for now and could leave while the magpies examined the new carcass steaming in the frozen air.

3

. . . .

DYLAN BAKER DREW BACK the arrow on his high-tech, compound-hunting bow aiming it toward the path. He fiercely wanted to kill these men, but the hunter in him kept his heart rate and respiration steady.

At any moment the butchers who had killed his girlfriend and hunted him throughout these woods, would step out into the clearing. They carried military-grade automatic M16s selected to full automatic fire, but these were Dylan's woods, and he was an expert with the bow.

Dylan's pale gray eyes coldly swept the clearing. He felt the arrow's fletching soft on his cheek and noticed the metal smell of the arrow. He used a high-tech hunting arrow with an aircraft aluminum inner body, surgical stainless steel blades and a titanium tip that would rip into the killers' bodies at over 320 feet per second. Six more of these arrows lay positioned to fire. He could fire all them with uncanny accuracy within four seconds.

He didn't understand why these men were shooting at him, or why they had killed Suzie. He was just a simple forest recluse. His principle asset was his expertise as a hunting guide and woodsman.

"Why are they hunting me?"

Ten years ago, he had guided a winter ascent of Denali that resulted in the loss of his fiancé and all his clients. The guilt and grief had propelled Dylan into a reclusive life in the wilds of Alaska. Just now he felt he had begun to heal and reemerge into society as a professional wilderness guide. But now this.

The first man stepped into the clearing. Dylan remained still on his rocky perch. He could fire, but wanted to kill at least three of them.

Just then a rifle shot rang out jarring Dylan from his reverie.

Dylan realized he was having a vivid flashback. This meant that soon his nightmares might return.

He hoped this did not mean his other PTSD symptoms would also return: anxiety, daymares, difficulty focusing, and depression.

Since the traumatic events several years ago, he and his counselor met regularly, and he took a daily, low-dose anti-depressant to treat his PTSD— post traumatic stress disorder.

The combination of the counseling and drugs had worked well. He found himself able to control his negative feelings and form positive relation-ships with others. He had fewer vivid, recurring memories about the attacks on him and his loved ones.

On this Shaman Mountain scouting trip, he had accidentally left behind his meds, and the flashback to the carnage in the woods was a reminder that he needed to continue his therapy regimen.

Other gunshots rang out, this time pistol shots. Somewhere up the mountain, Dylan guessed that someone was hunting. The second shots were likely used to euthanize severely wounded game. He'd been on the mountain a week and not seen any sign of humans, despite a small zinc mine operating just a few miles up the mountain.

Dylan emerged from his tent, stretched his 50 year-old body and looked down at his legs as he touched his toes. Some people might call him skinny, but Dylan kept himself fit so he could fully enjoy his hobby of rock climbing.

The difference between holding 165 or 175 pounds with just fingertips, could ruin a climb. He trimmed his beard short and left his still-brown hair long enough for a ponytail. A friend told him he could have leading-man good looks if his skin were not so craggy and weathered.

Shaman Mountain, which the Natives called Kila Ikpic, would become a great place to take clients on a wilderness experience. The area had the reputation of being haunted, but was actually a perfect place to take tourists.

Tourists generally loved the idea of a haunted place, and several articles in major magazines and a website mentioned ghosts. Dylan didn't believe in ghosts, but he was comfortable using the idea to promote a new wilderness excursion he was planning.

Besides the thrill of ghosts, Kila Ikpic had much to offer visitors. Dylan had noted a milky-green lake for a floatplane to land, a massive glacier fed by distant mountains, and a forest, full of springs, meadows, flowers, animals and even a hot spring for bathing.

Dylan also noted some strange wolf prints: too small for mature adults. If the small wolves were adults, then they might be a sub-species of the gray wolf. He decided to file a report with fish and game. If he had discovered a new wolf, he would be guiding trips to Shaman Mountain all summer.

What a beautiful place to guide trips! Despite the nearly perfect attributes of Shaman Mountain, Dylan felt uneasy about the place. Dylan attributed a vague sense of foreboding to his missing PTSD meds.

4

....

"MR. MEIJER, WHAT CAN YOU TELL ME about the origin of this nugget?" Rhett gestured at the iridium. Tiny blemishes on it told Rhett that Meijer's lab used an acid to evaluate the sample.

"Not much. I got an email from someone out of the blue. He says he knows I sell the most iridium in the world. He wanted to know if I was interested in this nugget." Meijer sat down behind a large computer monitor and waved to Rhett to come over. To Rhett, it looked like a master signaling a slave. He hated Meijer, but both men knew Rhett would accept the job and do whatever necessary to successfully complete it.

"Check this out. I'll forward all this to you, but look at this picture the seller sent me." Meijer pointed to the screen. "It's the nugget, and it's photographed next to a coin—a US dime.

"Our lab said the sample had zinc dust in all the crevices, as if it were mined in an area rich in zinc or stored in a lab that processes zinc.

"The guy who brought it talked in a harsh American accent and wanted 20 one-ounce Kruger-rands. I paid him 25 half-ounce coins, and he seemed happy with the deal. We marked all the gold with radiation tags."

Rhett knew that gold Krugerrands, were untraceable, but could be marked with low level radiation signatures which could be read with a cell phone sized device. *The seller should have used*

Bitcoin or some other crypto currency, thought Rhett. "What do you know about the seller?"

Meijer turned off his monitor. "He was paranoid. He said his name was John Smith and that he lived in Cape Town. An obvious lie."

Meijer walked over to a bar and held up a plastic bag with a whisky glass in it. "Here's the glass he drank out of. It should have his prints.

"I'll email you security camera photos of him. He's a big blond fellow who looks like he's former military."

Rhett looked at the glass. "Can you invite him back? I could follow him."

"I told him I'd buy as many nuggets as he can sell. He said he has crates full of nuggets like the one he sold me. He said he'd sell more when he needed the money. I think he plans to sell the rest on the open market."

"That would crush the price of iridium," Rhett observed. He already knew that Meijer squeezed the world supply of iridium to control the price. He had vaults full of the stuff that would lose much of its value if another seller flooded the market. This job was far more important to Meijer than he was letting on. A new mine rich in easily accessible iridium could destroy Mr. Meijer's business and result in the loss of millions.

"You need to make sure he can't sell any more and gain control of his source. Find him and anyone else who's in on the iridium, then do what needs to be done." Meijer gazed intently at Rhett.

"Mr. Meijer, why are you hiring me to do this job?" Rhett wanted the man to give his reasons aloud.

"You know why. You can go anywhere and do what needs to be done. You can blend in around rich white people because of your Swiss private school education.. All that training in the South African Special Forces taught you personal defense skills than none of my other employees possess. I know I can count on you to do what needs to be done."

Rhett returned the significant gaze and thought back to a conversation he had with his mentor, Father Mavuso. Before sending him on scholarship to a Swiss boarding school, the old priest told him that whites hated him more than they hated blacks because he was obviously mixed race: with delicate, almost feminine facial features like a white person, tightly-curled hair like a black, and a skin tone somewhere between the two.

Despite many women telling him his well-muscled body and pale green eyes made him handsome and exotic, he hated his appearance. He wished he were all black so he could belong to his mother's clan. He wanted to belong somewhere.

Father Mavuso had told him, "You want to know who you are? You are a man who does his duty. You belong to your duty."

Rhett thought about this assignment. He would make lots of money and probably kill a white man, maybe several.

Mr. God-damned Meijer wanted him to fix a problem, and the work would require Rhett to kill. Rhett would do this job. Doing his duty would make up for what he had done to Father Mavuso.

5

. . . .

AT THE BASE OF KILA IKPIC, the Kila Glacier grinds toward a pale shallow lake that's perfect for floatplane landings. Unlike most Alaska glaciers, Kila is seldom quiet. It groans eerily as the forces of gravity and friction seem to torture the massive ice flow. When the pressure becomes too great, concussive booms signal that thousands of tons of brittle ice have shifted.

Deep crevasses form and disappear over centuries or minutes, as seemingly capricious ice spirits cause the ancient ice to bend and tumble. During the day, the ice glows with many shades of eerie blue as if powered by some supernatural generator.

This wasn't daytime. In the late summer twilight, a dark figure wearing a homemade animal-skin parka, trimmed with wolverine fur, sharpened his pale walrus-tusk knife on a piece of silvery rock.

He lifted the sharp knife high and brought it down on the ankle of the naked body laid out on the Kila Glacier surface.

Kila seemed to rest as another long swing of the tusk knife hit the knee, then a hand and then an elbow. The cuts had to be just right and landed in time with a monotone song the knife-wielder sang.

Panting, the tusk-knife wielding figure seemed to pause, as if to listen to the glacier. He knew the glacier like a blind man knows his home. It would be about an hour before anything significant would change on Kila.

A final series of blows had nearly severed the head from the body. As Kila groaned, the knife-wielding figure lay down his weapon and rolled the body into a deep crevasse. As if on cue, the aura borealis danced overhead.

Satisfied, the singer cleaned his knife and began the trek that would lead him off the glacier and to his home on Kila Ikpic. The aura borealis's dance had made the trek worthwhile.

6

· · · · · · · · · · ·

THE PLANE LANDED under clear midnight skies at the Anchorage airport. As Rhett stepped onto the dark tarmac, he saw the faint northern lights dancing overhead—a rare sight in the light-polluted skies of the city.

The silent atmospheric show made Rhett pause as other passengers, apparently oblivious to the vague red and green surging lights, passed him by.

Rhett had traveled throughout Africa and Europe as a student and in his work as a member of the South African Special Forces and as a fixer for Mr. Meijer. He visited many strange places, but the city of Anchorage was the only place where he had seen the aurora borealis—those playful midnight lights moved like living sky spirits.

The fingerprints on the glass that Meijer had given him had led Rhett to this faraway and strange place. Rhett had used his sources, some white men with the police, to learn that John Smith's prints were in an international data base, but inaccessible to Rhett's contacts. However, he did find out that John Smith had flown from Johannesburg to Anchorage under the name G. Schechter.

A loud bang from a backfiring luggage truck caused Rhett to fling himself to the tarmac and roll for cover. He was up a moment later, hoping other passengers would ignore him as memories from a horrific battle in the Central African Republic momentarily flooded him.

His athletic roll on the tarmac caused a twitch in the muscles near his groin. This reminded him of a deep scar that often caused numbness near his genitals. Rhett shuddered involuntarily when he remembered how he got the scar.

It happened on a train ride through southern Italy. He and some high school friends had planned on seeing a concert in Naples, far from their elite Swiss boarding school. Rhett, as a poor scholarship student, did not have the money for a first class ticket, so he played a cat-and-mouse game with the conductor to dash out of first class and away from his friends whenever he saw the steward checking tickets.

Rhett, a slender, handsome teen, lounged near a luggage car as he waited for the next stop, when the conductor would be busy elsewhere. He looked through the doorway into the third class car where he was supposed to be riding.

A group of local, dark-haired, pale-skinned toughs had surrounded a terrified blond girl, obviously from the US, and were touching her hair and making lewd comments. An elderly woman stood up and cursed the rowdies who seemed to get bored and move on.

Then Rhett and the obvious leader of the group made eye contact.

Growing up in the Soweto slums gave Rhett a near sixth sense for danger and all his alarms were sounding at full blast. His only choices were to attempt to walk past the dangerous men, stand his ground, or retreat to the luggage car and attempt to hide.

Staying put, Rhett feigned interest in a train schedule posted at the back of the car, but the group closed in—forcing Rhett back into the deserted luggage car.

At knifepoint, the tall, pimply leader of the gang stripped off Rhett's clothes and removed his meager valuables, while the others held him down. Once the leader saw the slender, young African teen's lithe naked body, he sent the rest away so he could have his way with Rhett.

Falling back to his Soweto street survival roots, Rhett feigned cooperation, but made a grab for the leader's knife. After a skirmish, the blade nearly castrated Rhett as it plunged into the muscles of his leg, miraculously missing his femoral artery.

Rhett jammed the fingers of his right hand into the eyes of the rapist and felt something pop in the man's left eye socket.

Screaming, the man's hands went to his face. Rhett pulled the knife from his leg.

He shoved it deep under the white man's pimply chin then pounded it into the man's brain causing near instant death.

The amount of blood covering Rhett astounded him. Applying pressure to his leg wound with one hand, Rhett quickly arranged luggage to hide the body and blood mess. Rhett found a small WC at the end of the car and cleaned himself up as best he could.

At the next stop, Rhett fled the train before any luggage could be unloaded or any of the remaining gang could spot him. Even now, Rhett often woke, his pulse racing and visions of the would-be white rapist kneeling over him.

That attack changed Rhett. After he completed his Swiss education, he longed for home and returned to Soweto to hang out with his real friends, not the wealthy classmates who viewed him as their whip-smart pet. But there was no home for Rhett. All his teenage friends were gone or dead: consumed by the streets.

Searching for something solid in his life, Rhett applied for and was accepted into the South African Special Forces army unit called Recces, where his fighting skills outpaced the other elite trainees.

Outwardly, the other soldiers celebrated Rhett skills, but everyone knew that a mixed race man would never be a true comrade.

A battle wound sent Rhett back to the only family he still had: Father Mavuso, the man who had rescued Rhett as an orphaned street child. The priest, looking like a black Gandalf-the-wizard in his black robes and white hair and beard, stood by Rhett's hospital bedside ready to dispense comfort and advice. It was obvious to the priest that Rhett's body would heal, but not his angry heart.

"You need to pray and follow the teachings of the Church," the old man advised. "Did I do wrong by finding that scholarship and sending you to Europe for your education?" the old priest asked. "Should I have kept you with me?"

Rhett thought about the amazing education he had received in the Swiss Alps. A whole new world had opened for him: science, mathematics, European languages and so forth.

Afterwards, Rhett had become a fighting man of nearly preternatural martial skills and self-control. But despite his far-ranging skill set, Rhett would be unable to stop himself from destroying Father Mavuso.

The rattle of the luggage truck brought Rhett's attention back to Anchorage. He turned his eyes from the Alaska skies and the faint aurora dancing in the dark. It was time to find the man who sold iridium for gold.

7

....

RHETT'S RESEARCH had placed John Smith, aka Gideon Schechter in Anchorage, Alaska. Rhett decided this is where Schechter had probably turned his Krugerrands into dollars.

There were seven Anchorage shops where a customer could buy and sell gold coins, an amazing number given the size of the town. Rhett decided to start with the smallest and work his way through the rest.

The first few places claimed to have no half-ounce Krugerrands, but he learned that Alaskan pawnshops also bought gold. He got lucky when he went into the Greg's Coin, Gun and Small Engine Repair Shop.

Rhett walked in and saw a heavy, but well-muscled white man wearing a rainbow striped gay pride baseball cap with Greg stenciled on it. Greg stood behind the counter ringed with gun racks and dusty tools. Instantly and nearly unconsciously, Rhett planned how he would kill the big man.

Rhett wasn't fooled by the man's outwardly friendly greeting. Since everyone he'd seen in Anchorage was white, he knew a dark skinned man with afro-textured hair would be greeted with suspicion.

When Rhett asked if Greg had any Krugerrands for sale. Greg said he did, but they were expensive.

Rhett decided the asshole thought that, since he was dark-skinned, he couldn't afford to pay for a gold coin.

For a moment, Rhett thought about jamming his thumbs into the guy's eye sockets and pulling out his piggy little eyes. Instead, he pulled a baseball-sized roll of fresh 100-dollar bills from his jacket pocket and set the roll down on the counter.

"Greg, I want to see your Krugerrands," Rhett spoke softly, but suddenly aware of his South African accent.

"Why sure," Greg offered a false smile. "I can only show you one at a time. You know . . . insurance rules."

"Yes, of course. Bring one to me," Rhett pulled a small, cell phone-sized electrical device from his pocket and signaled for Greg to hurry.

When Rhett passed the device over the coin, the device beeped and displayed a number. "I'll buy this one. Let me see another."

Greg insisted that he get paid and hand over a receipt before bringing out the next coin, but this time he brought two. This went on until Rhett had purchased 23 half-ounce Krugerrands. Rhett knew how many Krugerrands Gideon Schechter was paid. There should be two more coins.

"Now Greg, where are the other two coins?" asked Rhett in a quiet voice as he pressed the coins into a tight paper roll.

"That's all I have. A guy comes in here in a hurry to sell these, and I bought 23 of them. The feller said he had 100 of them. Lucky guy. Now you have the 23 he brought in here." Rhett thought the man was either telling the truth, or had uncanny control over his heart rate and breathing.

Rhett looked down at the heavy roll of gold coins in his hand. "What was the seller's name?" he asked in an even quieter voice. He hoped Greg wouldn't tell him, so Rhett could apply some physical pressure on the big, white shit-bag.

Father Mavuso would have told Rhett not harm Greg unless it was in the line of duty. Rhett always did his duty. That's who he was.

"I can't tell you who sold these to me, privacy rules and all, but if you spend another $100 here at the shop, I'll leave my receipt book out here. You can look at it while I go in the back and get the next item. I have some Chinese gold coins back there." Greg's greasy long hair bobbed on the back of his neck as he imagined his profit for the night.

Rhett peeled off a fresh hundred-dollar bill. "Let me see the book."

Greg flipped the book to a page and pushed it over. Rhett saw that it listed the Krugerrands and the Shaman Mountain Zinc Mine as the address for someone named Gideon Schechter.

Rhett looked at the address. "So Gideon Schechter lives at a mine on Shaman Mountain?"

"I guess there's a zinc mine up there." Greg slid the book back behind the counter.

"How do I get there?" asked Rhett.

"Lordy, you don't want to go there. It's located in the Bermuda Triangle of Alaska. Planes get lost there. Hikers and hunters never return. There are stories about Shaman Mountain. I have no idea how that mining company can find anyone to work for them."

Greg pushed back his hat exposing more greasy hair. "Don't go there, Mr. Smith. You can have that information for free."

8

. . . .

WITH HIS UNLIMITED EXPENSE ACCOUNT, Rhett booked a corner room in the opulent Nesterov Hotel in Anchorage. It was surprisingly upscale and sophisticated, like the grand hotel in Dubai he often stayed in when traveling for Mr. Meijer.

From his room, he made a half-dozen calls trying to find out who owned the Shaman Mountain Zinc Mine.

What he learned was that he could get a full report from The Alaska State Division of Corporations, Business and Professional Services in just two weeks for only $24. All he wanted to know was the contact information on the owner or owners of the mine. He could have the report in one hour if he went in person to the office in Juneau and paid a copy fee.

After several hours of searching on his laptop, he learned that the mine was becoming less productive each year. He guessed it would be shut down in five years or sooner. This was good news. The owner would probably be interested in selling the lease—unless the owner was Gideon Schechter.

His next call was to an airplane charter service to find a fast way down to Juneau. It was surprisingly easy to book a powerful twin-engine propeller plane that could get him to Juneau in less than two hours. He would be at the Alaska state offices when they opened.

The next day Rhett enjoyed the rustic professionalism of the white pilot, an outwardly friendly chap named Flapjack. A slender man in his mid-50s and wearing clean work clothes and a worn blue baseball cap, Flapjack started the preflight checks with an Aerostar 703P.

"You're lucky this Aerostar was available," said Flapjack over his shoulder as he checked the fuel tanks. "Usually the company wants to use the single engine Beechcraft for a Juneau run. Saves fuel."

"And you'll stand by to fly me back to Anchorage after I'm done here in Juneau?" said Rhett.

"Of course, Mr. Seme. I'll have the plane ready to go when you are done with your business."

Rhett nodded and observed the practiced, confident motions of his pilot

"Yep," Flapjack nodded and closed an engine compartment, "this plane was built in 1979. It's equipped with Lycoming engines that together generate 700 horsepower."

"So it's fast," said Rhett.

"Fast? You bet. It set a speed record when it first came out, and in those days the engines only had 600 horsepower."

Sensing his passenger was not in a mood for conversation, Flapjack finished his preflight routine and quickly took the sleek, powerful airplane into a hazy sky.

Later, Rhett felt an unaccustomed awe as the Aerostar assumed a landing pattern over the Juneau airport. Surrounded by a bowl of heavily, treed mountains and framed by rivers, lakes and sea, the airport was unlike any Rhett had ever seen.

Soon Rhett found himself the only person in line to get a taxi. Everyone in the whole bustling city seemed to be white. Juneau, surrounded by mountains and glaciers and split by the Gastineau Channel, had a small town vibe that was disturbed by rows of tawdry tourist shops that likely thrived on the cruise ship trade.

Since Flapjack had made good time, Rhett stopped for breakfast at moose-themed restaurant that served outrageously large portions.

At 9 o'clock sharp, the State of Alaska Division of Corporations, Business and Professional Services opened its drab doors, and Rhett was first in line to get his information.

The young man behind the counter, who wore a gray, skinny tie and smelled like he had also eaten at the moose-themed diner, gave no outward clue that he noticed that Rhett was mixed race, as he copied the report that Rhett had come to get.

Rhett sat on a bench in a sunny children's playground and studied the report. He learned that the Shaman Mountain Zinc Mine leaseholder's name was Ursula Schiffmeister, and that she lived in Idaho.

Using a phone he purchased in Anchorage, he tried a direct call to the phone on record. He connected with her on the first ring.

"Hello?" Schiffmeister's confident voice boomed through the phone.

"Hello. Is this is Ursula Schiffmeister, the owner of Shaman Mountain Mine?" Rhett asked politely.

"Who the hell is this?" came the aggressive reply. "If this about those tailings polluting that little stream, we fixed it months ago."

"No, Mrs. Schiffmeister. My name is Rettief Seme. I'm a buyer's agent for a party interested in buying your interest in the mine."

"Someone wants to buy that mine?" Aggression morphed to confusion. "Huh. Buy the mine? Call me Ursula by the way. I can tell by your accent that you are from Australia."

"How perceptive of you . . . Ursula," said Rhett a quiet voice. "My wealthy client wants to invest in zinc mining, and your small mine seems just the right size for him to get started. Can we meet to discuss it?" Rhett allowed her to think he was from Australia since he knew of no iridium mining going on there.

"Did you say wealthy? Of course we can discuss it. I'm just now boarding a plane from Anchorage to my home in Boise. We can meet there tomorrow."

"Boise? That's a city in the American state of Idaho?" Rhett thought about the irony of Ursula leaving Anchorage when he could have made a deal with her there. Now he would need to travel to Idaho then back to Alaska.

"Yes, Idaho. Famous potatoes," boomed Ursula. "Can you meet me tomorrow morning? I'll have my lawyer draw up a contract."

"Tomorrow morning is fine," said Rhett thinking of the Aerostar flying at 700 miles per hour.

"Your client is lucky. That mine will make him rich." Ursula's voice took a conspiratorial tone. "But the price will need to be right."

"My client is prepared to make a generous offer for the mine, but first he wants me to inspect the mining operations." Rhett knew from his research that the zinc mine was producing poorly and might even be played out.

"And just so you know, I don't actually own the mountain, just the mining lease. And the lease is definitely for sale." said Ursula.

"Of course," Rhett knew that her lease on the pitiful zinc mine would run out soon. He pondered just stalling for a few months, then her mining operation would need to close down or the lease would come up for bidding. He had to talk to her face-to-face to see if she knew anything about the iridium.

"Let's meet tomorrow for lunch to discuss the details," said Rhett. "The inspection is a mere formality. We can talk numbers, and maybe even come to an agreement."

"Of course Mr. Seme," said Ursula. "I'll text you the address of a restaurant where we can have a drink and discuss the mine. I'll inform the Shaman Mountain Mine manager that he should call you to make an appointment to inspect the mine. I'll text you his phone number."

"That's perfect," said Rhett.

"And don't believe all the tales you hear about Shaman Mountain being a spooky place. There's nothing there to be scared of."

9

· · · · · · · · · ·

DYLAN BAKER'S LIFE as a wilderness guide was back on track. In a flooding disaster in Seward, Alaska, he'd lost everything. However, in recent months, Dylan had managed to scrape together enough money to start a new life in Anchorage.

Most of his business loan money went toward rent for the tiny storefront office and upstairs apartment, but he felt like he had regained some control over his life. This fresh start should have made him happy, but his PTSD tinged every good thing with anxiety. Something bad might happen.

Starting the new trip, which he called the *Shaman Mountain Tour*, captured the interest of adventure travelers. He was able to fully book his first tour and had two other tours filling up. He hoped it would go well since future bookings depended on the reviews he would get.

When clients first met Dylan Baker, they saw a sinewy, early fifties man whose granite-grey eyes and a tanned, weathered face that revealed a complex combination of maturity and boyish playfulness.

As his first group to experience the Shaman Mountain Tour gathered in his small Anchorage office, Dylan noticed it was an assembly much like others he guided.

A fit-looking, Asian-featured, middle-aged man with wearing a scuffed Seattle Mariners baseball cap, approached Dylan with an outstretched hand. "My name is Jun Lee, and this is my daughter Rong Chow." He spoke with a Jackie Chan Chinese accent as he gestured to a tall, confident-looking young woman with stylish short hair, designer outdoor clothing and expert makeup.

"Call me Jennifer," she said with a precise voice that sounded like a network newscaster. Dylan guessed she was in her late-twenties and a bit too pretty in a style magazine way and wearing too much makeup to be comfortable on a four-day wilderness trip. If Dylan ever allowed himself to imagine a romantic relationship with a client, this aloof and athletic-looking woman would be out of his league—too young and too pretty.

"She calls herself Jennifer; she not like to be Rong," joked her father.

Jennifer playfully pulled his Mariners cap down over his smiling face.

Besides the father-daughter pair, Dylan's clients included a couple of stocky red-headed brothers from Minnesota, who had recently graduated from high school, and a balding, forty-something photographer named Monty, who wore well-used, but high quality outdoor clothing. Dylan knew that having an expert photographer would mean the whole group would be most active when the sun was low, turning the sky warm with golden colors—which only happened very late and very early this time of the year.

Fortunately, the Minnesota boys, Bryce and Reggie, each wore different baseball caps so Dylan would be able to tell them apart. Bryce had a blue Twins cap and Reggie's cap was red with a Vikings logo. Dylan thought that, if they always wore their hats, he could tell them apart.

As Dylan went through his safety speech and checked each client's gear, his only real concern was Jennifer. She did not seem the type to sign up for a rugged outdoor trip where clients would study wilderness survival techniques and explore a remote natural area.

She looked like she would be most comfortable in a corporate boardroom, wearing a high-power business suit. He wondered if he would end up carrying her gear, digging her latrine, and washing her dishes. He wondered why he was thinking this because in the past, the girls with makeup were just as tough as anyone else.

Dylan knew that his trips were most successful when the participants made friends with each other. He had each person tell something about him or herself and explain why they signed up for the trip.

Jun Lee said he grew up in China and just retired from teaching at the Seattle police academy. He wanted to collect some rocks from the Shaman Mountain area. Jennifer explained that she was an attorney who was transitioning from a solo practice to applying to work at a major Seattle law firm, and that she was on this trip to spend time with her dad.

Bryce looked at his brother and pushed back his blue cap, "We signed up because we wanted some adventure before we start college in the fall."

"Yeah, are we going to see some supernatural stuff on this trip?" asked Reggie, an eager look on his face."

"You'll see super stuff and natural stuff, but I can't promise anything supernatural," smiled Dylan,

Monty held up his camera and said he was there to get some landscape shots of a remote area that no one else in his camera club had taken.

Just as he suspected, Monty had brought about 40 pounds of camera gear. Dylan explained that clients had to carry their own pack from the river to the camping area: a two-mile hike of uphill walking. The photographer expressed no concerns about the walk. "In Oregon, where I'm from, we have really steep hills," he bragged.

Jun Lee also had an overly heavy backpack, crammed full of scientific-looking instruments and tools. "I am a rock hound," Jun explained smiling, " . . . and a Seattle Mariners fan." He pointed to his well-broken-in cap. "My home collection includes a sample of nearly every possible element in the periodical table." He hefted his pack easily. "I have no problems to take this pack."

Jun would not agree to store some of his heavier gear in a locker.

Dylan did have some success with Jennifer. She decided to put her cosmetic case, a tablet computer, a large frisbee, and a pair of athletic shoes in a locker.

As they waited for the bus to shuttle them to the airport, Bryce gestured to a wall covered in framed awards, media articles and photos. "Whoa, Dylan! Are all these yours? Are you a famous rock climber?"

The other clients moved to the wall covered in impressive honors. They turned as a group and looked at Dylan with new respect: before them stood an internationally famous climber. Dylan just smiled and let the wall tell the story.

What he didn't tell his clients is that just because he could climb rocks like few other people in the world, that didn't mean he was a good wilderness guide. He kept the awards up to impress his clients so they would view him as an expert and be more willing to take his advice on safety issues.

As the group piled into the airport shuttle, Dylan told himself not to be anxious. Sometimes this self-talk helped him relax and enjoy his job. His friends often accused him of worrying too much.

He'd guided many small groups in the Alaskan wilderness, but this was his first time taking a party to Shaman Mountain. He hoped the trip would be successful. It had to be.

10

· · · · · · · · · · ·

SOLOMON QUIGLEY PREPARED to leave his office. Like most days, the sixty-three year old federal bureaucrat had stayed too long at work. His knees ached and a dull pain in his neck reminded him of his arthritis.

When he turned off his monitor, he saw himself reflected on the black screen: balding, sagging facial skin, neck like a plucked chicken and a nearly white goatee. It shocked him. He was once a dark-haired boy wonder and physically vigorous.

His secretary had left and nearly all the worker bees on his floor were home by now. The Anchorage summer sun sent slanting light through his corner office window and lit up the east wall of his large work area.

On that wall, hung photos of a 1959 New York Times article announcing Alaska statehood, a plaque from Alaska Opportunity Party, the AOP, thanking Solomon Quigley for his tireless devotion to Alaska secession, and a framed certificate for sustained superior performance from the head of the U.S. Interior Department.

To Solomon, it seemed ironic that he had worked his way to a top Alaska post in the Federal Interior Department, and still worked to get Alaska to secede from the union. With a shrug, he picked up his briefcase and started out of his office.

Ursula Schiffmeister charged past the empty receptionist's desk and ran nearly into Solomon Quigley.

"There you are," she said. "You owe me a favor, and I need it now." Her large bosom competed with her ample middle to burst out of a shiny fuchsia blouse tucked into a billowing black skirt. Gaudy plastic bracelets clacked against each other as if to compete for Solomon's attention. Her unnaturally black hair fit like a helmet on her round head and, to Solomon, looked like a wig.

"Mrs. Schiffmeister! How nice to see you. Our office is closed now, but if you call my secretary, she'll see if I have an open spot on my calendar for a meeting," Solomon backed away from her powerful floral perfume and into his office.

"Solomon Quigley, I'm in a hurry. I'm flying back to Idaho late this evening for a noon meeting tomorrow with a buyer. I changed my flight just so I could talk to you. I need your help."

Solomon looked at her with a dubious expression as Ursula puffed up her large chest. "I know you are up for reelection for your AOP presidency, and I know your secrets. Now you listen to me. I have a buyer interested in that underperforming zinc mine on Shaman Mountain. I haven't filed or paid the maintenance fees for the last few years, and I can't sell my lease unless I'm current. I need you to go into your computer and just click a box for me saying I'm current. This is urgent!"

Solomon noticed some red lipstick smeared on her startlingly white teeth. He assumed the teeth were not her own. "We don't do things like that any more. There are forms and fees. A computer program tracks everything. Why don't you come back tomorrow? My secretary will put you in touch with someone to help you."

"Don't you try and get rid of me," Ursula nearly shouted in the quiet office area. "Did you forget how I helped you when AOP funds you administered had disappeared? You and I believe in freedom for Alaska, but I'm the one who kept you out of jail. Without my help, you'd be just about finishing up a jail sentence for fraud."

The AOP elections were coming up soon, and he didn't need anything to ruin his reelection chances.

He hesitated, and she pounced. "Listen, you make me current with my federal mining maintenance fees, and I'll give a hefty donation to your reelection campaign and keep my mouth shut. I think the buyer is going to overpay, so I can make it worth your while."

"Mrs. Schiffmeister, you are asking a lot."

"I also want an extension on the lease. Once my buyer finds out the lease will expire in eight months, he will probably pull out of the deal."

"The lease extension will be tough. I'll see what I can do," Solomon hedged.

Solomon knew it would be a pain the ass to finagle her late fees, affidavit of assessment and claimant records, but he knew Ursula could derail his election plans. The party had some expensive projects going on now—including a wolf problem on Shaman Mountain. Maybe he could close down all mining on the mountain when the new owner came in. This might be an opportunity to shut down that feeble mine. It could keep pesky environmentalists from interfering with AOP goals.

"Of course, Mrs. Schiffmeister. Step into my office, and we'll see if we can land that fish for you."

11

. . . .

DYLAN FELT THAT THINGS STARTED to go wrong almost immediately. His reserved plane, a newly refurbished Cessna 206 that gave his clients a feeling of confidence with its new airplane look and smell, was unavailable.

The Cessna was actually built in 1968, but it was beautiful and handled 6 passengers and luggage. Shelia, of Shelia's Flight Service, told him the plane was unavailable due to an urgent flight to evacuate a sick guest from a remote fishing lodge.

Shelia and her husband Chuck, had started their air transport business about ten years ago. Dylan thought it aged her a lot more than ten years. She was thin as a post with a face full of wrinkles, blond-grey hair, and the air of a CEO used to making quick, unquestioned decisions.

The backup, a deHavilland Beaver, was actually a newer plane by a few years, but it needed to be renovated. Shelia used it mostly for flying cargo. It looked a bit shabby and had an Ivchenko seven-cylinder radial Soviet-built engine that smoked like a dragon and was the noisiest plane in the seaport. Passengers needed to wear ear protection.

"Dylan, I'm going to fly you myself," Shelia said. "I had scheduled Tim Clark to fly you, but he called in sick at the last minute."

Dylan could feel anxiety flooding him as he asked. "Do you think he believes those crazy rumors about the unlucky Shaman Mountain?"

"I doubt it, but I actually like flying the Beaver more than the Cessna. It has nearly twice the horsepower and is as reliable as an anvil. It will be ready soon. Get your clients down by the seaplane area in an hour."

"An hour!" Dylan winced. "I'll have everyone go through the aviation museum and try to make it seem like part of the service."

"We'll do the seaplane safety talk in the Beaver in an hour. I promise," Shelia said.

After the tour group had wandered the aviation museum they took a shuttle down to the seaplane dock. There, they dutifully listened to Shelia's safety talk and practiced boarding and exiting a seaplane. Dylan asked if there were any questions.

"OK," said Jennifer looking at Shelia as the group stood by the Beaver. "We are safe with you as our pilot, but what do you think of Dylan as a guide?" Jennifer smiled mischievously at Dylan.

"Dylan Baker? You don't know how lucky you are to go with him. He's a legend around here. He could be a professional climber or outdoorsman if he wanted to, but he likes being a guide. He'd be my first, maybe only choice, to lead a backcountry trip."

Bryce, his blue cap backwards, raised his hand as if he were in a class, "Where did Shaman Mountain get its name?"

"The popular press calls it Shaman Mountain, but the Natives call it Kila Ikpic. The Native term translates as Shaman's Familiar," said Dylan as he picked up a box and started passing out refillable water bottles.

Bryce accepted his bottle and said, "Shaman's Familiar! That's cool. Isn't a familiar some kind of demon animal that obeys its master? I got to see this place!"

"Native culture does not regard a shaman's familiar as something evil, but more as a magical helper. The medicine men often claimed to have special animals that would grant powers of healing and wisdom. These animals could be anything from a porcupine to a whale."

"Are there whales up there?" asked Reggie shoving his water bottle into his pack.

"No whales. Too far inland," Dylan resumed his talk. "About fifty years ago, someone got a mineral lease on Kila Ikpic to mine zinc. They named their business, Shaman Mountain Mine. It was probably an error in translation from Kila Ikpic. Later, maps started labeling Kila Ikpic as Shaman Mountain."

"Will we see any ghosts?" asked Bryce.

"I've never seen any there, but I can promise you'll see some amazing natural beauty. I know some of you may have heard stories about lost planes, ghosts, missing hikers and so forth, but these are overblown," said Dylan.

"Then will we see any wolves?" asked Reggie.

"Funny you should ask that," said Dylan. "Last week, when scouting for this trip, I spotted some oddly small wolf paw prints near a moose carcass. There are wolves on the mountain, but they are terribly shy. I've never actually seen one."

"That's all the time we have for questions," said Shelia. "The Beaver is ready, and we got a weather report of some storms threatening to move in to the Aleutians that will send gusts as far east as this airport. We gotta go now if we want smooth waters for takeoff."

Dylan leaned close to Shelia, "A storm? Anything I should worry about?"

"I don't think so. It's headed toward the Aleutians, then supposed to track directly northeast from there.

12

. . . .

SOLOMON QUIGLEY FINALLY GOT URSULA out of his office and immediately headed for the staff break room. He was several hours past his dinnertime, and he'd skipped lunch that day.

Maybe he could find a little something in the staff refrigerator to take the edge off his hunger. He found salad dressing, some mustard, and several crumpled brown paper bags with bits of partly consumed lunches. The least dubious bag had a half-eaten slab of lasagna that smelled fine.

Just as he was bringing it to the microwave, his personal cell vibrated. The caller ID read "Slade".

"Hello Slade, what did you find out?"

"Listen Superintendent Quigley, I got the DNA results back from that Shaman Mountain wolf I shot. Your concerns were justified." Slade talked fast, like he was on a timed call.

"OK, give it to me," said Solomon as he put the container of lasagna into the microwave. He was sure the heat would kill any bacteria from the person who had eaten the first half of it.

"Whoever told you there was something strange about the Shaman Mountain wolves was right. The DNA results indicate they are actually an unknown subspecies closely related to the Alexander Islands wolves."

"A new subspecies! That's like a worst case scenario," thundered Solomon as the microwave dinged. "What else did you find out?"

"Like the Alexander Island wolves, these animals are much smaller than the typical grey wolf. The wolves I saw probably only weigh about 30 pounds and the predominant color seems to be white with green eyes. The report has this line in it: *the mitochondrial DNA evidence indicates that the sampled wolf is genetically distinct from inland gray wolves and appears to be most closely linked, but separate from, the Alexander Island subspecies.*"

"Oh great. They are cute and rare," Solomon stuck his finger into the center of the pasta. Cold. He returned it to the microwave and set the power to max. "Anyway, how could they mostly be white?

I thought that was a recessive genetic trait, so the dark colors would show up more often."

"These wolves are probably isolated on Shaman Mountain by the big glacier called Kila Glacier. It's huge. So if most the wolves are white, all their pups will also be white. The dark wolves carry the genes for dark and white fur, so some of their pups will be white. It's kind of like why most Swedish people are blond and blue-eyed." Slade patted his dark pompadour.

"Slade, these wolves will likely turn out to be rare or endangered, or even if they aren't endangered, someone will file an Endangered Species Act petition. Small, white and cute wolves will get public attention. That could lead to the whole Shaman Mountain area made into a federally protected area. This could really delay our secession plans. The more the feds get involved with Alaska, the less likely we'll ever be able to break away."

Solomon's microwave dinged again. He opened the door to see the entire plastic container melted into a bubbling mixture of plastic and lasagna.

"That's not even the worst in my opinion," said Slade. "Since these animals are so pretty, they'll be made into a national treasure. Washington bureaucrats will control the mountain. I hate it when the lower 48 tries to boss us Alaskans around. Alaska needs freedom."

Slade appends the AOP slogan in every conversation, Solomon thought. "We need to keep this a secret. An Anchorage wilderness guide named Dylan Baker alerted my office to the possible existence of oddly small wolves. He was up there scouting for Shaman Mountain wilderness trips and saw some paw prints and unusual wolf scat that didn't make sense to him. Whatever that means."

Slade paused. "We need to discourage or stop this Baker guy, and anyone else from taking people into the Shaman Mountain area."

"Yeah, and we need to get rid of those wolves before their existence becomes public. They are a threat to a free Alaska." Solomon found himself eating a spoonful of ranch dressing to stop his stomach from hurting. "Here's what you do. Take a team in there and eliminate all the wolves. Do it with poison bait, not aerial shooting. Someone would notice all the commotion."

"OK." said Slade slowly. "It's going to cost a lot to put together and outfit a team."

"I'll take care of the money with AOP discretionary funds. Just get this done before the wolves become a national treasure. We Alaskans should decide how to manage our resources, not Washington."

If the feds get even more involved in Alaska while I'm in charge of AOP, I'll never get reelected, thought Solomon as he pulled another brown sack out of the refrigerator and sniffed it.

13

....

TO JENNIFER, SHELIA HAD NOT SEEMED worried about a storm moving toward the Aleutian Islands, "It's a thousand miles from here and moving northeast," she said confidently as Jennifer observed Shelia pumping water out of the plane's floats and inspecting the undercarriage of the deHavilland Beaver.

Jennifer had grabbed the co-pilot's seat, and everyone was given clunky green noise-canceling headphones with mics that facilitated conversation inside the noisy Beaver.

What surprised Jennifer was how long the safety briefing took. Sheila had everyone practice wet exits and listen to her strong admonitions against inflating their flotation devices prior to exiting the plane.

Sheila thrilled Jennifer when she swooped low and banked the plane to allow passengers to see some of the amazing natural sights of wild Alaska. Animals like white beluga whales, foraging moose and grizzly bears seemed set up just for the passengers' delight. Sheila gave a fascinating natural history lecture on the animals, glaciers and pristine lakes to make the trip special.

Jennifer found herself chatting with Sheila as soon as the talk was over.

"This looks just like the tape I put on my bicycle handlebars," said Jennifer looking at the black tape wrapped around the "steering" yoke hovering over her co-pilot's seat.

"It is. One of my hobbies is cycling. Do you have a hobby?" asked Shelia, her eyes flicking from gages to the Alaska sky and back.

"I play ultimate. Do you know what that is?" asked Jennifer.

"It's a team game played on a soccer field with a frisbee?" suggested Shelia as she used a black lever to adjust the throttle.

"It's something like soccer. Lots of running. I'm a cutter: someone who plays downfield and sprints around trying to find some open field in order to receive a pass when our team is on offense."

"Sounds intense. I like riding my bike on long, easy rides with my pup and a beer at the end. Sometimes my husband and I will ride our tandem."

Jennifer noticed a curled photo of a couple on a tandem bike that was jammed behind a dashboard magnet.

"There's our landing," Shelia pointed to a milky, green lake near the foot of a massive glacier. She took the Beaver low over the waters situated at the base of the Kila Glacier. Despite a speaker yelling *Caution! Terrain!* And red lights flashing among the flying instruments, Shelia looked satisfied, "The lack of ripples and floating ice means it's safe to land on this glacial lake."

Jennifer had never been in a seaplane, and was excited by the smooth touchdown onto the lake. Jennifer and the other passengers had their faces plastered against the widows taking in the pontoon spray and wild sights they would soon be exploring.

The impressive Kila Glacier terminus: 60 feet from base to blue/white ice towers, the bowl of rugged mountains from which the glacier flowed, and Kila Ikpic itself—with its virgin forests and eerie rock formations, snowy cap, and the darkening skies. Dylan's guests looked suitability impressed.

As Shelia taxied to a natural rocky pier, Dylan climbed out and perched on the Beaver's pontoon, a rope in his hand. He leapt to the shore and secured the plane as it rocked in the waves. Soon everyone pitched in unloading the packs and supplies off the plane as if they knew what they were doing.

Jun Lee pulled his battered Seattle Mariners cap over his short, spiky grey hair and appeared ready to charge up the mountain.

Jennifer standing on the rocks and looking back at the Beaver, she suddenly felt scared, like she did on her first day of kindergarten when her mom was about to leave her. She did not want the Beaver to abandon her and Jun. She had to restrain herself from climbing back into the noisy aircraft.

When Dylan cast off the ropes, and Shelia started taxiing away, Jennifer almost cried despite the thrill of being in such a remote area.

It seemed like Dylan knew exactly how she was feeling, and immediately distracted her by putting everyone to work. The group had to carry everything up a broad meadow to the camping area Dylan had picked out.

Three hours later, the camp looked even homey with a solar shower, latrine tent, and sleeping tents set up. With the thrilling view of the Kila Glacier on one side of the camp and the heavily forested Kila Ikpic on the other, Jennifer felt Dylan had chosen their base camp well.

Later, as the group foraged for the edible plants that Dylan had shown them, Jennifer did not see her dad slip away from the group. Had Dylan noticed, he would have immediately corralled the curious rock hunter.

FROM A ROCKY AREA, about 2,000 feet up Kila Ikpic, Snuffy Odgen, looked down at his Michael

Phelps swimmer's body gone-to-seed as he hung his battered binoculars on a belt clip.

"A bunch of goddamed tourists!" His small dark eyes formed into a scowl. "Gideon will not be happy. Looks like goddamned tourists. Their camp is set up like they're going to stay a week."

Snuffy swept off his baseball cap and scratched his scabby, balding head as he thought. He looked closely at his fingernails to see what scabs and loose skin he had pulled off and cursed his ever-present scalp rash.

Snuffy thumbed his walkie-talkie. "Gideon, are you there?"

No answer.

"Gideon, are you there? It's Snuffy."

No answer.

"Gideon, if you can hear me, there's a bunch of tourists camping down by the lake. I know you are going to want me to scare them off, but I'm just wondering how you want me to do it." Snuffy scratched his scalp.

Even after several other attempts at connecting with Gideon, the walkie-talkie received no response. *Just like Gideon*, thought Snuffy. *Always off somewhere or in the mine.*

Snuffy knew he should ask Gideon what to do. Once asked, Gideon would issue a series of unwavering orders would lay out very clear plans. He looked down at his Winchester bolt-action rifle and wondered what Gideon's orders would be. He hoped it wouldn't be to shoot at the tourists from afar. He hadn't been able to adjust the scope since he dropped the rifle a week ago. He'd have to get close to shoot them. That could be fun.

THIS DEEP IN THE MINE, the walkie-talkie on Gideon Schechter's tool belt received no signal. Slapping dust from his long blond hair, beard and wiping rock flakes from his deceptively innocent-looking face,

Gideon became aware of the difference between his six foot, four-inch muscular frame and the three small Asian-featured men attempting to move an awkward drilling machine into position.

Gideon gritted his teeth and turned his head toward the taller of the men. "Hey Kung, tell these shitheads to lift as they push. You can't just push." His intense dark eyes—so dark, that they appeared eerily black in low light, contrasted with his blond eyelashes, bangs and his albino-like skin.

Gideon stared hard at Kung, a tall, good-looking Chinese man with a strong chin and intelligent face, as he spoke in rapid, singsong Mandarin Chinese to the others. The men appeared to change their approach to moving the drilling apparatus while keeping their distance from Gideon. After much effort, he seemed satisfied with the placement of the drill. He checked his watch. "You gooks are two hours past your lunch break. Take 20 minutes, then open this fissure."

Kung looked up at Gideon then pointed to some dark rocks. "Mr. Gideon, shouldn't we drill closer to this igneous rock? Just above this burn line is where we've found most of the ore." Kung pointed to a dark stripe of rock about five feet across.

Gideon made a mental note not to ever let Kung off the mountain; he was hired direct from Taiwan as a mining engineer. He seemed to be the only one who understood that they were mining iridium. This iridium had to remain secret.

Gideon nodded to Kung. "Do what you think is best."

Kung then spoke to the others, and watched them relax with relief and trot up the damp tunnel toward their lunch pails.

"I'll be back in an hour," Gideon said. "I expect to see significant progress." He watched with satisfaction, as Kung appeared properly cowed.

The electric ATV Gideon used in the mining tunnels had about 300 pounds of iridium nuggets scattered among chunks of quartz and loose rocks in the bed of the vehicle. He imagined a room full of gold coins as he gazed down at the incredibly rare iridium nuggets. His future wealth depended on keeping this iridium mine a secret since he didn't own the mineral rights. He was essentially stealing iridium since he was the manager of the zinc mine, not an owner.

He also knew that the federal lease to allow mining in this area would expire soon. He had to extract as much iridium as possible before that idiot Schiffmeister found out she had a fortune just yards from her shitty zinc mine.

As Gideon strode out of the mine and into the mining camp, his walkie-talkie chirped.

14

· · · · · · · · · ·

RHETT'S PLANE TOUCHED down in Boise during a typical late summer heat wave. Flapjack announced it was 101 degrees at the airport, but

Rhett was unprepared for the shock of the hot air against his face. It was like being hit by a blast from a smelting furnace.

Rhett mentally reviewed his goals for the meeting: confirm Schiffmeister has no knowledge of the iridium, get her to lower her expectations for a large buy-out fee, and make sure she didn't sell out to anyone else.

As he walked through the molten Idaho heat from Flapjack's plane to the terminal building, Rhett found himself pulling off his jacket and shirt. Once in the terminal building, he noticed all the people were white and seemed to be looking at him with his outerwear folded over one arm.

The round girl in the airport clothing store reminded him of a termite grub with her nearly translucent skin. She asked him several times to repeat his request to buy a light, business shirt—as if she couldn't understand his South African accent.

The traffic-choked taxi ride to the restaurant, where he would meet with Ursula Schiffmeister, was slow and hot, despite the car's thundering air conditioner.

The overly cold air in the chain-style restaurant gave him a headache. A perky but hesitant teen, wearing a white waitress uniform, greeted him and showed him to a sticky red booth. "Your waitress is Millie, and she'll be here soon."

He had just seated himself, when an obese white woman with an absurd wig and flamboyant makeup approached him. He wondered if it was a set up. An assassin sent in using this clownish freak to distract him, so an attack could come from some other quarter.

Looking everywhere but at Ursula, Rhett eliminated the existence of possible threats and realized this woman was indeed Ursula Schiffmeister. *Maybe she is the threat*, thought Rhett. He immediately planned how to use improvised weapons at hand to defend himself and kill her.

Ursula thrust out her hand. "Mr. Seme, so good of you to come all the way to Idaho for this meeting." She gestured toward the booth he had secured. "This won't do. I want to sit in a chair."

He looked at her large middle and realized she didn't like booths due to her size.

Soon they were seated at a table in a quiet area of the restaurant. Although Rhett hated small talk, he recognized it was necessary to accomplish his goals.

Rhett forced a smile hoping he was able to hide his distaste for this woman. "Well, Mrs. Schiffmeister, hot enough for you?"

Ursula mopped her face carefully with a napkin so as not to disturb her abundant makeup. "It sure is, but you people are used to it, right?'

Rhett's hand moved to his fork as if it were a weapon, but kept his voice light. "Now what's that mean, 'You people'?"

"You know, African people. You are obviously not from Australia. All the movies show hot steamy jungles with elephants and lions. You know." She made feeble hand motions as she seemed to realize she said something inappropriate.

Rhett dropped his fork. "That's a common misconception. In my town, Johannesburg, we have mild summer temperatures. We are between two vast seas and at a high elevation. It's not a jungle, and we never have heat like this. Let's talk about the mine."

AN HOUR LATER RHETT PAID the bill, watched Ursula step out into the Idaho heat, then connected to his boss in Johannesburg. "Mr. Meijer, I'm certain the owner of the mine's lease has no idea about the iridium.

"She comes off like a fool, but she's wily. She agreed again to let me tour the mine if I made an offer within 10 days. I'm to wait for her manager— a man named Gideon Schechter, to call me." Rhett moved away from an overhead vent that pumped cold air down his back and stepped out of the restaurant onto a hot sidewalk.

"This Schechter person is the same fellow who called himself John Smith and sold you the iridium nugget." Rhett continued.

"I told her you need a business asset that will lose money at first to offset gains elsewhere. I think she believes me, so she gave me mostly straight information on the zinc mine; it's poorly perform-ing but has potential. It hasn't produced any ore the last six weeks due to a broken conveyer belt. I'm guessing she was lying about the potential."

"Great progress, Rhett. I'd like to have everything wrapped up by the end of the week, can you do that?" said Mr. Meijer.

"I can do it." As he spoke the words, he regretted them instantly. Father Mavuso had told Rhett the whites expected blacks and colored to lie. *You should never make a promise to a white man unless you are sure you can keep it*, the old priest's advice came back to Rhett.

Rhett paused to think about an impulsive promise he had made to Father Mavuso—a vow to protect the frail priest. Not only had he not protected his former mentor, Rhett had shattered everything the priest held dear. Rhett's destruction of Father Mavuso had been utterly savage and absolute.

As penitence for the sins he committed against the old man, Rhett conceded he would need to complete his duty to Mr. Meijer.

15

· · · · · · · · · ·

GIDEON PUNCHED THE TALK button on his walkie-talkie as he guided the ATV toward a padlocked shed stacked with crates full of iridium ore. "Snuffy, what's up? Blaster just told me something I did not want to hear. He saw a Beaver with floats in the area. Did another plane land in the glacier lake?" Gideon made sure his voice had an unmistakable ring of authority despite its higher than expected pitch.

"Yep. This time it looks like a tour group of about six people. This makes four landings in the last month. What do you want me to do?" Snuffy's voice sounded distorted as if he held the walkie-talkie close to his mouth.

Gideon stopped the ATV. "What the fuck? Why now? Why all these visitors? We got to stop all this attention to our mine. Time to show people that Shaman Mountain is a scary, haunted place."

Gideon put his mouth close to the walkie-talkie as his voice crept up an octave. "Wait until one of the tourists wanders from the group and kill him. Stash the body in the glacier like we did that gook miner that died last week. Try to make it seem like a ghost made the tourist just vanish."

"Shit! How am I supposed to do that? There's six of them and one of me? I'll probably get caught," Snuffy's voice sounded a bit garbled. Gideon could image him picking at his scalp. "I can just shoot one of them from a short distance. That would be easy and scare them away."

Gideon applied pressure to the ATV's accelerator and moved slowly toward the storage shed with his precious iridium. "Don't shoot one, you dumb fuck. That will bring too much attention. We just want one permanently lost. Keep an eye on them. I'll be down there when I can get away. We can figure out how to grab one without alerting the others. We're just now opening a fresh vein of ore, and I want to make sure it doesn't get screwed up. I'm going to call someone in Anchorage, and see if we can't get some extra help in keeping visitors away."

Parking the ATV near the generator hut, Gideon walked toward the aged metal-sided office/living quarters for the white mine employees. The front door was held on by just one hinge and more windows had plastic covers than glass panes. A blue tarp covered the sagging leaky roof on the west side.

Gideon shook his head sending rock flakes off his shoulder-length hair. *This whole fucking mine is just one big pile of deferred maintenance. If that tightwad Schiffmeister would just put some money into this place, it would be a halfway decent zinc mine, and a world-class iridium mine.*

Gideon walked into his private quarters, the sole room with its own bathroom, and the only clean place in the mining camp. Like many mines, dust covered everything—except Gideon's stuff. He kept his quarters with military-style neatness. It was the one place in the mining camp where he felt relaxed. As he walked to his bedside table, where he kept the camp satellite phone, he looked back into the workers' bunkhouse area and noticed someone had drawn male genitals on the China travel poster with the pretty Asian girl.

Schiffmeister saved a lot of money by recruiting laborers from China and Indonesia, but she sacrificed efficiency by introducing language barriers. They were often illegal so he had to keep them away from communication equipment. If they called the cops, he and Schiffmeister could get busted for human trafficking.

Gideon picked up the sat-phone. He checked the charge on the battery. Dead. He swapped out the dead battery for a fresh one in the base of the charger. By keeping the phone in the ready position, it ran down the battery in a day.

Looking at all the dust on surfaces in the common area, he imagined himself in a pristine new home in Seward. It would be right on the bay where he could fish anytime, take his big boat out to an island and hunt, or gaze at his chest full of gold coins.

None of this would happen if word got out about the iridium strike. He'd need to give all the iridium to that bitch Schiffmeister. There is no way in hell he would let anyone or anything steal his dream.

IT TOOK A FEW CALLS to get through to Solomon Quigley, head of the Alaska Opportunity Party and bigwig federal mucky muck. After hearing Solomon's voice, Gideon reminded Solomon of their time together in AOP meetings and functions.

Once the small talk was over, Gideon got to the point. "Superintendent Quigley, I need your help. We're trying to run a mine up here on Shaman Mountain, and suddenly we got all kinds of visitors taking time away from our operations. Can you figure out a way to ban recreational visitors? Shaman Mountain Mine is a leased parcel on federal land. Hikers are in danger. We got avalanches, blasting, and mine shafts. It's dangerous up here."

"Did you say Shaman Mountain?" Solomon's voice revealed interest.

"Yes, and I know you can issue some federal regs to keep people away," said Gideon looking up at his collection of traditional and fantasy weapons hanging on his wall.

"Have you seen any wolves up there?"

"Wolves?" *What the fuck is he talking about?* wondered Gideon. "We hear them all the time, but I've worked here for two years and only saw a couple of really young white ones last summer. But the wolves aren't the problem. It's the visitors. Right now they got a campsite less than a mile from our operations. There's also Kila Glacier. That place is super dangerous for tourists."

"The wolves are more of a problem than you know," said Solomon. "And we can't have visitors taking note of them. I'd like to take a look at that campsite. Maybe there's some federal regulations they are violating."

"What? No. You don't need to come up here. We are swamped. I can't spare anyone to show you around." Gideon couldn't believe his ears. *Not more visitors!* "I'll take a picture and email it to you."

Gideon heard Solomon tapping on his computer keyboard. "OK, I brought up our file on Shaman Mountain Mine. My notes say you have an Indian caretaker who spends the winter months looking after the mine. Why can't he show me around? He may know more about the wolves."

"You mean Aguta, that crazy shit?" Gideon's voice rose. *What's with his obsession about wolves*, wondered Gideon. *The guy's nuts*.

Gideon noticed his voice was rising and consciously brought it down, "That Indian doesn't know anything about tourists. He manages the avalanche problems in the snowy seasons. Does a hell of job, too. But we hardly ever see him in the summer unless he has game to sell us. I'm not even sure where he lives. Probably a dirty old cave. He just shows up when the snow starts to fall."

"Send me the coordinates for your landing strip. I'll fly my own plane and be there mid-morning tomorrow. I'll try to find Aguta to show me around."

The call ended. Gideon stared at his sat-phone. "What the fuck!" Gideon's voice rose as he yelled at a Klingon sword hanging on the opposite wall. "Now I need to clear the logs off the landing strip. Another interruption to the mining! Quigley might see the iridium storage area. Fuck! Fuck! Fuck!

Pissed, Gideon grabbed his "baby", a Sig Sauer P320 chambered for 9mm. With a polymer frame and grips, it was light, accurate and deadly.

Before the army kicked him out for "accidently" breaking the jaw and facial bones of a fellow soldier during hand-to-hand training, he had qualified as marksman with the P320.

If he had remained in the army, he would be close to retirement now. It wasn't Gideon's fault that the guy he was sparing with didn't know how to fight.

As a teen, his religious parents had sent him to Israel to "straighten him out". Instead of getting religion, Gideon enrolled in a Krav Maga fighting school.

After seven years, the school expelled him for nearly removing the fingers of his instructor. *That was his fault*, mused Gideon. He trained me to attack preemptively and target the body's most vulnerable points. *The asshole was lucky I didn't attack his liver*.

Before heading down the mountain to join Snuffy, Gideon found Blaster, wearing his old Harley Davidson hat, by the main camp generator involved with replacing the oil filter.

Years ago, Blaster had been working on a truck when a small explosion tattooed his face with black specks. He always looked like he needed to wash, and the look wasn't helped by his long greasy dreadlocks and his unruly brown beard.

Blaster started nervously when Gideon silently came up behind him and spoke. "Blaster, take some of the gooks down to the runway and roll the logs off."

"Jesus! You made me jump," said Blaster as he dropped a filter wrench.

"Everything makes you jump. Just get that strip cleared off. I'm expecting a visitor." Gideon turned to leave.

"I thought you didn't want anyone but the scheduled supply planes landing here? You were all bent up about a plane I saw approaching the glacier lake last week," said Blaster, his prominent Adam's apple bobbing as he cleared his throat.

"An important guest is coming," called Gideon from across the yard. "I'll be gone for a couple of hours helping Snuffy with a project down the hill near the glacier."

"Why can't Chewy or Leo do it? I'm busy," complained Blaster.

"I have something special for Chewy and Leo," answered Gideon.

16
. . . .

BETTER THAN MOST PEOPLE, Blaster knew that Alaska could be hard on a bush plane. Multiple landings on gravel, ski or float landings, exposure to salt water or touchdowns with big bouncy tundra wheels can take a toll on a plane built in the 40s or 50s.

The unfamiliar plane coming in low to the freshly cleared Shaman Mountain Mine landing strip looked to Blaster as if it had been through a lot. Gideon had said he was expecting someone, but Blaster did not expect that the plane would come in moments after he finished clearing the strip.

Gideon liked to keep the strip "under repair" to discourage visitors, so usually they only saw scheduled supply flights.

The high-winged Cessna 180 made a low pass before making an awkward touchdown that ended in the gravel on the far side of the strip about 2,000 feet from Blaster.

Hand shading his eyes, Blaster waited by the staff buildings at the opposite end of the strip and watched as five men got out and unloaded packs from an improvised cargo hatch.

This Cessna was definitely a beater long past a needed paint job and who knows what else needed attention. The 230 horsepower Continental engine appeared to run smoothly from far across the landing strip, and it surprised Blaster that the pilot left the engine idling as passengers and cargo were unloaded. Blaster, not known for his curiosity, wondered about these guests of Gideon.

The pilot climbed back into the plane and took off, ascending into the Alaska summer sky and banking south. Blaster looked to where the men and their packs had deplaned and saw they had hiked into the woods leaving a small box at the end of the runway.

The engine sound faded as Blaster nervously approached the box. In it were four bottles of expensive bourbon and a note thanking Shaman Mountain Mine for letting them land. This is weird, thought Blaster as he admired the bottles. Fancy whisky was rare at Shaman Mountain Mine.

AFTER WATCHING THE BATTERED 180 take off, Slade led his helpers into the woods near the landing strip. Slade's team, who introduced themselves as A-B-C: Able, Bonner and Charlie, was selected partly because they were small in stature.

Their smaller bodies would allow Slade to take more gear on the bush plane. He could take more gear, but he worried about these little guys.

They were all members in good standing with the AOP and had attended many militia trainings, but he wasn't sure they had the juice to live in the wilderness and kill wolves. One guy, Able, said he worked at a car wash for Christ's sake.

As soon as they had set up a camp, Slade would brief them on their mission. The mission goals were clear: kill wolves and don't get caught. This meant killing some prey animals to set carrion traps, salt the carrion with the poison packs, and repeat until the wolves were all dead. He figured it would take them a week at most to kill the wolves on Shaman Mountain.

Slade looked over his team. The men dressed alike in black Carhartt work clothes, but new looking. Their gear had probably been supplied by the AOP. Able was the most muscular with his gymnast body but Charlie was built like a middle school boy with sticks for limbs. Bonner seemed to fit between them in build.

In one of their backpacks, freshly unloaded from the plane, was a solar battery charger and a folding Mavic Pro drone fitted with an infrared camera to find game and wolves. It wasn't sporting to hunt and kill animals when you knew exactly where they were, but sport was outside their mission.

UNSEEN BY SLADE'S TEAM, and concealed by brush and shade, a figure with a compact build, Asian features accented by high cheekbones and stubby teeth observed the team. Aguta, wore clothes he'd made himself mixed with some high-end outdoor gear. Aguta watched uneasily as the four men prepared their hunting camp.

Aguta had lived on the isolated mountain he called Kila Ikpic for eleven years working to recapture the long-forgotten spiritual truths and powers of his native culture.

He lifted the pant leg of his caribou-skin trousers to touch the wolf tattoo on his ankle. He might need some of that power now that so many strangers were coming to Kila Ikpic. Until the last several months, only the Shaman Mountain Mine people and a tour guide had visited the area.

The mine people had hired Aguta to perform avalanche mitigation to keep their buildings and infrastructure safe from the seasonal snow/rock landslides. This job had provided Aguta with money and access to their supply planes.

Aguta brought his Swarovski 10 x 42 binoculars to his eyes and gave the hunter's camp a careful examination. He noticed that instead of traditional hunting rifles, the men all carried Colt model 604 military-style weapons—called M16s by the Army. In his former life, Aguta had served in the US Army and had trained on the deadly M16 long gun and other weapons. He found it odd that all four of the men had the same expensive gun, as if they were equipped from an armory.

Training the binoculars on the camp, Aguta noticed four small boxes stacked up near the largest tent. Their labels said: Sodium Fluoroacetate, Formula 1080, Small Mammal Poison, Product of Australia.

Why would they bring so much of that nasty stuff? Aguta wondered. Animals killed with that powerful toxin were also toxic to scavengers—his wolves. These men were not hunters. They were exterminators.

Aguta felt a surge of anger and fear. These men would try to kill his wolves.

17
· · · · · · · · · ·

"IS EVERYONE READY FOR A HIKE to see the hot spring and our bathing place?" Dylan smiled at the group. They looked fresh after their breakfast and clean up.

"I'd like to see the glacier this morning," said Jennifer shrugging into a light jacket.

"Me too," said Jun looking up from his samples and rock-testing equipment.

"Well, I hadn't planned on anyone bathing, I just want you to know where everything is." Dylan had planned to take his group to a natural hot spring bathing place where warm shallow water cascaded and pooled over smooth black rocks.

Monte hefted a huge camera, "I'd like to see the glacier and scout some photo locations I saw from the plane."

Dylan looked at Bryce and Reggie, "How about you guys? Want to see the glacier first this morning?"

Bryce shrugged, but Reggie said, "I'm down with seeing the glacier. Can we touch it?"

"Ok. Glacier it is. And everyone will get to touch it."

Dylan glanced up at a darkening sky. "We are going to pack light, but bring rain gear. We move out in 10 minutes."

After about a half-mile of hiking, a loud, concussive glacial boom startled everyone. The group jumped in surprise.

Dylan mentally slapped his forehead for not warning them of the sounds Kila Glacier made. "It's OK everyone," Dylan said.

"The Kila Glacier is quite active and sometimes a 60-foot column of 3,000 year-old compressed ice is 'bent' by the pressures. Since ice isn't very flexible, it makes a lot of noise under pressure. It can make an explosive sound much like a shotgun or artillery shell exploding.

Jun laughed. "I know that not shotgun, but it loud!"

"Are you former military?" Bryce asked Jun. "You reacted fast."

"He's a retired cop," said Jennifer. "He trains recruits at the police academy. They are supposed to know what to do in an emergency like a random gun shot."

Reggie pulled off his Vikings hat and bowed in an exaggerated way. "An expert! Hey can you show me how to do the choke hold?"

"That hold is too dangerous. Too many people have died when law enforcement used it," said Jun good-naturedly. "But later I'll teach you to how to deal with assailant who attacks you from behind."

"Cool!" said Reggie.

As they got closer to the glacier, its other noises became audible. Deep, eerie groans and close and distant booms could be heard. Dylan knew many inaudible sounds were also coming from the glacier. These could be felt as a deep, penetrating throbbing or as vibrations caused by hidden interglacial rivers.

Dylan pointed to a spot about a half-mile to the west on the terminus of the glacier. A large shelf of blue-white glacial ice started to slide into the water below. Moments later a sustained crashing sound reached the hikers, followed by loud booms that thrilled the group.

"Was that icefall a calving?" asked Bryce, who couldn't take his eyes off the place where the calving occurred.

"Yes, it happens every day, but you need to be lucky or patient to see it. The sound of calving is loud, but sometimes the sound doesn't reach a viewer until it's too late to see the calving since sound travels so slow," said Dylan.

Dylan led the group to a safe place he had scouted the previous week.

Monty pointed with his camera to part of the glacier that had a particularly dramatic look. "Can we go over there? I see some blue ice towers."

"You would never want to get close to those towers. They are called seracs, and are very dangerous. Fractured ice like that can fall or even explode outward. Photograph the seracs from a distance using a long lens."

Monty looked disappointed. "Does that mean we can't hike close to the end of the glacier?" He pointed to the high cliffs and towering seracs at the glacial terminus.

"Not this glacier," said Dylan. "It's too active. You can see all the water flowing out from under the glacier; Kila Glacier is full of flowing water. The flow pattern can change at any moment and a hidden lake could burst out of the glacier. It's very dangerous."

"Can we hike on it?" asked Bryce.

"Not today, but I will take you up there later," said Dylan. "We need to bring our crampons, ropes, ice axes and a crevasse probe. After a safety lesson, we'll hike on a more stable part of the glacier."

Dylan did a mental count of everyone. *Where is Jun*? "Jennifer, where's your dad?"

Jennifer looked alarmed. "He went down there." She pointed toward an area with some smaller seracs.

"Stay here, everyone," Dylan said as he threw off his pack and trotted down the hill parallel to the glacier. Moments later he saw Jun picking up a black rock sample in a place where the glacier had cut away part of a rocky hill.

"Jun, you can't wander off," Dylan's chest heaved as he caught his breath.

"Look what I found. Igneous rock randomly distributed in a metamorphic area! Metamorphic rocks surrounded this igneous rock quite some time ago. There has been no volcanic action here, so what melted these rocks?" Jun pointed to a black line in a place where the glacier sheered a cut in a hill. "Look here, this line of black runs through this hillside. There was a heavy burn here a long time ago. I also found this," Jun pointed to what looked like a religious alter arranged on a log with carved figures of animals, small pouches and some animal bones. "Are these ancient Indian relics?"

"Nope," said Dylan. He pointed to a shiny ten-foot aluminum ladder, a beautifully polished ice axe and a well-used crevasse probe nearby. "Someone put these here recently." That ladder looks new and could serve as a bridge across crevasses or work as a sled. Very handy on a glacier walk."

Dylan peered closely at some of the animal bones. "This is a canine skull, probably a large coyote or small wolf. Don't touch them. We need to leave this place unmolested. This looks like a spirit altar. It's special to some native people."

As soon as the pair returned to the group, Jennifer held Dylan's satellite phone out to him. "This keeps beeping and showing text messages from your pilot, Shelia saying unexpected storms are moving into the area, and that we should evacuate."

FROM HIS HIDING PLACE on the rocks, Snuffy handed his binoculars down to Gideon and said, "There, you see? Tourists!"

Gideon looked and handed the glasses back. "We'll stick with the plan. One of them will disappear in the next few hours." A sharp gust of wind shook the trees nearby. "You go down and burn their camp while they are at the glacier. Make it look like lighting or ghosts."

"Storm's coming. I got to do this fast," observed Snuffy as he started down the hill toward the campsite.

18

· · · · · · · · · · ·

THE HIGH-PITCHED BUZZING sound of a small drone seemed to annoy the woods. Thin trees tossed and shook in the pre-storm gusts.

"It's too windy," said Able, a small man whose thick upper torso made Slade think the guy spent hours lifting weights. "I need to bring it down."

"That's OK," said Slade. "We now know where the game hang out, and we can get one of the caribou on the other side of this ridge. That drone is handy." Able tapped the return to home button on the cell phone screen where they were watching the animals. Moments later Able packed up the small drone, his thick arms moving quickly. The others gathered around Slade for a quick strategy meeting.

"I've been here before and shot a small caribou in this same general area. There's some snowmelt just above this ridge that waters fresh new plants. The drone confirms game in that location. Charlie, you go up high. Then after Bonner and I are in position, you move down the draw slowly. You don't want to startle the caribou, just make them uneasy so they walk past us."

"There's caribou in this forest? I thought they needed big rangelands?" asked Charlie, a small man who reminded Slade of a gullible middle-school boy.

"This forest has really small caribou. I don't know why," said Slade. "Maybe for the same reason these wolves are small. Perhaps the glacier and tall mountains form a special climate here that favors smaller animals and prevents migration."

Slade signaled Charlie to move out, then he and Bonner started in the opposite direction.

An hour later, the four men hiked back to their camp, a fresh caribou hindquarter over Slade's back, leaving the rest of the caribou carcass sprinkled with poison packs. Able acted so excited, his voice sounded giddy. "That was so cool! We get fresh meat tonight, and a bunch of dead wolves in the morning."

"We don't know if the wolf pack will find the carcass tonight. Sometimes the carcass needs to ripen before they find it. That or the magpies will tell the wolves where the free dinner is at." Slade wished he had asked Able to carry the meat.

The four men walked right past Aguta without seeing him standing in some deep forest shadows. After the men were over the hill, Aguta followed their tracks back to the caribou carcass.

Carefully, Aguta used a gloved hand to pick each poison pack out of the carcass and place them in a burlap sack. After that, he pulled down the front of his pants and urinated over the caribou carcass. No wolf would touch it if marked by Aguta's urine. When he finished, Aguta removed any trace of his footprints as he left the area.

On his way back to his cabin, Aguta tried to figure out why anyone would come onto Kila Ikpic and try to kill the wolves. Aguta knew that the wolves drew their power from the mountain, and he gained his power and wisdom from them. He would do anything to save them. He looked down at the sack of poison packs.

Anything.

19

. . . .

DYLAN GATHERED HIS CLIENTS around him. "Look, this rarely happens, but sometimes we get powerful late summer storms. This one is a doozy. Already, the Aleutian Islands are getting 45-foot waves and the central low pressure is 928 millibars!" Dylan held out his black satellite phone showing a message from Shelia.

"What does that mean?" asked Jennifer.

"Hurricane Katrina was only 920 millibars. Since the trajectory of the unexpected storm has shifted toward us, we need to evacuate. Shelia will be here in an hour."

"Why didn't you tell us about this before we left" asked Monty putting his camera under his rain jacket.

"The storm was headed southeast. NOAA told us the storm wouldn't be a problem," said Dylan.

"I heard Shelia, the pilot, tell Dylan not to worry," said Jennifer pulling her rain hood up.

"What about our camp?" asked Bryan.

"We will need to pack up in a hurry and get down to the lake. We'll only take our personal items. I have insurance to cover the loss of my equipment." As Dylan spoke, he had an uneasy feeling about the camp. Maybe it was the tiny hint of smoke in the air that alerted him.

As the group approached their campsite, billows of black smoke hid their tents. Throwing down their daypacks, the group ran toward the flaming camping area to see what they could do. Orange, windblown flames licked from every tent. A strong smell of camp fuel hung in the air.

Dylan couldn't believe it. One tent catching on fire would be a rare event, especially since he had inspected each one. But to have all of them in flames made no sense. Arson?

"Let's get down to the river," said Dylan. "We'll wait for the plane there."

Monty hefted his pack and started down toward the lake. "Good thing I have my main camera body. It has the memory cards for the shots I've taken. My long lenses are in that flaming tent. I hope that's insured."

I hope so, too, thought Dylan.

Jennifer pulled out her cell phone and took pictures of the burning area. This seemed to frustrate Dylan. He cupped his hands to his mouth. "Everyone, we need to gather at the landing area. The Beaver will only be here long enough to load. They need to get away before the really big winds come."

That seemed to do the trick. In no time, the group was standing in a shivering cluster near the rain-swept rocks where they unloaded just the day before.

"Dylan, why didn't you tell us about this?" Monty wanted to know. "I paid you a lot of money and used up my vacation time for this trip."

The rest of the group seemed to suddenly realize their wilderness trip was about to end. They looked to Dylan for an explanation.

Dylan, like the others, felt disoriented. It seemed that moments ago, the trip was going fine, now their camp was smoldering and a dangerous storm was forcing emergency evacuation. For a moment, he tried to remember if he'd taken his PTSD meds that day as he found himself feeling unreasonably nervous.

"First of all, I would never take anyone on a trip where I knew they would lose their money. I'm a highly-rated guide because I take good care of my clients," the wind blew Dylan's hair around. "Everyone will get a credit for another trip."

"Credit? I want my money back and replacement camera gear," yelled Monty through the wind.

"Hey!" yelled Jennifer. "Where's my dad!" She spoke as she started running up the hill.

Dylan looked through the rain at the smoking ruins of their campsite to see the distant figure of Jun jogging back on the trail to the glacier. This was the opposite of what Dylan needed.

"Damn!" whispered Dylan. "Everyone, stay here! I'm going after those two. My guess is that Jun forgot his rock samples." As he spoke, the distant, noisy Beaver could be heard approaching."

Dylan yelled ahead. "Jennifer! Come back! I'll get Jun. You wait here." But his voice seemed to be lost in the wind and the vast wild area around Kila Ikpic.

Jun was nowhere in sight, and Jennifer ran up the hill with startling speed.

Dylan caught up to Jennifer near the path to the glacier. As they approached the glacier, Dylan felt an odd sense of unease. Jun's rock hammer lay near the place where he had found the odd igneous rocks and the small altar. His baseball cap was near the pack, but there was no sign of Jun.

"Jennifer, you need to go back with the others," Dylan panted. "I'll find Jun. It's not safe here. Icefalls can hurt or kill people. I've personally known people who died from an icefall."

"I need to find my dad. You don't understand, he came on this trip to look at the rocks, not to enjoy wilderness camping."

Kila Glacier made an eerie groan and baseball-sized chunks of ice fell to their feet. Dylan glanced up nervously at the glacier. "Quick! We must move away from the glacier. It's not stable and those seracs above us could fall."

"But my dad," cried Jennifer looking around.

The glacier groaned again as hidden pressures deep inside the massive river-of-ice exerted themselves. High above Jennifer and Dylan, a towering serac leaned and fell. Somewhere nearby a loud explosion startled some ravens in a nearby tree. Looking up, Dylan could see a cascade of softball-sized ice chunks about to fall in their direction.

He pushed Jennifer away, but it wasn't far enough. A pile of blue/white ice soon slammed into Dylan and Jennifer.

"GO FASTER, OLD MAN," yelled Snuffy as he prodded Jun.

"Why are you doing this? I'm not doing anything wrong," panted Jun as he trotted on stiff legs up the hill followed by Snuffy and Gideon. Trees bent and swished in the rain and wind.

"We caught you trespassing on Shaman Mountain Mine property. We're taking you to the police," said Gideon.

Jun stopped abruptly and turned to face the men. "There's no police up here. I'm a trainer for the Washington State Police Academy. You are not law enforcement. Let me go. My party is leaving now. I just came back to grab my rock samples."

"Rock samples!" echoed Gideon, his voice sounded oddly high in the gusty winds. "Why are you collecting rock samples? Who put you up to this, some mining company? What do you know about Shaman Mountain?"

Ignoring the questions, Jun lowered his voice but spoke with authority. "Let me go, now. Or I will bring in the authorities."

Snuffy knew they needed to get Jun farther away from the tourists. Gideon's plan was to make one of the tourists disappear and have it look mysterious. That meant they needed some distance from the others. Snuffy put his hand on Jun's chest and pushed. It was a mistake. Jun parried the force of the push, and Snuffy found himself on his back with Jun standing over him—the old man's fists cocked back and ready for a fight.

Gideon laughed from behind Snuffy. "You just got thrown by that old man half your size. What's the matter? Can't you take him?"

Fuming, Snuffy stood up and sarcastically shouted. "Oh that karate stance really scares me." Snuffy's meaty fist shot out fast at Jun's face, but by reflex, Jun deflected the blow and instantly landed a rib-cracking double-counter punch to Snuffy's side breaking some ribs. Snuffy fell to his knees his arms hugging his chest.

Jun looked from Snuffy to Gideon. "I'm very sorry to hurt your friend, but I must go now."

Gideon eyes widened with anticipation. It had been a long time since he had hand-to-hand combat with a trained fighter, even if it was an old man. "You need to take me down if you want to leave," said Gideon as he pulled off his jacket letting the rain soak his shirt, his heavily muscled chest showing through the wet undershirt.

"We don't need to fight. I didn't want to hurt your friend, but he left me no choice." Jun spoke with a quiet, soothing voice.

"Take off your pack, unless you want to fight me while wearing it."

Stiffly, Jun turned and hung his backpack on a nearby tree limb then pulled off his jacket.

Gideon assessed Jun's style as defensive and relying on disabling counter punches. Gideon's martial art, Krav Maga, a merciless Israeli attacking style with the goal of maiming or killing would be completely unexpected by this old man who taught police how to defend themselves without causing their opponents permanent injury.

Jun, up on the balls of his feet, knees slightly bent with his fisted hands near his waist, appeared utterly calm as he faced Gideon.

Gideon just smiled, "This is going to be fun."

Jun did not wait for a strike to counter punch. He hurled his coiled body directly at Gideon, his wiry old man's fist aimed for a nose-crushing strike.

Without conscious thought, Gideon moved to the side and pushed Jun past, unbalancing Jun. Jun's momentum and the push by Gideon, sent the old man down to his hands and knees in the mud.

Panther quick, Gideon leaped on Jun slamming the old man hard onto his stomach. With his hands on Jun's shoulders, Gideon brought his legs up high as if to start a handstand and came down forcefully with his knees onto Jun's spine. A sickening snap followed by crunching sounds as Gideon's knees broke Jun's back and several ribs. Instantly, Gideon's lethal hand, formed into a deadly blade, snapped down onto Jun's neck breaking his spine in a second place. The entire kill took less than a couple of seconds. Of course, Jun wasn't exactly dead, just completely paralyzed and quickly dying.

"Shit!" yelled Snuffy over the wind. "That's the most amazing take down I ever seen! And you did it to a trained fighter." Snuffy bent down to peer at Jun.

Blood and mucus clogged Jun's labored breathing as his body struggled for air. Snuffy ended Jun's labored breathing by picking up a nearby baseball-sized rock and caved in Jun's skull with several vigorous strikes.

"That will teach the little asshole to mess with me," said Snuffy rubbing his lower ribs.

"I doubt if he's in any condition to learn something," said Gideon wiping his hands on his pants.

WELL HIDDEN IN SOME WINDSWEPT bushes but close enough to hear Jun's spine snap, Aguta watched Gideon and Snuffy drag Jun's body through the rain and down to the Kila Glacier. He watched them stuff the body into an ice cave, then hide it with gravel and ice.

I will have more work on the next clear night, thought Aguta.

HOURS LATER IN AN anchorage hospital, Dylan awoke to recall a powerful headache, and Shelia's face above his. Sounding far away and faint, he heard her voice telling the campers to get Dylan and Jennifer away from the glacier and down to the plane.

Rain, snow and wind emphasized the chaos. Dylan was aware of excited voices around him. Later, he wouldn't remember the bumpy take off as Shelia crabbed the wings to account for the winds coming down from Kila Ikpic.

Dylan would have no memory of landing in Anchorage or of leaving Jun behind.

20

· · · · · · · · · ·

RHETT STILL FELT STRESSED even after his second hour-long workout. Alaska was so strange with so many white people who act like they've never seen a man with his skin color. It reminded him of his first days in his Swiss boarding school.

Rhett wanted to go home. He didn't really belong there either, being somewhere in the no-man's-land between the black and white worlds, but it was so much better than Alaska. Adding to that stress was a collapsing time line. That white clown, Ursula, told him to expect a call from Gideon, but then he heard nothing for two days. When he called in a report to Mr. Meijer, he had to listen to the impatient white man berate him for his tardiness.

Now there was a huge late summer storm cloaking the Shaman Mountain Mine, so travel was impossible for who knows how long. Rhett felt like he was a caged jaguar longing to be free.

In his extravagant room at the sparkling Nesterov Hotel, Rhett turned on his tablet and logged into the website for his internet phone service. He knew it was risky to program his phone software to show Ursula's name on the caller ID when he called Gideon, but he needed to make progress. Gideon could be angry at being tricked into answering his phone and refuse to see him, regardless of Ursula's wishes. This could be especially true if Gideon was intentionally avoiding Rhett.

After completing the simple task of manipulating the Caller ID information that Gideon would receive, Rhett called the sat-phone number Ursula had provided. The call was answered almost instantly.

"Yeah, Ursula. What's up?" said a high-pitched voice Rhett assumed was Gideon.

"Gideon, this is Rhett Sims. I'm using Ursula's phone. I just want to give you a heads up that I'm visiting Shaman Mountain Mine as soon as this storm abates."

"Let me talk to Ursula."

"Too late for that. Just get ready to show me the mine and all its assets. If there are any delays, Ursula will fire you and have you thrown off the mining site. She is in a hurry to sell her zinc mine. I'll be there as soon as the weather allows. Don't call Ursula back. Her mind is made up." Rhett terminated the call before Gideon could say anything. *That went well*, Rhett thought. *Even in the storm, the call went right though. The bastard has been stalling.*

Restless, Rhett knew needed some action. After a computer search, he decided to get a drink in the Fairview area of Anchorage. It had a crime rate over 100% higher than the national average, and criminals don't call the cops when there's a bar fight.

Just in case he needed it, Rhett checked his back holster for his ceramic throwing knife. This razor-sharp, superbly balanced blade fit between his shoulder blades and could be whipped out and thrown with stunning accuracy. Since it contained no metal, he could easily take it through metal detectors.

An hour later and after assuring the taxi driver that he wanted to go to the biker bar called Prospector's Sluice, Rhett walked calmly into the noisy bar.

It smelled of beer and sweat. Amongst the harsh metal rock soundtrack, a loud clack of billiard balls penetrated the smoky haze.

Rhett was the only black face in a room full of rough, white biker-types with big biceps and bellies. In contrast to Rhett's tight designer workout clothes, most of the patrons wore leather and denim.

Rhett walked right up the bar and ordered a Shirley Temple—a drink guaranteed to bring derision from the locals.

The bartender looked nervous. "Hey buddy. I can tell by your accent that you're not from around here. I suggest you leave."

"Just give me the drink," said Rhett.

An obese, potato-faced woman wearing a leather vest over her bulging breasts spoke in a loud voice. "Hey Darky. Are you sure you belong here?"

"You mean because I'm not dirty?" answered Rhett.

The woman turned to the huge man next to her. "Hey Ricky, did you hear what that nigger said to me?" She turned back to Rhett. "Darky, you'd better leave."

"I'm staying here until I finish my drink," answered Rhett. Before coming to this place, he had decided not to inflict any permanent injuries on anyone. It could bring unwanted scrutiny and delays. He just wanted to hit someone who hated him based on race. He got his chance when big Ricky approached Rhett and stood inches away. An obvious dare.

Rhett picked up his drink and moved it side-to-side in front of Ricky's face. By Ricky's odiferous breath and the big man's eye movements, Rhett could tell he was drunk. *This will be too easy,* thought Rhett as he put his drink down.

Ricky moved his hand toward Rhett as if to grab his throat. Rhett batted it away and said, "Just leave me alone. I don't want your dirty hands on me."

Instantly Rhett detected a narrowing of the pupils, and increased respiration and heart rate in Ricky's big body: a result of a rush of adrenaline. Ricky was preparing to attack.

Rhett let his vision go wide taking in the room, including the mirror behind the bar where he could watch others.

From this visual standpoint, Rhett would be able to see the slightest moves from any part of Ricky's body as well as other patrons. People around Ricky were putting down their drinks and coming over, presumably to watch Ricky beat up some uppity black guy.

Rhett licked his lips, and his thought processes became hypervigilant. When his mind did this, Rhett's brain could take in information and process it so quickly that it was as if he was viewing the activity in the room in slow motion.

Rhett saw Ricky bring a low fist upward as if to land a fierce uppercut to Rhett's chin. Rhett grabbed Ricky's wrist and, using Ricky's momentum, brought the fist up high, then back behind Ricky's head and held it there. Ricky looked ridiculous with his hand painfully pinned behind his head looking like he was trying to scratch his own back.

When Ricky brought his other fist up, Rhett used the pinned wrist to spin the big man around so his back was to Rhett. Placing his foot on the biker's back, Rhett pushed the big man forward and kicked him harmlessly in the butt sending Ricky facedown to the floor.

"That nigger just attacked Ricky! Get him!" yelled the potato-faced woman.

This was what Rhett had come for: beat up some racist assholes. He hoped he would not lose his temper.

Rhett's mind continued to slow down all the action in the room. He calculated all the risks and prioritized his actions. He had only two other assailants at first, probably Ricky's drinking buddies. But after they were down, one with a broken sternum and the other with a broken cheek, three more bikers came at him.

One of these had a knife. Rhett had to allow a glancing blow to his shoulder from one man, in order to grab a beer bottle and shove the small end into the knife-wielder's mouth breaking dozens of teeth.

When the knife clattered to the floor, Rhett stood over it as he disabled the next three with joint-destroying blows to knees and nose-flattening strikes. So much for no permanent injuries.

With the floor covered in blood and writhing, broken bikers, Rhett picked up the knife. In just moments, Rhett had incapacitated six men, and the barkeeper was leaning down to pick up a shotgun from behind the bar. *Time to leave.*

Rhett backed himself out the front door of the bar brandishing the biker's knife. Once he had closed the door, he jammed the knife into the door crack slowing down anyone who might want to open the door.

A sharp, well-placed kick to a line of shiny motorcycles toppled six of them like dominoes. Another kick to a bike's gas tank resulted in a gasoline leak. Rhett used a lighter to ignite a wet stream of gas near the leaking bike. While he vanished into the stormy night, a roar of burning bikes and angry cries leaped into the sky.

As the darkness enveloped him, Rhett knew Father Mavuso would not approve of this type of recreation. Father Mavuso understood the urge to strike out at white men, but not at the poor and foolish. *Alas, Father Mavuso wasn't perfect*, thought Rhett. *And neither am I.*

21

. . . .

THE STORM HAD PASSED leaving the night clear. Aguta knew it would be the perfect time to send Jun into the afterlife.

According to the stories told by the old women of his village, Aguta knew that if a man approached the afterlife as a warrior, he would be allowed to become one with the aurora borealis and play in the night skies forever with friends.

It was usually women's work, but since there were no women here, Aguta took it upon himself to inflict post-mortem wounds on a good man's body, so he could live forever and play in the night skies with the other warriors.

Aguta's family was gone; lost to poverty, domestic violence, depression and suicide. The bad times had started a century ago when the government took all the children from the village and sent them to boarding school.

There, the children were forbidden to speak their own language and taught to distain their culture and native knowledge that had allowed the villagers to thrive in a harsh environment. Adrift, and without belonging to any culture, the whole tribe seemed to collapse.

After running away from school, Aguta depended on his rarely sober mother and a disabled grandmother for his formal education. He had to learn to hunt and fish from his uncles. But the women taught him the songs and stories of the village. The women told him how to send a deceased man to play forever in the aurora.

Aguta felt his age as he dug Jun's body out of the ice cave where the miners had buried it. He lashed the body to his shiny aluminum ladder and dragged it up onto the glacier. His eyes were not what they used to be, and he was grateful for the brilliant starshine reflected off the glacier to see where he was going. Using his ladder, he was able to cross some dangerous crevasses and find a suitable ice-alter to perform the ceremony.

Kila Glacier, eerily quiet at the moment, seemed to wait in anticipation for Aguta to carry out his gruesome chore.

After removing Jun's clothes, he sharpened his walrus-tusk knife on a piece of silvery Kila Ikpic rock and began singing the monotonous women's mourning song. Aguta brought his knife down on Jun's ankle. Continuing with the song, he worked his way up the body delivering cuts that the gods would mistake for war wounds.

When Snuffy had buried a Chinese worker, killed in a mining accident, on this same glacier; Aguta had sent that honorable man to the heavens as a warrior.

Now it was time to wound Jun's head. These were the most important cuts. After some savage blows to the face, scalp and neck, Aguta dragged the nearly decapitated body to the edge of a deep crevasse and watched it slip over the edge. Kila Glacier trembled.

Aguta, nearly out of breath, felt satisfied when he heard the glacier moan and saw the beginning of the aurora overhead.

"Who will do this for me when I am gone?" Aguta whispered.

22

. . . .

JENNIFER STOOD BESIDE HIS BED and started shaking Dylan, despite the hospital staff's prior warnings not to disturb him. "Wake up, Dylan. God damn it!"

From far away Dylan could hear her voice, but could not remember where he had heard it before. Her voice sounded harsh and caused a painful headache to erupt in the front of his skull.

"Dylan, do you hear me? Wake up!" Jennifer continued to shake him. A wave of nausea overcame him and he threw up in Jennifer's direction.

"Oh shit! You barfed on me!" Jennifer whined as she backed up.

A painful bright light flashed in his eyes. A nurse had turned on the room light and entered the room. In a quiet but firm voice she said, "If you want to talk to him, you'll need to wait. He's had a concussion. He will heal faster if you just give him some quiet."

Jennifer turned to the nurse. "But he is our guide, and he left my dad up on Shaman Mountain. We need to go back and get Dad!"

"This man is in no shape to go to Shaman Mountain or anywhere else. Besides, until that storm blows over, no one is going to that part of Alaska." As the nurse talked, she led Jennifer from Dylan's room and out into a hallway. "If your dad is lost on Shaman Mountain, you should call the police. They will alert the various rescue organizations."

"I've talked to them. They contacted the Shaman Mountain Mine and told them to keep an eye out for my dad, but the mine people said they couldn't do anything until the storm calms down." Jennifer looked as if she was about to cry.

"There, you've done everything you can," the nurse patted Jennifer's hand. "Now you just wait until tomorrow, and Dylan should feel better."

IT WASN'T UNTIL three days later that Dylan could leave the hospital with instructions to return if his symptoms got worse. Jennifer dogged him all the way home. "Dylan, you've got to help me find my dad. The search party organized by the mine couldn't find him or any sign of him."

"Jennifer . . . your dad. I'm so upset about this." Dylan thought back to when he lost his fiancé and two clients on a winter ascent of Denali many years ago.

"We've got to go back," said Jennifer. "The authorities have changed their goals from a rescue to a recovery situation. They are sure my dad is dead. If that's so, we need to get his body. My family is going crazy."

"I'm pretty woozy right now. It's hard for me to think," Dylan said in an overly quiet voice. "I want to help you, but I'm sick. Besides worrying about your dad, my business is in trouble. I've had to cancel my next trips. That cost me a lot of summer income. I'm just getting my Anchorage guiding business off the ground. I have bills to pay.

"Plus, some guy from Department of Interior called to say they are going to pull my guiding license due to gross negligence. If they do that, it will kill the rest of my summer income." Dylan held his head in both hands as if trying to figure out the connection to his guiding license and the DOI.

"Dylan, I can pay for your services. Plus, you owe me. You left my dad on Shaman Mountain."

Shaman Mountain, Dylan thought. *It's like that mountain has it in for me.*

23

. . . .

"HEY BLASTER, IS THAT LANDING STRIP ready? I just got a call from the visitor I'm expecting. He should be here soon," Gideon yelled from the kitchen.

So that plane that landed hours ago with the whisky wasn't the expected flight? Blaster ran his hand down his beard greedily and called out from his bunk. "Yes boss. I got it all cleared off. That storm put some blow-down on it, but me and the gooks got it cleaned up."

Blaster nervously checked under his bunk. *The whisky is still there.*

"The guy that's coming is a big shot with DOI. He's just checking into the zinc mine, so don't mention any other minerals if you talk to him. Also, he's curious about those wolves we hear at night." Gideon's mouth was full of food as he walked into the bunkroom with a bowl containing a cube of butter and a pile of saltine crackers. "You should get your lunch so you don't eat in front of this DOI guy. We don't have enough extra rations to feed him, too."

"Sure thing, Boss," said Blaster, thinking about the whisky.

IN HIS CESSNA 180 SKYWAGON, Solomon tried again to call Slade on the sat-phone.

No answer.

Solomon punched the button to leave a voice message.

"Slade, this is Superintendent Quigley. I'm guessing you are hunting wolves and have your phone turned off. I'm going to land at the Shaman Mountain Mine landing strip soon, and I want to see your wolf extermination progress. Find me at the landing strip."

Solomon terminated the call as he scouted the area around the mine looking for the hunters' camp. If he couldn't get a guide, he'd find the hunters' camp himself.

BLASTER LOOKED UP. The Skywagon flew a pattern over the woods. Blaster had already made sure all the Chinese workers were hidden in the iridium mine, so the zinc part would be clear for inspection. It wouldn't go well if some DOI guy saw some undocumented workers.

Solomon's high-winged tail-dragger did a fly over above the landing strip then banked to start a landing pattern.

Gideon looked up and admired the pristine red-on-white paint job. Someday he'd have his own pretty bush plane and learn how to fly it.

After the plane bounced to a landing on its oversized tundra tires, Solomon taxied it over to the office area of the Shaman Mountain Mine.

Solomon got out and approached Blaster. "Where's Gideon?"

"He's coming. I'm Josh, but they call me Blaster," said Blaster extending his hand.

"Mr. Quigley," Gideon's high-pitched voice cut through the diesel exhaust and campfire smoke of the mining camp. He waved as he walked toward the Cessna.

"You can call me Superintendent Quigley," said Solomon looking around as if to see some wolves.

"Certainly, Superintendent Quigley. Like I said on the phone, we need to make our meeting brief. I'm short-handed at the mine, and the end of our mining season is near. The snow gets so deep here, we can't get anything done in the winter. We have some things to discuss."

"I understand," said Solomon. He reached into his plane and pulled a box of donuts and a fresh, daily paper to hand to Gideon. "This is for you and your crew."

Blaster's eyes lit up expectantly.

Solomon went on. "I know you are busy, but I didn't come to check out the mine. I want to know more about the wolves in this area."

Gideon looked confused. "The wolves . . ."

"Yes, I want to see them if possible," said Solomon.

"I've only seen them once, and I've been here for five years," said Blaster.

"I've never seen them," said Gideon.

"I saw some a couple of years ago when I was hunting. They were around a caribou carcass, but my view was across a canyon, and they looked like white puppies. They ran away when they noticed me," said Blaster.

"Have you spoken to my guy, Slade? He and his hunters may have contacted you," asked Solomon.

"Who?" Gideon was more confused than ever. Blaster looked at his feet.

"Never mind," said Solomon as he reached into his Skywagon and pulled out a contraption that turned out to be a folded rifle. Gideon recognized it as a Kel-Tec Sub 2000. A small carbine that shot pistol ammo and can fold small enough to fit into a briefcase. Did you contact that Native guy who lives up here in the winter? He could show me around."

"You mean Aguta?" said Gideon. "We never see that crazy fucker until the snow starts to fall. He is our winter caretaker. He's nuts, but he has a way of reading avalanche danger. Until we hired him, we'd lose a shitload of our infrastructure every winter due to slides." Gideon pointed in the direction of the Kila Ikpic summit. "He uses a bazooka that fires a concussive artillery shell to get the snow moving before it's heavy enough to cause any damage."

Seeing that Solomon was about to march off into the woods, Gideon blurted out, "Superintendent Quigley, remember? We were going to discuss how to keep so many people from coming here?"

"I've already taken care of it," said Solomon over his shoulder. "Dylan Baker will not be bringing any more tourists up here. I made sure he lost his guiding license."

"We also need the mining lease extended. It's going to expire soon," said Gideon. "I have the papers in my office."

"I don't think you need it extended. You are hardly producing any zinc now. I'm closing down this mountain." Solomon turned away and started marching toward the woods.

Blaster pointed toward the other end of the runway where Slade and his hunters had gone. "Superintendent Quigley, I heard some wolves over there last night."

"Fine. I'll look there. You can go on with your work," said Solomon checking his Kel-Tec. "I'll only be here a few hours, I have a ton of meetings back in Anchorage late this afternoon."

"Sir!" shouted Gideon at Quigley's rapidly retreating figure. "Sir, you can't close down this mountain."

All he got back was a shrug from the Superintendent as he disappeared into the woods.

24
· · · · · · · · · ·

A TAXI DROPPED DYLAN off at the tiny apartment above his office. There he found three very disturbing items. One was a letter informing him about the revocation of his guiding license.

Another was an article in the local paper that made it seem like he was at fault for the loss of Jun on Shaman Mountain. A recovery mission mounted by mine employees had failed to produce Jun Lee's body or any sign of him. Ghosts were mentioned.

The third item was an astronomical bill from the mine for the costs of the recovery mission to search for Jun's body.

On top of this, Dylan's insurance company was holding back funds pending an investigation of gross negligence on Dylan's part.

Dylan received the recovery bill since someone in power had decided it was his fault that Jun was lost and presumed dead.

The storm that forced him to evacuate his clients brought in three days of freezing weather, thus the police determined Jun could not have survived the elements. Dylan agreed with the assessment of Jun's chances of survival but not with the bill. It seemed like someone in authority was trying to put him out of business.

The newspaper article, full of inaccuracies, made him seem like a terribly irresponsible guide. Dylan understood that the loss of Jun had been out of his control, yet he still felt guilty. *Any time a client is injured, it's the guide's fault*, thought Dylan. His headache started to intensify, but he had to make a call.

An hour on the phone with a bureaucrat in Juneau did little to shed light on the decision to pull his guiding license. All he got was that "someone very high up" had ordered this. He could apply for another license in five years. Given the bad report in the newspaper, his guiding business had received a fatal blow. The article made him seem completely irresponsible for taking clients to such a dangerous place.

When a knock came on his downstairs office door, Dylan was feeling depressed, and his head ached. He almost didn't look out the window to see who it was.

Jennifer's voice floated up to his open window. "Dylan, I just found out the hospital let you out. Time to plan a trip back to Shaman Mountain. You owe me."

Dylan wanted to sit in his dark room and rest, but he felt he did owe Jennifer. He put his head near the window and told her to come up the back stairs.

When Dylan opened the door to let her in, he was again surprised by how pretty she was, and how well dressed.

Her face and makeup conveyed an interesting mixture of innocence and womanly confidence. Her clothes told anyone that this person had money and style. Even with just shorts, a cute top, and sandals, she looked amazing standing there holding two paper bags of groceries.

"Jennifer, I'm so sorry about the loss of your father," Dylan began.

"It wasn't remotely your fault. I checked. When we embarked on the trip, the weather forecast was just for a few rain showers and gusty winds. You had no way to know a huge storm would appear. No one did. It's this damn climate change.

"Besides, Jun went back to get something, and you got hurt trying to find him. Falling ice knocked us both out, but your head must not be as hard as mine. I feel nearly normal," Jennifer held up the groceries. "I figured you haven't had a chance to go shopping."

She started unloading the food and putting everything into the wrong places.

"Thanks for the food. How much do I owe you?" asked Dylan as he watched her move about his small kitchen.

He felt a strong attraction to her, but knew anything but a professional relationship was out of the question. And there was the fact that she was too young and way out of his league.

"You owe me a trip back to Shaman Mountain, or should I say Kila Ikpic. I want to find my dad's body and bring it back to Seattle for a family burial." Jennifer put a carton of dishwasher pods into the cupboard with the dishes and opened a box of cereal.

"I just heard that state police and volunteers had returned this afternoon after a recovery mission and still found nothing," said Dylan.

"I read that. But that article blaming you for the disaster was so full of shit, I don't trust that the state police did a good job. It took them a whole day to call and tell me they couldn't find his body. I had to learn it first online. Part of me hopes he's still alive. We need to leave as soon as you are able." Jennifer pulled a handful of cereal out of the box and started nibbling.

"If I guided a client back to Shaman Mountain, I could be arrested. The state pulled my guiding license."

"What bullshit! I'll have an attorney friend call someone in charge, but can't we just go as a couple of tourists instead of guide and client? We just ask Shelia to fly us in back there." said Jennifer reaching for more cereal.

"Jennifer, I'm broke." He waved the recovery bill. "My summer earnings get me through the winter, and I've basically lost my job and got a huge bill for the costs of sending that team to Shaman Mountain search for Jun."

"Dylan, I'm rich. As a rookie attorney, a running shoe I bought hurt me. Through a friend of mine who worked there, I found out that the shoe company knew the shoe would hurt customers, but sold it anyway. As a job-seeking, thirty-something attorney, I started a class action lawsuit that settled for tens of millions. Just plan the trip. I'll cover all the costs and pay you well." Jennifer pulled out her next scoop of cereal and continued.

"And I'll find a local attorney to contest this search and recovery bill. It wasn't your fault that Jun disappeared. You shouldn't have to pay for it, and you shouldn't lose your license. This seems like someone is trying to put you out of business." Jennifer put the box of cereal, still open, in the cupboard with the pots and pans.

"I thought women's shoes were supposed to hurt. How did you ever win a suit like that?" Dylan stopped himself from retrieving the cereal, closing the box and putting it in the right cupboard.

"I know, right? I won because of the health assertions the company made were made with full knowledge that their claims had no merit, that and I brought in a top law firm to help me with the suit when it got too big for me." Jennifer picked up a newspaper. "I want to see that article again."

"That newspaper story made it seem like I was a negligent guide," said Dylan as he quietly closed the cereal box and moved it to the pantry.

"Well, this article is bullshit. I'll write a letter threatening a lawsuit if they don't print a retraction and give you free advertising."

"I appreciate it, but I'm already out of business. I'm finished," said Dylan plopping into a chair and holding his head.

"Then you are free. You can take us back to Kila Ikpic. Start packing."

25

· · · · · · · · · ·

BLASTER TIMIDLY KNOCKED on Gideon's door. While he waited for the door to open, Blaster glanced back at Kung standing several paces back.

The Chinese miner wore a dusty yellow hardhat and dirty work clothes. Kung's impassive face and Asian eyes made the white workers wonder what the Chinese man was thinking.

When Gideon opened his door, he winced at the pungent smell of human body odor. He tried to decide who smelled worse, Blaster or Kung. He made a mental note to give the Asian miners some time for personal hygiene.

"What do you want?" barked Gideon. "Don't tell me someone else is coming for a visit. We had a hell-of-a-time time keeping that state police search and rescue team away from the mine."

"Kung here tells me that Way is gone. He thinks Way has run off," said Blaster. "Want me to get Chewy and Leo and go find him? Chewy and Leo can read tracks like no one else."

"Is that true? Did Way run?" asked Gideon looking at Kung.

In a strong Chinese accent, Kung agreed. "Way is much sad. He want go home and run away."

"Well he can't get to China from here," said Gideon.

Gideon pulled the walkie-talkie from his belt. "Hey Leo. We have a runner. Get Chewy and find the guy. It's Way, that skinny gook. Do you copy?"

A scratchy voice came back through the walkie-talkie. "They're all skinny, but I think I know who Way is. We'll go get him."

Gideon put the radio to his lips. "This time don't injure him, we need him to work, but you can rough him up so's the others don't get the idea to run."

"Sure thing, Boss," said Leo. "Chewy will find him. We'll have Way back before dinner."

Gideon knew Leo was right. Chewy had grown up as a subsistence hunter just a few hundred miles from the mine. He could track anything and anyone.

"What if we find he's dead? That last runner fell into a canyon and broke his back," Leo's voice sounded scratchy.

"Then bury him in an ice cave in the glacier like we do any of the dead gooks," said Gideon.

Behind his emotionless face, Gideon thought he saw a hint of rebellion in Kung. Gideon really needed Kung, the yellow fucker seemed to know where to look for iridium and was the only Chinese worker who could speak some English.

"Kung, tell your guys to take the afternoon off to bathe and wash clothes. This time I'll heat up some water," said Gideon. "You can wash your bedclothes, too."

"That will be very much appreciated Mr. Gideon," said Kung. "But why not give us one day off a week to do these things? And internet access so we can communicate with our families?"

"Don't push your luck. I told you, no one here has internet," growled Gideon. *Show these yellow dogs some kindness, and they see it as weakness.*

26

. . . .

SLADE WAS PISSED. He'd missed the visit from Solomon and a chance to show him their operation. He looked at the brief note Solomon had left on a log near their campfire pit and listened to the camp sat-phone for messages.

Why hadn't Solomon made arrangements ahead of his visit? Was he trying to surprise the wolf-eradication team to check on them? In addition to the note, Solomon had left a sat-phone message and texts explaining that he had tried to make contact.

Slade looked over at the solar battery charger with his satellite phone battery slowly gaining a charge. He should have brought more solar chargers since the drone took all day just to get a partial charge. All his batteries were low.

Slade winced when he heard Able, Bonner and Charlie arguing and complaining over by the solar charger. They griped about the storm, the food, their work, and about anything else they could think of. No matter how carefully he explained the importance of their work, the three men always saw the glass as half empty. Today might be different. They were going to try something new.

In the past, they killed game, cut open the gut and sprinkled poison packs around the internal organs the wolves seemed to prize.

Each time they checked the carcass for dead wolves, all they found was a rotting carcass covered with magpies and ravens. Often they would find wolf tracks, but no dead wolves.

One time they did find a dead red fox nearby. By the foam near the fox's mouth, they decided that he'd died from the poison. But the poison packs were gone, it's like the wolves liked to eat them.

This time, Slade decided they would stake out a carcass and shoot the wolves from a blind. The men complained about building the blind, but after it was done, Able and Slade killed a porcupine, cut it open and left it within 100 yards of the blind across an open meadow.

Able had made a mistake and cut open the scent gland on the dead animal. The stink of the porcupine amazed him. It already smelled like rotting flesh.

Slade hoped the smell would attract some wolves. What came first were the magpies and ravens. It looked like they were going to get all the soft parts. A bald eagle surprised Able when it perched in a tree to watch. It was as if it was waiting for the other birds to leave. It looked so mighty; it didn't make sense that it would let the other birds eat first.

From about 1,000 yards away, Slade spotted three wolves, looking like white specks, trotting across an open area and heading in the general direction of their kill zone. What he didn't see was Aguta about 500 yards away watching them with his binoculars. Slade also didn't notice Aguta put down his binoculars and hurry away.

Soon, Slade saw four more wolves cross the open area. Maybe they were all coming to the trap. He hushed the men and told them to hold fire until at least four wolves reached the kill zone. Slade fretted that someone would shoot the first wolf that showed up and all the others would get away. A gunshot would cause all the wolves to vanish.

As the birds quarreled noisily over the carcass, Slade pointed to a silently approaching adult male white wolf with green eyes. It squatted to urinate, so Slade knew it was a subdominant pack member. "Only the alpha male and female wolves lifted their legs to pee," Slade whispered to the men. "We want to prioritize killing the alpha wolves since they are the only ones who will breed."

From somewhere in the woods, a softly musical wolf howl floated into the kill zone, but the only wolf visible was that first subdominant adult male. The magpies harassed the wolf, but the ravens took to the trees when they saw it come close to the carrion.

Two more white wolves stepped carefully into the clearing keeping close to bushes.

Slade could tell that his men were trembling with excitement. He hoped they would wait and remember to take the targets they had agreed upon.

Suddenly, from high up on the mountain, a huge concussive explosion echoed off the rocks and forest. The two wolves near the edge of the clearing vanished like vapor, but the nearest wolf, fell to a crouch at the sound, then burst into a run. Slade and the others opened fire on the wolf. The sound of automatic fire filled the air, but the wolf zigzagged as it ran to the forest edge.

Slade saw a tuft of fur fly up on the rump of the beautiful, graceful animal. "I got it!" yelled Able. But the wolf kept running and in an eye blink, was out of sight.

They tried to follow its blood trail, but lost it in the woods. Bonner and Charlie talked about the possibility that these wolves were magic. After all, how could a wolf dodge all those bullets?

Slade decided to call it a kill anyway. He also wondered who was firing artillery on this mountain.

27
. . . .

JENNIFER FELT HAPPY when the loud Beaver airplane landed on the choppy shallow lake at the foot of Kila Glacier. On this trip, Sheila had flown directly to the shallow lake and not bothered to show Jennifer and Dylan Alaska wildlife.

To Jennifer, it seemed she and Dylan had rushed in a manic way to complete preparations for this trip, and then rode in the noisy Beaver as Shelia flew through the Alaska skies. No longer timid about leaving civilization behind, Jennifer jumped off the airplane's pontoon ready to move.

Dylan decided they would set up camp close to their previous, now burned campsite. It surprised her that, after their own camp was ready, Dylan went through the burned area collecting recyclables, trash and perhaps clues, to take back to Anchorage.

She watched him work and it bothered her that he was so deliberate, since she was ready to go out and look for Jun.

Looking around at the forest, mountain and the huge Kila Glacier, it seemed to Jennifer that this place was filled with a terrible, wild beauty that attracted her. The landscape also conveyed a sense of danger that made her uneasy. She couldn't remember ever seeing so many shades of green, from the blue-green forest to the milky green river flowing into the lake from the glacier.

The intense blue sky, cotton-ball clouds and the atomic-soft blue of the glacier seemed to fill her with energy and a vague longing. She felt like she understood what wild could be as she looked down at the groaning glacier. Her chest filled with energy.

Her thoughts turned to Dylan. In the past days her feelings about the handsome older man confused her. *Why do I feel this way? Is it because I miss my dad? Am I falling in lust with Dylan? He is good-looking and capable . . . and also wild.*

She found Dylan's presence comforting. He moved so confidently in this strange and beautiful place. He called to her from up a hill. "I'm setting a snare for rabbit. Maybe we'll have fresh meat tonight. Then we can start a preliminary search."

She felt like a little girl when she picked some flowers and arranged them in front of her orange tent as Dylan set traps.

Dylan's voice close by startled her. "Nice flowers. The yellow ones are edible. Let's go down to the glacier first and look there for signs of Jun. If there's a body, we might see magpies and ravens.

They are first to find carrion." Dylan suddenly looked stricken. "I didn't mean to say that your dad was carrion."

"It's OK. We need to know what we are looking for," grimaced Jennifer. Her eyes brimmed with tears.

As they started the trek toward the glacier, part of Jennifer wanted to find her dad's body and part was afraid she would.

28

. . . .

RHETT WONDERED IF THESE racist Alaskans could tell he was dark-skinned over the phone. He'd called nearly every charter airline service in the area. Everyone said they had no pilot available for a flight to Shaman Mountain.

He learned that one company, Shelia's Flight Service, had just flown in a pair of visitors the day before, but could not find any openings through the next week. Rhett figured no flight service would want to fly a man with his dark skin unless they could cheat him with exorbitant fares.

From the call to Sheila's Flight Service, he found out that the landing strip at the mine was under repair. That would mean he would need to charter a float plane to land on the glacial waters near Kila Glacier and hike a few miles uphill to the mine.

Rhett felt the pressure from his boss to complete his task quickly. Father Mavuso would have told him not to give up. The whites would expect to wear a black man down with hurdles so he could be easily controlled. Rhett would not give up. He owed that to Father.

By hanging out at the seaplane base, he found a beautiful yellow and black single-engine de Havilland Otter float plane that had just dropped off a passenger who'd flown up from Orcas Island and could take Rhett to the Kila Glacier Lake on his way back to base in Seattle. The fee would be under the table and paid in cash, so the pilot would not want any complaints to his company. Rhett thought the stocky, pale pilot charged a fair price.

"How are you going to get back to Anchorage?" the pilot asked. "You have a sat-phone?"

"No, but the people at the Shaman Mountain Mine have one. I've called them." Rhett tossed a small but heavy daypack into the Otter's rear seat.

Rhett settled into the co-pilot's seat and memorized how the pilot operated the plane. If he had to disable the pilot, he wanted to be able to fly the plane. After an hour or so of flying and watching, Rhett had confidence he would have few problems flying the Otter, but had no idea how to land it.

Rhett also thought about his decision to come on this trip armed only with the knife hidden between his shoulder blades. If he came armed, he would look less convincing as a rich buyer's agent from Australia and more like an assassin.

Hours later, the pilot made a short pass over the milky green Kila Glacier Lake, then assumed a landing pattern.

FROM A FEW MILES AWAY, Snuffy, Blaster and a beaten and bruised Way noticed the yellow and black Otter and watched it land on the glacial lake.

It surprised them to see light-skinned black man dressed in outdoor-gear chic, hop from the Otter's pontoon to the shore rocks.

They also spotted a fresh campsite near where they had burned down the other one when the tourists camped there a few weeks ago.

Snuffy pushed his hat back and called Gideon on the walkie-talkie. "Gideon, another plane just dropped off a passenger. A black guy who's all dressed up."

"Scare him off," ordered Gideon abruptly.

"Can't. He don't got no place to go. His plane is leaving," said Blaster scratching his head though his hat.

"Then you know what to do. When you're done, put his body in the glacier."

"Why do I got to do it? I'm busy. Leo and Chewy are gone, and they left me and Snuffy in charge of taking Way back to camp," Blaster twisted his hands as he talked.

Snuffy took the walkie-talkie from Blaster. "Gideon," said Snuffy. "It looks like a campsite is already set up for this darkie. It's right in the same spot where we burned out that last bunch of tourists."

"How could there be a site already set up?" Gideon demanded in his high voice.

"How should I know? We can't hear every plane that lands down there. We were just lucky to hear this one while we were bringing back Way," said Snuffy.

Gideon paused, then repeated himself slowly. "You know what to do. Kill the black guy and put the body in the glacier. I've never heard of a black guy traveling alone in the backcountry. No one will miss him. They'll say it was another Shaman Mountain mystery."

Gideon ended the transmission. Snuffy looked down at Blaster. "You do it. I need to take Way back to the mine. Besides, Cookie is making cinnamon rolls and I want a fresh one."

"Me? I don't do stuff like that. I want to take Way back to camp," rattled Blaster as he cleared his throat.

"You got your name from being such a good shot, right?" Snuffy pulled a small handgun from his pocket.

"Hell no. They call me Blaster because of my loud truck," said Blaster looking at the gun.

Snuffy handed Blaster a revolver, a small Taurus DT.357 Magnum, five-shot handgun. "This small revolver has a hell of a kick. Use two hands when firing it. Don't lose it. And don't shoot it just for fun, I only have one box of .357 shells."

Blaster nervously took the gun and admired its modern appearance with a black rubber grip, chrome cylinder and 2-inch black barrel. Then he turned his eyes down the slope toward the slender, well-dressed dark-skinned man gracefully stepping from rock to rock.

He's too dressed up for Alaska, thought Blaster. *He won't be for long.*

"OK, I'll do it," said Blaster caressing the gun. "Can I keep this?"

Snuffy laughed, "Get close before you fire. The short barrel makes this gun hard to shoot straight."

29

. . . .

DYLAN CHECKED JENNIFER's daypack and found it nearly perfect. However, instead of clipping her bear spray on her belt, she had buried it in her pack where it would not be ready in the unlikely event of a charging bear. Dylan clipped it to her belt, and smiled at her.

They practiced drawing their cans of bear spray and pretending to fire at trees.

Seeing she had Dylan's approval, she found herself feeling confident in her ability to enjoy hiking in the wilderness. On this warm day, they both wore cargo-style hiking shorts, baseball caps and light shirts with front pockets.

"First I'm going to show you to a natural bathing area. It's really on the way to where we should start searching for Jun. Clean, fresh water comes down rocks, mixes with a hot spring, and pools over smooth black rocks. I'm guessing you enjoy a daily bath," said Dylan.

"Great. Maybe you can wash my back," taunted Jennifer grinning mischievously at Dylan.

This confused and excited Dylan. He had found himself daydreaming about sitting with Jennifer in the evening, but to think of naked frolicking in a warm pool with such a beautiful woman, was not anything he thought remotely possible.

It was unethical for a guide to take advantage of a client. He decided she was not serious and tried to push the thought of her nude, soapy body out of his mind.

Once at the pool, Jennifer looked enchanted. Dylan could tell she loved the small waterfall, the warm pool, and the idea of being au naturel in such a wild and pristine place.

Jennifer found herself becoming very aroused as she looked at Dylan's lean, masculine body clothed as it was in hiking gear. She took off her pack, then her boots to sit on a warm, black rock and put her feet into the water. It was amazingly sensual to her, warm and flowing and so impossibly clean.

"We can drink this spring water as it comes down these falls. The aeration and UV rays from the sun adds purification to already clean water," said Dylan putting his cup under the falls and trying not to look at Jennifer's pretty legs.

As the waterfall splashed noisily nearby, neither of them heard Rhett's plane fly over and land just a mile away.

"Jennifer, put your boots on. We need to get to the glacier where we last saw Jun's hat. You can take a bath here this evening. I brought special soap and shampoo that won't hurt the environment," said Dylan indicating she should get ready to leave.

Soon they found themselves near the place where the glacier had dropped ice chunks on them. Both were exceedingly cautious as they scouted the area for signs of Jun. When Jennifer approached the place where Jun had found the ladder and the spirit altar, Dylan looked surprised to see everything had been moved around. The ladder lay on its side and some more objects adorned the altar.

Looking around, Dylan found a place where the ladder had been used to scale the glacier. It was a perfect place to climb since there was no danger of falling ice, and the top of the glacier was fairly close to the gravel base. "Stay here," he said to Jennifer. "I'm just going to see what's on top of this part of the glacier."

"I'm coming, too," said Jennifer. "He was my dad."

Moments later, the pair stood atop the Kila Glacier able to see it wind upward toward a distant wall of knife-edged mountains. Jennifer caught her breath; the power and beauty caused a flutter in her chest. She pointed to a smaller glacier to the east flowing into Kila Glacier. "What's that called?"

Dylan pointed in the direction, and Jennifer leaned her head against his arm to see where he was pointing. She could tell her touch was electrifying to Dylan, but he spoke in a normal voice. "That's a tributary glacier. I don't know the name. See the main glacier comes from the west side of those mountains. It's called the trunk glacier."

Jennifer's hand remained on Dylan's arm. He kept his arm up, and pointed to a dark line on the glacier where the tributary and trunk met. "That dark line in the middle of the glacier is made up of debris that falls from the mountains. It's called a medial moraine."

Jennifer, moved by the sight and her hands on Dylan's strong arm, looked up at Dylan and parted her lips.

He wants to kiss me! she thought. *I hope he doesn't go all professional on me.*

Dylan moved away and pointed to some scraping marks on the glacier's surface. "It looks like a sled or something made these marks."

"Let's follow it," said Jennifer her hand now by her side.

"Too dangerous. We would need a crevasse probe, crampons, and we would need to be roped together before I'd try following these marks. I don't think Jun made these. He didn't have a sled or crampons." Dylan looked at his watch. "We should be getting back to camp. I can check the snares and see what we will have for dinner, and you can have your bath."

"Couldn't that ladder be a sled?" asked Jennifer.

He looked down at her sparkling eyes and smiled warmly. *He wants to hold me. I can tell by his look.*

"Why yes. Ladders are useful as sleds when crossing a glacier like this. You are really observant, but we need to leave. You have that bath waiting for you."

"And you are going to wash my back," Jennifer threw her naughtiest look right at Dylan. She could tell his feelings were strong. Just then she wondered if the glacier was moving beneath them or was it emotions?

30

· · · · · · · · · ·

BLASTER WATCHED the well-dressed man take a compass out of his backpack and check it. Then he started hiking up the hill, but not right toward the mine, he was going more to the north parallel to the cliff that ran along the glacier.

This would take the man very close to Blaster's position. When the glacier made a loud explosive sound, Blaster watched the man dive to his stomach and roll. *This guy is really jumpy,* thought Blaster.

After watching the man climb for about 40 minutes, he was close enough for Blaster to see he wore some kind of designer hiking clothes, and not business attire. His shoes were black low-top hikers.

Blaster hunkered down behind a large rock, held the revolver in his hand and waited for the man to get close. *It shouldn't be long now.*

When the dark stranger didn't arrive, Blaster rose up, pointing Snuffy's pistol down the hill. Just to his right, some bushes bounced.

Forgetting to use a two-handed grip, Blaster fired two shots into the bushes. Despite the generous rubber grip on the powerful revolver, Blaster's wrist hurt like hell from the small pistol's recoil.

Certain that he had hit his target, Blaster stood up and stared hard into the bushes as he held the pistol two handed. "Alright, come out of those bushes, or I'll shoot to kill," yelled Blaster.

Suddenly, from his left side, the sound of a rock loudly colliding with another rock caught Blaster's attention. Carefully, he put two more quick shots in that direction.

"Let me throw another rock into the bushes so you can use up your last round in that five-shot revolver," Rhett's calm voice whispered into Blaster's ear.

Blaster was so startled, he yelped and fired the pistol into the air as he turned to face the whisperer.

Rhett reached over and grasped Blaster's sore wrist bending it painfully downward. The empty pistol fell to the ground. Keeping Blaster's wrist bent, Rhett reached down, picked up the gun and threw it deep into some bushes far down the hill.

"Ouch! Let go of me," shouted Blaster. "You messed up throwing that gun. Snuffy's going to be pissed if he doesn't get it back."

Rhett looked Blaster up and down, "You are ill. I can tell by your odor and pallor."

"What are you talking about?" coughed Blaster. "You a doctor or something?"

"I'm no doctor, but I can tell you have something wrong internally. You might not even know you are sick."

"Let me go," Blaster twisted to try and relieve some of the pressure from Rhett's grip. "I wasn't going to hurt you. Just scare you a little. We don't want people snooping around our mine."

"I'll let you go, but you need to answer some questions I have about the mining camp," said Rhett putting more pressure on Blaster's wrist.

"Oh my god! That hurts!" coughed Blaster. "OK. What do you want to know?"

"I need to know all about the mining camp and the staff composition." Rhett released Blaster, and turned him so they were facing each other.

"If I tell, are you going to let me go?" asked Blaster rubbing his wrist.

"We'll see. It depends on your answers," answered Rhett.

31

. . . .

ON THE WAY BACK to their camp, Jennifer accidentally dropped her water bottle when they stopped for a break. It rolled downhill over some rocks and through some bushes. When she disappeared into the bushes to find it, Dylan thought she was gone a long time.

Being discrete, he said nothing, but waited patiently at the side of their trail. Suddenly he heard her cry out. "Dylan, come here!"

Running downhill and crashing through the bushes and not knowing what to expect, Dylan came upon Jennifer pointing to a blue and white daypack hanging on a tree limb.

"This is Dad's pack! I know it," said Jennifer holding a small notebook she'd obviously removed from the pack.

Dylan looked at the familiar pack. "It looks like his pack. It's the blue and white waterproof Columbia pack. Let's take it back to camp."

"No, I want to look through it first. Maybe there's a hint of why Daddy thought it was so important that he had to go back for it."

The pack, stuffed with rock samples labeled with Chinese characters, also held a complex kit for testing mineral samples. Dylan had never seen anything like it. It was a whole lab in a box. They also found several other notebooks with brief notes written in Chinese.

"It's close to mealtime," Dylan said. "Let's take all this back and you can look at it while I fix something to eat." He knew she would feel better if she ate something.

Her eyes brimming with tears, Jennifer nodded.

Dylan slung Jun's absurdly heavy pack onto his back, and they continued the brief journey back to camp. Exploring Jun's pack would keep Jennifer busy and her mind occupied while Dylan cooked.

It wasn't long after they returned that rabbit stew and wild vegetables bubbled merrily on Dylan's camp stove. Jennifer had spread her sleeping bag over some sand and put each item from Jun's pack on it. She was scowling at a notebook when Dylan approached. "Dinner will be ready shortly. So what did you learn from examining Jun's pack?" said Dylan.

"OK, look at this," she handed Dylan a small zip bag with a jagged piece of what looked like platinum, but very shiny, almost wet-looking.

"It looks like a big piece of aluminum," said Dylan hefting the small nugget. "Whoa! It's heavy. Like gold or platinum."

"Daddy's notes said he thought it was platinum, but he tried to tarnish it was a mixture of nitric acid and hydrochloric acid, and it didn't tarnish."

"Your dad brought those chemicals on this trip! Holy cow! They are really dangerous!" said Dylan.

"He knows how to handle chemicals. He calls the acid mixture acid regia. He made a note here." Jennifer pointed to some Chinese characters. "He thinks this sample might be iridium, but there's a question mark next to his note. I guess he wasn't sure."

"Acid regia? Isn't that the nasty stuff that can dissolve gold?" asked Dylan.

"Dad expected it to dissolve platinum or at least to tarnish it, but it had no effect on this piece of iridium."

"What's iridium?" asked Dylan. "I mean I've heard of it, but what is it?"

Jennifer flipped through Jun's notebook. "It says here that it's the densest element known to exist, and it's extremely rare and expensive. It's the only noble metal that can't be tarnished by acid regia."

"If it's so rare, how did your dad find a piece of it when we were here only a day?" asked Dylan.

"Maybe it's not rare on this mountain. Maybe this whole mountain is full of it," said Jennifer wide-eyed.

"Wow," said Dylan. "Well it's time to eat."

"Not yet. See this other notebook?" Jennifer held up a smaller spiral bound pad that looked like a detective's notebook.

"My dad came to this mountain looking for my cousin. My dad has a sister who lives in Taiwan, and her son is a mining engineer. Someone from Alaska hired him to come and work in this state. If my cousin is here, we need to look for him."

"Is that something your cousin would do? Look for a job in such a remote place like this?" Dylan asked.

"I've never met this cousin, and it doesn't make sense that he'd want to work in a place like this. Dad had reasons to look for him here, but Dad often chased down weak leads."

Jennifer turned a page in the notebook and looked up. "My dad writes that my cousin was very secretive about the new job. He had to sign a confidentiality agreement not to tell anyone about it, but he let it slip that he was working at a secret mine."

"So that's why Jun came on this trip? To find his nephew?" asked Dylan.

"My dad's a cop. He knows how to find people. I wish he had told me why he booked this trip. I'm guessing his sister told him to find my cousin," said Jennifer closing the book. "As good as Dad was at finding people, I think he made a mistake on this one."

"What's your cousin's name?" asked Dylan glancing over at his stew.

"Kung Lee—a common Chinese name."

"I've been thinking about that iridium," said Jennifer. "It's probably really valuable. Do you think that's what they're mining up there?" she pointed up the mountain.

"I thought they mined zinc. We should hike up there and ask if they know anything about Jun and Kung Lee," said Dylan. "And they would love to know about the iridium if they don't already know about it."

32

· · · · · · · · · ·

AS SOON AS BLASTER had finished answering all of Rhett's questions, Rhett put Blaster into an eternal sleep quickly, then pushed his body down the cliff toward the glacier.

As he watched it bounce and tumble over the rocks, he thought that anyone examining Blaster's body would guess he accidentally fell over the steep cliff. The man would probably be dead or in the hospital within a week if he hadn't been pushed off the cliff.

Rhett puzzled over Blaster's response to the question about whose campsite was down by the glacial lake. Blaster thought the site belonged to Rhett. The African man felt uncomfortable not knowing who else was in the area. He would need to look into who was on this mountain, and who knew about the iridium.

His goal was very clear: prevent news of the iridium from getting out and preclude anyone else but Meijer from mining it. If the campers knew about the iridium, they would need to die.

Rhett felt uneasy about killing some white campers who bore no guilt, but his path was clear. As he walked, Rhett decided that surely Father Mavuso would understand that Rhett must do his duty.

Rhett was certain Blaster had been sent out to kill him. He wondered who would send such an incompetent individual on such a dangerous job. If the Shaman Mountain Mine people were trying to kill visitors, then it could be that everyone there knew about the iridium. Perhaps they knew that Rhett wasn't actually a buyer's agent from Australia or South Africa.

Rhett thought about the map of Shaman Mountain he had memorized. Since someone at the mine had sent out Blaster to kill him, Rhett decided to survey the area and gather information before presenting himself to Gideon as the buyer's agent Ursula had mentioned. He didn't have the luxury of taking a day or two to do it. His boss was getting edgy, and every day increased the chances that news of the iridium strike would get out. Rhett had to move fast. He started quietly trotting through the woods.

THE FIRST ODD THING that Rhett found was a tidy, hand-built cabin on the southwest side of the mountain. It looked like a subsistence hunter lived there.

Very little evidence of modern tools was visible except a large solar panel array on the roof. To Rhett, it seemed like the entire log cabin was made using hand tools.

The windows had no glass, but instead an animal membrane was stretched across the openings letting in light, but keeping out the wind and cold. Rhett kept a good distance away, since he didn't know if the owner had dogs.

Rhett decided that whoever lived in the little cabin, liked living there and would probably not be interested in iridium. Still, he made a mental note to learn more about the cabin's occupant.

Continuing his forest jog, he heard the wolf hunters long before seeing them. They appeared to be drunk and quarreling. He gathered from what he heard and his reconnoiter of their camp, that they were strictly hunters and not miners. By their vocabulary, he judged only the boss as well-educated.

Grateful to be jogging downhill, Rhett slowed as he came near the mining camp. From the forest, he could look across a gravel landing strip to two decrepit mining operations.

One was obviously active, and the other shuttered up. He guessed the closed one was the old zinc mine. Between the two mine shafts was an office, work buildings and bunkhouse area.

Staying in the woods, and using his binoculars, Rhett spent several hours patiently observing the mine. Besides noting the operation was in a shocking state of decay, he could see that Blaster had probably told him the truth about who was there.

He counted six white men and four men who appeared to be Asian. *The tall, blond man is Gideon*, Rhett thought. Rhett observed the deference the others showed the blond man.

At one point, one of the white men took a length of rebar and banged an old five-foot tall metal acetylene tank hanging from a tree limb near the mine entrance.

The amazingly loud gong sound must have echoed all over the mountain. It was likely the signal that the workday had ended. The Asian workers appeared to clean themselves up and start preparing a meal on an outdoor campfire.

All the whites walked into the buildings except for Gideon. He took off his shirt, put on some leather gloves and started a martial arts workout routine near an improvised exercise course.

The workout impressed Rhett. Gideon's large, well-muscled body moved incredibly fast—delivering killing-force blows to the padded logs set vertically in the workout area. Rhett decided he would not allow the deadly man to hit him.

He also noticed that the man's fighting style favored nearly all blows delivered by his upper body. Maybe Gideon neglected to work on his footwork—a potential vulnerability. Still, this man was dangerous.

Rhett put down his binoculars, and stashed his pack up a tree. It was time to chat with the miners.

33

· · · · · · · · · ·

JENNIFER AWOKE HEARING DYLAN outside fixing breakfast. Jennifer had always imagined herself as an urban girl. She liked the bustle and stimulation of a vibrant city, she liked stylish clothes, pick-up ultimate frisbee games in a local park, and she liked to bike to work and arrive at appointments in time to fix perfect hair and makeup.

She had pictured the wild outdoors as pretty but boring. There would be no wifi, nothing to do and everything would be dirty. Dirt was everywhere, but somehow the mountain seemed incredibly clean.

What she found was that being on Shaman Mountain, and seeing Alaska though Dylan's eyes opened up a profound world she didn't know existed. Jennifer became aware of natural contrasts: dynamic creation and destruction, of absolute silence and a symphony of chaotic forest sounds, of a night sky so black yet so full of brilliant stars.

The forest, the glacier, and the mountain all seemed like one integrated organism: forever changing yet retaining an n intense wild character.

She felt herself physically drawn to Dylan despite their age difference. He had to be in his fifties, still he seemed alternately boyish and yet projected wisdom earned from suffering.

His body was rodeo-cowboy lean and muscular, but his grey eyes looked soft and kind. She recognized he was a complex mix of passion and self-control, and strength and vulnerability.

And she found the immense privacy of the wilderness erotic. The woods care not if a person is naked or clothed, or if a couple made love in a forest. She had wanted to climb into his tent the evening before, but didn't want to rush things. She could sense Dylan was keeping a professional distance from her.

After breakfast, Dylan had strung Jun's backpack up in the tree with their food out of range for curious bears. They decided to continue their search for Jun near where they found the pack the evening before. After an hour of hiking, leaving the Kila Glacier behind them, Dylan suddenly stopped and listened. "Why are we stopping?" whispered Jennifer.

"Listen," Dylan whispered back. "Can you hear it?"

Jennifer didn't hear anything other than normal forest sounds: the breeze in the trees, a clatter of a small brook somewhere, and birds. After a moment, she could hear a harsh bird call that sounded like a rapid-fire repetition of At-At-At-At. She looked at Dylan and smiled an acknowledgment that she could hear the new bird sound. They both listened.

"Magpies. Over there," Dylan pointed to a grouping of trees about 200 yards away.

Her heart leapt to her throat. She felt her pulse quicken and her knees become weak. *Could it be my dad's body*?

Dylan started walking toward the trees. She followed tentatively. He noticed she was not keeping up. "Do you want me to look, then tell you what I find?" he asked gently.

She took his hand; it was warm and rough. "No. I'll look." A wave of dread came over her as they walked closer to the trees. She found herself gasping for air.

As they approached the trees, the magpie noise became harsher, as if the black and white magpies resented this disturbance to their meal.

Jennifer felt herself captured for a moment by the beauty of the birds. Their most distinctive feature, besides their loud, quarrelsome calls, was their strong black and white patches of feathers. Such dark, iridescent blacks and bright whites! Surely she had never seen such contrasting colors anywhere in her life. And she couldn't recall ever seeing a wild bird with such long tail feathers.

Soon they were standing close to a curious forest phenomena. She paused; then encouraged by Dylan's hand in hers, she walked up to the trees. The grouping of pines looked eerie to her. It appeared as a ring of same-sized trees arranged around a flattened circle of forest floor, but the body inside the ring was not her dad's. Inside the ring lay the carcass of a small white wolf, its belly opened by the birds.

Dylan entered the ring and examined the dead wolf. "It looks like a pup or a juvenile," he said as he stood over it.

Jennifer found her dread had vanished, and her heart rate started to return to normal. In a whisper she asked. "Is this . . . Is this a fairy ring? It looks so magical: a perfect ring around a pure white wolf. It's like woodland fairies made a perfect circle."

"No. The fairies don't dance in a circle here on magical nights. These trees grew up around an old stump. The stump decayed and is long gone, but the ring of trees is still here. Look, there's another small ring just over there by the creek," Dylan pointed up the hill about 10 yards. "But check out this wolf. It looks like it was shot, see here." He pointed to a wound on its hip."

"This place looks supernatural to me," whispered Jennifer.

"Hey," said Dylan looking in the wolf's mouth. "This is not a juvenile. Look at these teeth. It's a full grown adult."

"You can tell by the teeth?" asked Jennifer.

"Yes, young wolves have baby teeth just like humans." Dylan lifted the head off the forest debris. "Look at this. A green eye! The other eye has been pecked out, but this one was against the ground where the magpies couldn't reach it."

"Green eyes are unusual for a wolf?" asked Jennifer as she knelt down to see the eye.

"Usually their eyes are a shade of amber. I've never seen a wolf like this. The Aleutian Islands have a population of smaller wolves, but they are seldom white and have normal eye colors. This one is really special."

"Should we bury this body?" asked Jennifer.

"No. The forest will take care of it. It will feed birds, foxes, weasels and the small rodents will gnaw the bones to get calcium."

Jennifer looked around nervously, "Are there other wolves nearby?"

"I don't know. This may be an adult male wolf that lives outside a pack."

"Wait. I thought all wolves were pack animals."

Dylan pointed to the carcass, "This is a sexually mature male wolf. Often these animals leave their birth pack and go off to form their own pack. Every fiber of this wolf's mind was likely focused on belonging to its own pack. It hates being a lone wolf."

Jennifer looked up into the branches where the noisy magpies continued to complain about the humans disturbing their meal. "These birds are beautiful."

"They sure are. They are members of the crow family. They are so bold, that they will land on a moose and eat the ticks. They will steal food off your picnic table if you aren't careful," said Dylan straightening up. He looked at the circle of beautiful trees that formed a magical-looking ring around the carcass of the once amazing creature.

"It really does look like a fairy ring," said Jennifer. "Can we explore the smaller ring, too?"

The second, smaller ring had flowers growing in the center and still, flower-perfumed air. To Jennifer, it looked truly paranormal. "I'm going to name this place with the sweet flowers, Magic Ring."

Dylan smiled. "Good name. We should get back to camp. Tomorrow we go to the mine. We can ask them what they know about your father and this wolf," said Dylan turning away from Jennifer's fairy ring.

"Maybe they will know about the iridium," asked Jennifer. She looked over at the ring of trees containing the beautiful broken wolf carcass. "I wonder who would shoot a gorgeous creature like that?"

34

. . . .

SLADE OPENED HIS MEALS READY TO EAT
to find it was another jambalaya meal. It had to be
the worst MRE ever made. He knew he bought the
mixed selection of MREs for this trip.

One of the guys must have taken out all the good
meals and left the nearly inedible jambalaya meals
in the box. Bonner and Charlie were out in the wolf
blind waiting for the pack to return, so he could
safely search their tents.

As Slade approached Bonner's tent, he could tell
someone was in it. "Hey. Who's in there?"

Able's voice came out. "It's me. I'm looking for
something."

"What'er you looking for? Bonner's vibrator?"
Slade pulled back the tent flap to see Able
rummaging around in the back of Bonner's tent.

"No. It's just that I'm getting sick of this
jambalaya meal. I saw Bonner eating the
hamburger steak meal yesterday." Able held up a
box. "Ah ha! He has a shit load of the good MREs
hidden in his hip waders."

"That asshole!" burst out Slade. "Let's fill those
waders full of jambalaya."

The two men giggled as they switched out the
meals Bonner had stashed. "Why would he do
that?" wondered Slade. "He should know he'd get
caught. It's bad for morale."

"He said something about being borderline pre-
diabetic and needing high protein meals," said Able
zipping up Bonner's tent.

"That doesn't make any sense. If you are on the border of being pre-diabetic, then you are not pre-diabetic. Let's see what's in Charlie's tent," said Slade.

"I'll tell you what's bad for morale. We've only killed one wolf in all the time we've been out in these stinking woods. The whisky's gone, and all we do is argue with each other and steal shit from each other's tents. I can't even stand to take a shift with Bonner," said Able.

Slade knew Able was right. They were doing something wrong. The wolves were wary around the hunting blind, and they seemed to eat all the poison packs and not die. They found some dead magpies and foxes, but no dead wolves. Forest creatures, other than wolves, gobbled up the poison trap carcasses. *Could someone be sabotaging our project out here*?

While Able searched Charlie's tent, Slade stood outside. "Have you seen anyone leave camp after we've put out a poison trap carcass? I wonder if Bonner or someone is ruining our traps."

"Why would they do that?" asked Able. Slade could hear some glass break. "Oh shit, I broke a bottle of whisky."

"Charlie had a bottle in there? That asshole. He never offered to share," said Slade looking in the tent.

"It's not bourbon like you brought, it's Irish. He must have brought it himself. Whew! It really stinks like whisky in here. But there's no stashed MREs." Able backed out of the tent.

"I think those guys are untrustworthy. I'm going out to check on them. Maybe they are napping out there," Slade shouldered his rifle. "And don't go into my tent."

35

· · · · · · · · · ·

THE ASIAN MINERS SEEMED ASTONISHED to see Rhett. Whenever a visitor came to the camp, the miners worked where they would not be observed. Rhett saw evidence of bad nutrition, poor health care and overwork.

He thought of his mother's people: forced to work in the South African diamond mines years ago.

Rhett hated whites. He hated the part of himself that was white. It kept him from being a true part of his Zulu family. It kept him alone. These miners were alone and abused.

He controlled his emotions and politely asked if anyone spoke English. No one answered. He tried Afrikaans, Zulu, and various European languages he had learned in his Swiss school. One of the workers, a tall man with an intelligent face finally spoke up. "I speak English. Are you hungry? Do you want to share our meal?"

Rhett looked at the pitifully small meal that the four workers were preparing. "No thank you." Rhett dug in his pockets for some energy bars and offered them. "Would you like these? What's your name and where are you from?"

The tall man accepted the bars with gratitude and passed them to his comrades. "My name is Kung, and I'm from Taiwan, but my friends are from a part of mainland China you would call Inner Mongolia."

"I'm Rhett and from South Africa. My boss is thinking of buying this mine. I need a tour, and don't tell any of the whites I'm here."

Kung translated for the other miners who exchanged fearful glances. "If questioned, they must tell. Mr. Gideon will put them in the hole if he finds out they lied."

"OK. Tell them just not to volunteer information about me. Gideon is expecting me to visit, but he just doesn't know when. If my boss buys this mine, you will get paid well and given good food. I need a tour of the mine before I talk to Gideon."

Kung looked down. "If they catch me taking you into the mine, the trackers will beat me."

"Trackers?" asked Rhett.

"Yes, two big men who patrol the mine looking for anyone out of place. If one of us tries to run away, they can follow our tracks and bring us back. They love to find a reason to beat us," Kung said.

One of the workers said something to Kung. "He wants to know if you can get us out of here now. They promised us good wages and working conditions, but so far, we have not been paid, and we can't communicate with our families."

Rhett fumed internally.

"Maybe you have a sat-phone?" asked Kung.

It saddened Rhett to think these men probably knew about the iridium. If so, he might need to kill them.

"I have no phone," said Rhett. "But I might be able to borrow Gideon's. First tell me, what are you mining here? Can you give me that tour? I will not let the trackers harm you."

Rhett watched Kung internally process the promise of protection. "I can guide you, but the trackers are very big and mean. They will beat you, or even kill you since you are not needed to work in the mine," Kung said.

One of the other workers handed a bowl of rice covered with a brown sauce to Kung. As he ate, Kung led Rhett toward the mine. As they entered the mineshaft, Kung removed two hard hats with headlamps and handed one to Rhett.

Just outside the mine, Rhett noticed bins full of iridium nuggets waiting to be moved to storage, some the size of apples. Never had he seen anything like this. If these went to market, it could put Mr. Meijer out of business for good.

As they entered the mine, Kung and Rhett turned on their hardhat lights. Kung pointed up at dark overhead lights, "Those are run off a battery, but sometimes they work and sometimes not. We use the hardhat lights in the evenings."

Walking down a gently sloping path past side tunnels and avoiding stepping on small gage railroad tracks, the tunnel opened high up into a large black cavern about the size of a high school gymnasium. The walls were smooth and black as if burned, but shiny and translucent. Rhett felt as if he could see through the smooth walls into the rocks. From the walls and ceiling, thousands of tiny, sharp lights twinkled as if disco-ball mirrors covered the entire cavern.

Kung pointed down to the floor of the cavern about 20 feet below. "We need to go down this ladder to get to the floor area. Careful, it's not easy," gesturing to a rough wilderness-made ladder.

"I've never seen a natural cavern like this," said Rhett.

"It's a bubble formed when the rocks were very hot. The walls are basically glass with shocked quartz. Do you like the sparkles?" said Kung as he descended the rickety ladder. "We call this big room the Glass Dome."

The flat floor of the dome, about the size of an athletic court, seemed to be an area filled with debris that had filtered down from the ceiling and walls. It felt like walking on sand-covered-concrete.

Kung stopped before a steep-sided pit about 20 feet deep. "When the zinc miners found this bubble and the iridium, Gideon started workers digging here thinking they were finding platinum. This floor is very difficult to mine. The fallen debris has formed chemical bonds that make it like concrete." Kung turned around and faced Rhett. "Do you know what iridium is?"

Rhett nodded, but inwardly winced when Kung said *iridium*. He did not want to harm this miner. So many of his mother's family had worked in mines and suffered abuse by rich white mine owners.

"Gideon hired me online to supervise his iridium mining operations. I have a degree in mining. When he brought me here, I showed him a better way to get the iridium, and work stopped on this pit. Now Gideon uses this pit to punish lazy miners. He puts us in it, and it's impossible to get out. It's the worst kind of punishment—being shut up in a completely black cave and a floor of sharp stones and discarded mining equipment. He always gets his way."

Rhett thought about being trapped in the black hole with no way out. The walls were nearly sheer and steep. It would be the worst kind of solitary confinement: sensory deprivation and isolation. True mental torture.

"In the last few months, the upper edges of this glass bubble have produced the most ore," Kung led Rhett back up the rickety ladder to a path cut into the side of the dome.

They walked until reaching a side tunnel dug into the wall of the glass bubble. It opened into an area about the size of a large kitchen.

"We've been doing this for three months now. Here's where we are working today," Kung pointed to a flat place near a pneumatic drill.

Rhett brushed some rubble away and pulled out an iridium nugget the size of a walnut.

"Can you do something for me?" asked Kung shyly. "I need you to get a message out to my family. No one has heard from me or any of the other miners for months. Just an email saying you saw me would be wonderful."

Rhett looked sadly down at the eerily heavy iridium nugget in his hand. Kung was a dead man, but before ending Kung's life, he had to gain control over this mine. There might be a way to spare the miners.

Father Mavuso would have advised Rhett to find a way to spare Kung and the other miners at all costs, but Father Mavuso would have also told Rhett to complete his duty. This second precept made Rhett's path clear.

Never. Not once since the day of his precipitous confession to Father Mavuso, had Rhett ever let down his commanding officer or boss.

That confession! How Rhett wished he could take it back!

Rhett couldn't take back those destructive, dark moments in the confessional booth. But he could do something about the present.

Surely completing an agreed upon assignment was his duty. It had to be. *Father Mavuso would understand I must do my duty*, thought Rhett. *If I neglect my duty, then who am I?* Rhett felt lost and alone, and knew he must cling to his rock: duty.

"Kung, show me the other parts of this mine. I'm especially interested in other areas where you think we could find iridium."

Kung nodded. "We need to leave this shaft and hike up the mountain for a kilometer or two before it gets too dark. I show you some other places I have planned to sink shafts, but one is near a wolf den, so we must make sure they are gone.

A few minutes later, the two had emerged from the mine using a side entrance, and began hiking up a hill thick with forest undergrowth.

Kung spoke in a quiet voice over his shoulder as he led Rhett through the woods. "Watch out for the trackers who will beat me if they see I am away from my area. They will beat you, too."

"They won't beat me, I'm a potential buyer, but a wolf den?" asked Rhett.

"Yes, strange white wolves. Sometimes the wolves use a den near a potential iridium deposit. The men from Mongolia say the iridium gives the wolves special powers like spirits. And the trackers, Chewy and Leo, will beat you when they find you."

NOT FAR AWAY, the two trackers started on an intersecting path to Kung and Rhett.

36

· · · · · · · · · · ·

THE HIKE UP TOWARD THE MINE was much steeper than Dylan had thought. A human-made path made the hiking a bit easier. It was clear that miners hike down to the Gila Glacier River some-times—maybe to meet floatplanes.

It made Dylan uneasy when he found a place that resembled a hunting blind, where someone had spent hours behind a log that overlooked his campsite. He wasn't going to point it out to Jennifer, but she noticed a pile of human waste, toilet paper and candy wrappers near a small stream.

"Eww. Someone doesn't know enough to bury their waste? Gross!" she backed away.

Dylan took a small shovel from his pack and cleaned up the site. "Someone doesn't know any better or doesn't care. This should be buried at least 200 feet from a stream. Whoever left this mess didn't even bury it."

Gingerly, Dylan put the candy wrappers into a zip bag and stood up. He knew he would need to bring this up with the people at the mine. He could not bring clients here if the streams became polluted by human waste and garbage. First he would ask them about Jun.

After several hours of hiking, Dylan noticed they were getting close to the mining camp by the number of trails they crossed. The miners would likely hike around the mining camp area for various reasons, but not go any father than needed. Soon he could hear the clatter of a diesel generator sounding a discordant note in the soft air of the woods.

"What's that engine sound?" wondered Jennifer aloud.

"It's a diesel generator most likely," said Dylan. "We are close to the mine." Dylan slung off his pack and hoisted it up on a tree limb. "I'm leaving my pack here. No sense carrying all this stuff up the last quarter-mile."

"I'm keeping my daypack," said Jennifer. "Maybe there's a washing machine at the mine. I have a few things to wash out." Jennifer pointed to a sack near Dylan. "What's in there?"

"It's a bag of apples. Anyone bringing fresh fruit is welcomed into a remote mine," said Dylan picking up the apples.

Emerging from the woods, Dylan and Jennifer entered the Shaman Mountain Mining Camp. What struck Jennifer first was the utter dreariness of the place. Surrounded by pristine emerald forests, the camp was a single color: gray. Piles of rubble pushed back the forest and ugly disorganized piles of garbage were the only bright spots of color in the gray monochrome camp. A loud outhouse-sized diesel generator labored under the sagging roof of a shack and belched stinky, black smoke into the air. This created a low-lying cloud of malodorous exhaust that the pair had to walk through.

Approaching the office building, its pitiful condition shocked her. If ever she had imagined an abandoned mine building, this would be far worse. It appeared that little or no maintenance had ever been done on the property. A dim porch light that pulsed in time to the generator's metallic clanking was the only sign of life.

"This place is a dump," Jennifer said to Dylan as they approached the building with the light bulb.

"It sure is. I've never seen an operation so poorly run. It looks like it's going to shut down any day now, or it shut down several years ago and is now occupied by squatters. Don't comment on the condition of the mine, this is home to the people who work here." He hefted the bag of apples and handed it to her. "You offer the apples when we meet them. Let's knock on the door and make some friends."

Standing near the door, they could hear loud voices inside. A rowdy group of men were obviously having dinner. Dylan knocked on the door, but inside there was no sign that he was heard. He tried knocking louder, but no response. Trying the door, Jennifer walked into the building before Dylan could stop her.

She wrinkled her nose at the smell of unwashed male bodies and followed the sound of the men's loud voices to a large room containing a long trestle table covered in open cans, many with eating utensils protruding. Dylan trailed behind her.

As if hit with a stun gun, all talk and movement stopped as the men, dressed in dirty work clothes, looked up and saw a beautiful woman with a bag of apples standing before them.

The contrast to the drab surroundings and Jennifer's vivid feminine presence must have thrown the men off balance.

First to speak was a large, heavily muscled blond man who appeared to be the cleanest.

"How did you get here?" he asked looking at her bare legs. "Didn't anyone try to stop you? Where's Blaster? I thought you were a black guy not a Chinese chick."

Just as Dylan came up behind her, she brushed aside Gideon's questions and held up the bag. "Who wants an apple? Hey, can I take a hot shower and do a load of wash? I brought a change of clothes." She added the last part of her request as if that would surely get approval to use some of their hot water.

Gideon pointed to his private bedroom across the hall. "There's a shower in there, but we don't have a lot of hot water, so make it quick."

Dylan edged around Jennifer as she handed him the apples and headed for the room with the shower.

"We entered because no one answered the door when we knocked." Dylan extended his hand to the man with the blond eye lashes and dark pupils. "I'm Dylan Baker."

Confused, Gideon shook Dylan's hand. "And why are you here? Just to do a wash?"

"We're camped down by the glacier lake. We wanted to ask about Jennifer's father, Jun Lee. He got lost in this area about two weeks ago. We're also trying to find out if her cousin is here."

"Before we talk about those guys, I want to know a few things starting with, why did you come here in the first place?"

Dylan handed the bag of apples to Gideon who took one and passed the bag. "I'm a guide. My clients know this area as Shaman Mountain and are curious. I lead wilderness excursions."

"Take your clients somewhere else. This area is dangerous. Maybe the little lady's dad got lost and died. It's not the first time that's happened."

Gideon took an enormous bite out of the apple and resumed talking with his mouth full of apple bits. "Anyway, we got a call from the police about some missing guy. We haven't seen him. One of my guys, skinny with a big beard, reported a black guy coming up the hill. Have you seen either of those guys?"

"Nope. You are the first people we've seen since we've gotten here." Dylan looked around the room at all the white faces. "I don't see anyone here who could be Jennifer's cousin. Mind if I ask your men about Jun Lee?"

"Don't bother my men. They are busy." Gideon turned to an unnaturally skinny man wearing a battered white hard hat. "Hey Bones, go find Blaster. Last time he called in, he was at the glacier lake lookout."

As Bones left the room, Gideon turned to Dylan. "And after your wife showers, I want both you out of here. I don't want to be responsible for your safety."

Gideon grabbed another apple from the bag. Gideon knew that Shaman Mountain was a large area, and it would be entirely possible to have people all over the mountain and one party would not know about the others.

The other miners gradually adjusted to the shock of seeing Jennifer and her apples, and started talking. Soon the room was as noisy as before. Dylan munched on an apple and answered Gideon's barrage of questions. Abruptly Gideon asked a question that would land Dylan and Jennifer into hot water. "What do you think we do here?"

"You are miners. You mine," said Dylan.

"Yeah, but what do you think we mine?" Gideon looked closely at Dylan.

"Iridium?" Dylan pointed to a tennis-ball sized nugget on the table. In the dingy, dirty room, it shone with a soft, pure silvery light.

37
. . . .

KUNG AND RHETT HAD FINISHED the tour and started back to the Chinese camp, walking through woods that dripped with moisture.

Long strands of moss hung from the evergreen trees and deep forest debris cushioned their steps. Their movements were nearly silent but Rhett heard some male voices behind them on the trail. After another minute, Kung heard them too.

"Those are the trackers," whispered Kung. "If they see us, they will beat me." He looked scared. Rhett noticed his eyes had widened and the pulse in his neck quickened.

"Let me talk to them," said Rhett calmly. "They won't bother me. Why don't you find another way to return to your camp? Keep all your footprints on rocks so they can't track you. They're just following our footprints."

Kung looked doubtful. "They will beat you. They only beat us workers a little because they want us able to work, but they could beat you hard."

Rhett motioned Kung to leave as the voices became louder. As Kung disappeared into the woods, Rhett stepped around a bend in the trail and nearly ran into two rough men and their prisoner, obviously a Chinese worker who had run away, but hadn't gotten far.

One tracker stood tall and large as a refrigerator with a three-day growth of black beard and a round crew cut head. His hands and arms looked as if the man bent crowbars as a hobby.

When he saw Rhett, his big hand drifted toward a wicked black combat knife strapped to his thigh.

The second guard was about five feet tall but thick with muscles and wore smudged wire-rimmed glasses in front of a rat-like face.

Rhett noticed a Nazi SS symbol tattooed on the neck of Refrigerator and crude prison tattoos on the hands of Rat Face.

Between them a very slender man with Asian features walked with his hands bound behind his back. The Asian man was undoubtedly one of the Chinese miners, and he had clearly been recently beaten. Congealed blood covered the man's upper lip and left eyebrow.

The two white men appeared astonished to see Rhett walking in their forest.

"What the hell are you doing here?" asked Refrigerator, stopping short, his hand resting on his sheathed knife.

"I'm completing a survey of this property. What's your name?" asked Rhett in a quiet, confident voice. "I'm looking over my new mine. So if you boys work here, I need to know what to call you." His first impulse was to kill the two men. White African mine employees, who saw the black miners as having less value than a mule, had mistreated his mother's people.

However, if he killed the men, it might make it much more difficult to get information from Gideon and could draw attention to the iridium if outsiders found out about it.

"I'm Leo," said the small, rat-faced man with a remarkably deep voice.

Rhett could see no reason why people would call a dirty, rat-faced man, Leo. The men were close enough now, that Rhett noticed they smelled like they had recently eaten peanut butter. He also noticed the large combat knives strapped to both men's thighs looked clean and well-used.

"This here's Chewy," said Leo gesturing to the refrigerator-sized man. "What do you mean, 'your mine'?"

"I'm buying this mine," said Rhett planning his non-lethal assault on the men. He had to deal with the knives right away. "You can let that man go now. He's my employee as are you."

"The hell you say," said Refrigerator in a horse voice. "We're taking you into custody. You're trespassing on private property."

Leo pulled a black zip tie from his pocket. "Put your hands behind your back. You're under arrest."

"OK, I'm under arrest. I asked nicely for you boys to let that man go." Rhett decided that they would attempt to restrain his hands, then beat him. Judging by the marks on the Chinese worker, that's what they did to him. He noticed no marks on either tracker so the Chinese man had not defended himself.

Chewy lunged at Rhett and attempted to grab his arm, but Rhett swept his hands up knocking the larger man's hands away, then threw his shoulder into the big man's chest sending him backward over a log. As the refrigerator man fell, Rhett yanked the large combat knife from its scabbard on the big man's leg.

Rhett flashed the expensive kabar knife at the little man. "I'm going to cut the zip tie from the wrists of your prisoner. I'm not going to hurt you unless you attack me."

Rhett stepped up to the worker, turned him around and used the knife to cut the zip tie. Afterward, Rhett tossed the deadly combat knife deep into the tangled mossy forest where it would probably be impossible to recover.

"That was a big mistake, Asshole," said the smaller man pulling out his similar knife from its scabbard.

To Leo, Rhett appeared to move at super-human speed, but to Rhett, his brain's ability to quickly process input, had simply slowed down everything around him.

Leo appeared to move in slow motion, and Rhett perceived his own actions at normal speed.

Rhett grasped the knife hand of the smaller man, and drove the butt of the knife into the man's face crushing his nose and knocking him to the ground. That knife soon spun into the woods in the opposite direction of the first knife.

Shocked at seeing both of his captors on the ground, the worker hesitated, and then ran off into the woods, apparently to resume his escape attempt from Shaman Mountain Mine.

Standing, Chewy swung his huge fist right at Rhett's face, but Rhett batted the blow away. "Listen to me. I'm not going to hurt you unless you persist on this aggression."

Ignoring Rhett's words, the refrigerator-sized man put his head down and charged Rhett. The big man would cause real damage if he were successful at tackling someone, but Rhett grasped Refrigerator's arm and used the big man's momentum to propel him past Rhett and headfirst into a spiky devil's club bush.

Refrigerator screamed with pain and fury as dozens of the wicked needle-like thorns pierced his scalp and arms.

Leo stood far from Rhett and assumed a subservient posture. "He's going to kill you. You know that."

"If he does, he'll be out of a job," said Rhett calmly. "I'm his boss. Now after you get all those thorns out of his face, I want you to bring back that Chinese worker, but don't beat or harm him in any way. I need his labor."

"But it will take us all day to find him. He's tricky," whined Leo in his deep voice.

"Then you best get started," said Rhett stepping past him and continuing on his way toward the mine.

It was time to meet Gideon.

38

· · · · · · · · · ·

JUST THEN JENNIFER POKED her head out of Gideon's bedroom door. "Honey can you help me with something?"

"You wife wants help," giggled a chubby beard-ed man with a large soiled cowboy hat "Want me to help her?"

Dylan ignored the comment and hid his bewilderment as he slipped into the bedroom. It was surprisingly clean and orderly, but very stark. No decorations softened the room aside from a display of martial arts weapons on one wall. Dylan decided they didn't soften the room, either.

From the rustic, but tidy bathroom, Jennifer motioned him toward her. She appeared naked and wet from her shower.

Dylan didn't quite know what to do. Her urgent gestures to come into the bathroom moved him uneasily forward. Dylan wanted Jennifer to feel utterly safe with him, so he wanted to treat her like a daughter, but, he wondered, did she want something else?

In a harsh whisper Jennifer said, "I don't like it here. These guys seem like criminals. They scare me."

Perhaps by accident, Dylan noticed Jennifer's lithe athletic body. Her pert, perfect breasts jiggled as she spoke, and, without directly looking, it seemed she had no pubic hair.

He found himself consciously looking at her face and not looking down at her chest . . . or lower.

He nodded in agreement keeping his eyes locked on her face. She appeared utterly unembarrassed by her nakedness.

"Let's pretend we are husband and wife so they leave me alone," she wrapped a towel around her head like a turban. Her pretty breasts rose up and Dylan noticed her nipples were erect. "And stay close to me so they don't try anything," Jennifer said leaning over and kissing his ear.

"Oh. Your hair had a wild smells like coconut and campfire smoke. I like it," she smiled.

Dylan gulped nodded again. Forcing him to think about something besides the beautiful naked woman in front of him.

He had to agree that these were not the hearty, friendly Alaska miners he had expected. "These guys give off a bad vibe. I'd say we go back to camp as soon as we can."

Jennifer stepped into some shiny black panties as she talked. "Take my dirty clothes to the washing machine and put them through on delicate with the warm cycle. Dry them on the permanent press low temp option." She handed Dylan a wad of clothes that looked perfectly clean to Dylan.

"I doubt they have a dryer. In fact, if they do have a washer, it probably has only one cycle and no warm water. These miners would not use precious diesel fuel to warm water for clothes washing."

Dylan noticed Jennifer had slipped a clean top over her bare breasts, then she gave him a sharp look.

"Well, you could have told me that before I got this top on." Jennifer pulled off the top and held her hand out to Dylan.

Not knowing what to do with Jennifer's outstretched hand, he avoided looking at her breasts and shook her hand.

"You goofball, don't shake my hand, give me my bra from the dirty clothes I gave you," Jennifer smiled at his discomfort. "Why do you act so uncomfortable with this situation? Haven't you ever seen a bra?"

Dylan felt oddly voyeuristic as he pawed through her clothes looking for a bra.

"It's a black sports bra," Jennifer pointed to a garment that looked like all straps to Dylan.

Just as she put it on, the door burst open, and Gideon burst into the room holding his Sig Sauer pistol with Rusty and his cowboy hat following close behind.

"Get your hands up, you did something to Blaster," shouted Gideon.

39
. . . .

JENNIFER SHOUTED, "GET OUT! Can't you see I'm changing?"

This time Gideon was not caught off balance by Jennifer's assertive manner. He brandished his gun. "You are here to sabotage our mine. You've done something with Blaster, and when I figure out what you did, it's going to go hard on you."

"Nonsense," said Jennifer, seemingly unembarrassed at being caught standing in her underwear. "We don't know what you are talking about. Do we, honey?" She nudged Dylan.

"She's right," said Dylan stepping in front of her as she dressed. "I'm guessing Blaster is one of your employees. You and the men in the mess hall are the first people we've seen since we got here. I'm sure there's a reasonable explanation for your missing man."

"Blaster isn't answering his radio, and he didn't come back when we rang the gong. He always comes back for dinner." Gideon reached for the bear spray canisters from Dylan and Jennifer's things.

Rusty, trying to see around Gideon's large body, pushed back his cowboy hat and leered at Jennifer. "Blaster is never late for a meal, that's for sure. Bones couldn't find him anywhere."

A half-hour later, Dylan and Jennifer stood before a seemingly bottomless black pit dug into the floor of the Glass Dome. Behind them stood Snuffy, Rusty and Gideon. At a signal from Gideon, Snuffy and Rusty lowered a long, bouncy wooden ladder into the blackness. Dylan noticed the pit was about 20 feet wide and 20 feet deep with very smooth walls that narrowed as they came closer to the opening.

"No. You are not going to put us down there," said Jennifer firmly. "It's completely out of the question. Now you told me I could do a wash. I demand you stop this nonsense and take us up back up to the surface."

Rusty looked pleadingly at Gideon from under his cowboy hat. "Why don't I take the girl up and leave this guy here? I can help her with the wash."

"Yeah, and I can help her next," said Snuffy picking at his scalp.

Gideon looked sharply at the two men. "Ok. You guys can help her with her wash." Gideon put the word *help* in air quotes. "Rusty's first. But don't screw this up or there will be hell to pay."

Dylan stepped in front of Jennifer, his chest touching the barrel of Gideon's pistol. "No one is going to harm my wife. She stays with me."

"That's easy to arrange. I'm within my rights and can execute you both for the murder of Blaster," said Gideon pushing the barrel of his gun to Dylan's chest. "Now get into the pit, or you both die right now."

"You have no rights like that," said Dylan.

"I do in this remote mine. I'm like a ship's captain," growled Gideon.

Dylan had met killers before, and this large man seemed very dangerous. Snuffy was bigger and heavier, but Gideon projected an aura of cold malevolence that Dylan recognized. It might be best to follow his directions and attempt an escape later.

Jennifer's eyes got big as she watched Dylan slowly descend into the blackness. As the blackness took him, raw fear flooded her.

He left her alone in a cave with bad men who wanted to harm her. She suppressed tears as Rusty and Snuffy pulled the ladder out of the pit. When the men's headlamps shone away from the pit, it disappeared as if it wasn't there, but she could still feel its utter blackness.

Rusty pushed back his soiled cowboy hat and called down to Dylan. "And don't worry. You can't escape from this pit. The sides are too steep and smooth. Even if you did, we have expert trackers here who could find you."

Rusty put his rough hand on Jennifer's shoulder and spoke to Gideon. "Let's go out the west tunnel exit. It's faster to get outside that way."

It was obvious to Jennifer that he spoke with urgency.

Her heart jumped in her chest. This terrible dirty man was going to rape her! A powerful feeling of dread pushed down on her. She wished she had heeded the warnings to never come to Shaman Mountain.

She felt a rough hand push her forward up the path. Now, perhaps the dirty man might even kill her. She could feel herself hyperventilating. She needed to keep her wits about her.

In the past, when she was unsure of herself, she had always put on a false confidence that got her through tough situations. It had worked for her during her high school drama auditions, job interviews and courtroom appearances. She had to put on a confident front.

Dylan's voice came out of the darkness as the men led her past the work site and up the west tunnel. "Jennifer, I'll meet you back at the Magic Ring."

To Jennifer, his distant but confident voice gave her a bit of courage to face what she would have to endure.

40

· · · · · · · · · ·

GIDEON HAD LEFT THE MINE listening to Rusty and Snuffy quarreling about who was going first. Their height differences made them look like a fireplug quarreling with a lamp post with Rusty's cowboy hat tilted back so he could see Snuffy. Gideon quickly left the shaft and turned south toward the dusty bunkhouse.

Twenty minutes later, he closed the door to his room and thought about the Shaman Mountain Mine visitors: people like Solomon, Dylan and his tourists. News of the iridium would get out soon. He wondered how much the Chinese laborers knew. He was fairly sure they thought they were mining platinum.

Kung knew what they were mining. He wished he had gotten more information out of Dylan. How had he figured out they were mining iridium? He was just a shithead tour guide unless he was lying. Could he be a spy for another mining company?

Gideon pondered gathering up all the iridium he had stockpiled and making a run for it. If he sold his cache before word came of how rich the iridium mine was, he could make a killing.

Even if he disappeared with 100 pounds sold at international prices, he would never have to work again. It was the rarest mineral on Earth—until the world found out about the seemingly endless supply in this mine. Gideon needed to make a decision within hours.

He heard a loud knock on the door of his office. His first thought was, *Who would knock at the office door? There's no visitors up here*. Then he expected that Rusty would answer the door, but he remembered Rusty was out having fun with Dylan's wife.

The knock sounded again even louder. Probably Snuffy couldn't get the door because he was spying on what Rusty was doing to Dylan's wife. Blaster had not come back, and the trackers were busy chasing a runner.

Gideon left his orderly bedroom, crossed the chaotic common room to the door where the knocking came even louder. What he saw when he pulled open the sagging door shocked him.

There was a well-dressed black man standing there—smiling like an idiot.

"Are you Gideon Schechter?" asked the black man. "I'm Rhett Sims from South Africa. My boss wants to buy this zinc mine. I believe Ursula Schiffmeister told you I was coming."

Among the hundred thoughts that flashed though Gideon's mind were: *A black man here on Shaman Mountain? How did he get here? Can I just tell him to go away and come back in a month? By then I'll be long gone and rich. Is this the black guy Blaster said he saw? He looks athletic but a bit small; could he have beaten up Blaster and sneaked in here? No, he looks too citified. Does he know about the iridium? I sold that nugget to a South African, but he was white.*

Gideon regained his voice. "Yes, Mr. Sims . . ."

"Call me Rhett," said the black man offering his hand in a relaxed gesture.

Rhett noted the look of puzzlement on the tall, blond man.

What surprised Rhett was how such pale, blond eyelashes surrounded Gideon's dark eyes. There was only a very slight difference between the man's pupil and iris—like the baked goat heads for sale in the slums of Soweto.

The rest of his unlined and youthful face displayed a false innocence and a hidden hardness Rhett had seen in a few soldiers. This man would easily kill without remorse or second thoughts. He was no youthful innocent.

Rhett looked at the man's huge scar-covered hands, appearing like the grilled pig knee joints sold at summer outdoor grills often stacked up next to the baked goat's heads.

By the quiet pulse in the man's neck and the relaxed muscles around his eyes, Rhett knew there would be no attack until the man had decided Rhett was a threat or an obstacle.

Rhett put his hand down when Gideon did not appear to understand the gesture offering a handshake.

Rhett had prioritized the parts of this mission. He had promised his boss he would have the deal complete in just a few days, and his self-imposed deadline had nearly lapsed. He wanted to find out who knew about the iridium. If it was a small enough group, they could all be silenced. He had to find out what this man knew.

It would be best if all the information came out voluntarily, so he could close the deal on the mine to take all the iridium off the market.

If everyone on the mountain died, it could delay the mining lease for Mr. Meijer. Rhett stood at the door with exaggerated vulnerability to allow Gideon to drop his guard.

So far, it wasn't working. He could see Gideon's pupils contract as his neck pulse increased as Gideon sized up Rhett. Gideon's body was preparing for action. Rhett was always ready for an attack. It was who he was, but he wanted to avoid or postpone a fight with Gideon.

Rhett overcame his caution to turn his back to Gideon and sweep his hand over the mining camp. Turning his back left his body open to a strike from Gideon's dominant right hand, but the risk of exposing himself could be outweighed by the possibility that Gideon would relax and not strike before Rhett could get the information he needed.

"So this is the Shaman Mountain Mine," said Rhett turning back toward Gideon.

The big blond man's pupils were a bit smaller and the obicularis oculi, the muscles around his eye, were relaxing. Gideon had begun to relax. Maybe he wanted information before he started a fight.

"Yeah. So what?" said Gideon.

"Well, how about a tour? That's what Mrs. Schiffmeister told you to provide," said Rhett grinning, while watching Gideon closely. "If you want, I can explore on my own." Rhett held up a map and list of assets Ursula had given him.

"No," blurted Gideon.

"No to what? To the tour or self-exploration?" Rhett put on a puzzled expression for Gideon. It was obvious to Rhett that Gideon was openly racist.

Gideon pushed away from the door. "I'll show you around, but I'm busy, so this has to be short, then you need to leave."

"Wait. What's that?" Rhett edged into the building and pointed to the tennis-ball sized iridium nugget shining on the table behind Gideon.

41

· · · · · · · · · ·

DYLAN WATCHED THE BOBBING shadows quickly fade as the miners escorted Jennifer out of the Glass Dome. Panic began to close in on him. Not panic caused by being imprisoned in an inescapable black pit deep in an eerie mine, but panic that there was nothing he could do to protect Jennifer.

If he had refused to go into the pit, he had no doubt they would have just killed both Jennifer and him. *The men have no internal limits to their cruelty*, thought Dylan.

Years ago he had met men like this when he lived in the small Alaska town called Seward, and he recognized the type.

He had allowed his fury to combine with his outdoor knowledge to defeat a group of trained mercenaries. He would need to call on that fury and knowledge now to save Jennifer.

I must escape and help Jennifer. I must!

Everything about the Shaman Mountain Tour had gone wrong. Instead of helping Dylan's fragile new guiding business get on secure financial footing, his clients had to put up with delays, were put in danger by weather and Jun was probably dead. No positive reviews from this tour.

Now Jennifer was in serious physical peril, and Dylan was stuck in a hole. Dylan knew his tenuous new business and his life in Anchorage was toast.

He felt terrible worrying about his business when he should focus on saving Jennifer. *What kind of man worries about his business life when someone is in danger?*

Jun had dragged Jennifer on the trip to find her cousin, and now it's possible she'll lose her life. Dylan worried that he would gain a reputation for killing clients, and probably also loose his own life.

A wave of guilt swept over Dylan. *How can I worry about my stupid business when Jennifer is in danger?*

He recognized that negative thoughts were pounding him and preventing logical thinking. This kind of thinking could cause depression and paralysis.

He would stay stuck in a hole. Jennifer would be horribly assaulted. And they would both likely be killed. He recognized that he was playing a loop of negative thoughts that would lead to depression and inaction.

Dylan knew he had to force positive thoughts into his mind.

Alaska miners were the most touchy and aggressive when they had located a promising mineral deposit but before they had made a legal claim to it. That couldn't be the case with the Shaman Mountain Mine, since it was a fairly big mining operation.

They had to have state approval to extract and market the minerals, or they would be shut down, fined and possibly imprisoned.

Why were these miners so harsh? Could it have something to do with the iridium Jun had found? Maybe they only had a permit to mine for zinc. Maybe, as soon as the iridium permit went through, they would let Dylan and Jennifer go.

This thought buoyed Dylan. It could be a matter of hours before everything would be resolved. The iridium-mining permit would be issued by the state, and Dylan and Jennifer would be released. Dylan realized he was grasping at straws.

Then Dylan had a terrible new thought, *Maybe they are conducting an illegal mine and don't want anyone to know about it. If this was the case, they could never let Dylan and Jennifer go.*

Dylan felt the pit suddenly became even blacker.

42
. . . .

RUSTY HAD TROUBLE WALKING with his erection pushing against his rough overalls. He needed relief and wanted to have his way with this skinny girl right there in the mine, but he knew he'd need to get her at least into the bushes outside before he could have his fun.

He thought he saw tears on her cheek. Maybe it was concern for her husband back in the pit, but maybe it was tears of joy. She wanted it. Even if she cried and screamed, he knew that, deep down, she probably wanted some rough sex.

Once outside the mine, she seemed to change her attitude. She walked with a pronounced swish, and would toss a sly smile back at him. He'd been at the mine for weeks and needed this hot girl. *She wanted it, too*, thought Rusty.

"Let's go over here," she said indicating some tall bushes. Rusty followed her as Snuffy went on ahead and disappeared down the path.

As soon as they were alone, Rusty knocked her down with an open-handed slap to her head. Jennifer went down hard, as if she had collided with another ultimate frisbee player while both were diving for a disc.

Jennifer quickly stood and shook her head. Pretending the slap was foreplay, she tried to sound brave. "Wait until everyone's gone, then I want to see what you have for me," she smiled even though her voice sounded shaky and a bright red image of Rusty's hand appeared on her cheek.

Rusty smiled and figured her voice was shaky with desire. Maybe he should hit her again. She probably liked chubby bearded men who smelled masculine—like a hard rock miner who seldom showered or washed his clothes. It did seem odd to Rusty that she wanted so much privacy. They seemed to go further than necessary into the woods.

"OK, I want to see what you have," she spoke as she tugged at his belt. As soon as his pants were at his ankles, she threw her shoulder into his gut sending him flat on his back. For a moment he seemed stunned.

"Remember, if you fuck up, Gideon is going to make you pay hell for it. Don't tell him I got away." She kicked a mass of dirt into his face as he slowly sat up.

"I'm a cutter on my ultimate frisbee team. You don't know what that means, but if you did, you'd know I could outrun and out-dodge other players for hours. You don't stand a chance of catching me." She raised her voice. "And neither do you, Snuffy!"

"Hey! Stop. You can't get away," Rusty yelled trying to get to his feet despite his tangled pant legs.

But she had vanished—gracefully leaping over logs, and dodging tall bushes. The woods were suddenly empty in the direction where she had run. Snuffy burst out of some bushes nearby. "Get her!"

"You were watching us!" Rusty yelled as he fumbled with his pants and followed Snuffy into the woods.

A half-hour later, the two men stopped and labored to catch their breaths. After that last glimpse of her leaping into the Alaska woods, they never saw her again.

"We need to get Chewy and Leo to find her. She's hiding somewhere," said Rusty, his sides heaving.

"You need to tell Gideon you lost her. Be sure to duck after you tell him. He's going to kick your ass," said Snuffy, straightening up.

"How was I supposed to know she cut frisbees?" whined Rusty. "Tell Gideon it wasn't my fault."

"I'm staying out of it," said Snuffy breathing deeply. "This is your problem."

"Ok. But let me tell him on my time. I want to wait until he's in a good mood," Rusty stood up straight catching he breath.

"Right. When does that happen?" said Snuffy looking around the empty woods.

JENNIFER RAN IN A ZIGZAG pattern until she reached the cliff overlooking the Kila Glacier. She noticed tears streaming from her eyes, and loud painful gasps escaping from her chest.

She was crying and wailing in fear. Suddenly all her false bravado vanished to be replaced with fear and horror.

Her chest heaving, she looked back—terrified she'd see a group of angry men following her. Peaceful, uncaring trees were all she saw.

Knowing she had some time, she moved more carefully and deliberately. She paused by a stream to vomit and wash. Her cheeks and arms, slashed by branches, were crisscrossed with congealing blood mixed with dirt. At a place where a cold, clear spring burst out of some rocks, she drank deeply. Her whole body trembled as adrenaline left her muscles.

Once the sun set, it would get cold. And her little daypack had only a light windbreaker and the emergency items Dylan had insisted she always carry. As the chill deepened, her dirty clothes would be welcome now, but they were all in Gideon's room back at the mine.

She looked out over the Gila Glacier: its breathtaking beauty unimportant to her now. Dylan was trapped in a hole deep in the mine, and bad people were after her. I hate this place!

From this position, she knew she just needed to go downhill for about a half-mile to find the fairy ring: the Magic Ring. As soon as she saw the magpies, she would know she was close to the place where Dylan had told her to meet. *But how will he get out of that pit? I'm alone in this hostile place. Why did I ever come to this horrible mountain*!

Just then, a soft rain began. From a distance, she heard a wolf howl penetrate the large, cold raindrops. "I hate Alaska," she heard herself say through sobs.

43

· · · · · · · · · ·

DYLAN HAD CLIMBED ROCKS his whole life. As a teen, he sought the most difficult routes. As a young man, the renowned climber, Sid Green, had chosen him as a mentee.

Sid had viewed Dylan as a talented prodigy and helped the young man develop near supernatural climbing skills.

Dylan had climbed for thousands of feet on granite, sandstone and everything in between. He'd climbed in over 40 countries and made scores of solo first ascents.

As a young man, he worked as talent for several climbing and outdoor magazines surpassing the skills of his mentor. Dylan's specialty was solo climbing on impossibly difficult routes.

Dylan made it look easy, but actually he spent many hours planning and memorizing a route before actually climbing it. Other climbers claimed he had a photographic memory in order to know that if he leaped blindly to his right at a certain point, there would be a ledge or toehold to grasp. Despite his long list of accomplishments, few people in Anchorage knew him as a climber. They just thought he was an accomplished guide and outdoorsman.

In the blackness of the hole, Dylan felt a sharp, cold river of fear running down his back. Of all the difficult climbs he'd done, he'd never climbed in total blackness without time to plan and memorize a route. Even on his night climbs, he had had some starlight.

He thought back to the walls of the pit that imprisoned him. A flash of a headlamp had briefly illuminated them. Would it be enough information to plan a route? If he fell, he would land on sharp shards of volcanic glass boulders and discarded rusty metal that lined the bottom of the pit like dragon's teeth. The likely injuries would preclude his escape from the pit.

Trying to recall the dimly illuminated image of the pit in his mind, he stood in the complete darkness to plan his climb. He did not understand why his brain was able to put a picture of a wall in his mind and permit him to plan a climb, but for years, it had worked for him. Dylan knew he had to trust his brain.

Standing among the sharp stones and old mining junk thrown into the pit, Dylan ignored some lingering foul odors—probably from previous occupants, and imagined his route. He pictured each hand and toehold, each resting place, each move that would take him out of the pit.

As he planned, he tried to push thoughts of Jennifer's problems out of his mind. She must be in terrible danger. The urgency of her situation kept interfering with his plan.

Despite the intrusions, Dylan finally had his route planned. It was utterly clear in his mind. Even in the inky blackness, he knew if he put his hand on a certain place on the wall, there would be a small rock or crack that would allow him to move upwards.

Dylan felt his way to the wall and reached up to grasp his first handhold.

It wasn't there!

Confusion washed over him. Hadn't he seen the handhold in his memory of the wall? Why wasn't it there?

Delicately moving around the pit, Dylan searched for the handhold, but it wasn't anywhere he thought it would be. He cut the back of his hand, not on the sharp rocks, but on some rusty old iron mining equipment that someone had thrown into the pit.

The confusion he felt earlier changed to doubts and then began a feeling of hopelessness. Blackness filled Dylan's mind. He despaired for Jennifer, and ached that he couldn't help her. Perhaps the route he had planned came from a mental picture of another place.

It would be terribly dangerous, and maybe even suicidal, but Dylan knew he had to see if he could climb the wall completely blind.

If only I had some light! Dylan inwardly shouted.

Blindly feeling the wall, a possible handhold, a grapefruit-sized rock Dylan had found, came off in his hand when he attempted to put weight on it. It was hard and sharp edged. He threw it across the pit where it hit something iron and threw off a metallic clang and a bright yellow-hot spark of light.

44

· · · · · · · · · ·

MOVING PAST GIDEON, Rhett took several steps into the building and picked up the tennis-ball sized nugget of iridium. "What's this? It isn't zinc. It weighs about a kilogram."

Rhett hefted the nugget and turned to study Gideon's reaction. By the micro muscle twitches in Gideon's face, it was clear to Rhett that Gideon knew what this was. Rhett also noticed a new musky odor coming off Gideon. *Was this big man scared or just uneasy*?

Gideon's face showed anger. "It's none of your business. Come on, I'll show you the assets of this mine, but you shouldn't buy the lease. It's just about paid out and it will expire soon anyway."

"We'll renew it," said Rhett. In the background of his mind, Rhett noticed nearby items that could be improvised as weapons, the number of exits—including windows and a leaky skylight above the trestle table.

"Renewal is unlikely. Too much opposition from Native groups and tree huggers."

"What's this mineral?" persisted Rhett. "If it came from this mine, it is my business."

"It's silver, low grade. Contaminated with lead," Gideon lied. "One of the guys found it in a glacial erratic bolder brought down by the Kila Glacier and left in the valley. No telling from which of the dozens of upstream mountains it came from, or how many thousands of years ago the boulder was deposited in the valley. It's a one-off. There's no more."

Gideon's eyes twitched as he snatched the nugget out of Rhett's hand with amazing speed and tossed it back onto the table with a loud thunk that knocked over some partly filled coffee cups.

Rhett had known the grab was coming from a change in Gideon's pupil size and posture, but allowed Gideon to think he was surprised. *So that's his tell—his pupils. Too bad they are hard to observe in dim light.*

As they walked toward, what looked like to Rhett, an apparently abandoned zinc mine on the opposite side of the landing strip from the active iridium mine, Rhett looked sharply at Gideon. "Are you sure it's silver?"

Gideon stopped in the dust and looked at Rhett aggressively. "What else could it be?"

"Well, it's very dense and, by its luster, resistant to corrosion or oxidation. Platinum could be a good guess. Did you test it?" Rhett wore his innocent face. He needed to keep Gideon talking to find out what he knew, but avoid making him unduly suspicious.

"What test? We don't have testing facilities out here. We just mine zinc." Gideon had resumed walking toward the zinc part of the mine.

"Platinum reacts strongly with hydrogen peroxide. Did you try soaking it?" asked Rhett.

"We don't have a drug store nearby to buy shit like that. Maybe it's not platinum, but just dirty silver."

"Silver ore usually has a bluish tint," countered Rhett.

Gideon stopped and obviously changed the subject. "Look around. If you take over the lease, which will expire soon, you'll get these three shitty buildings, that diesel generator, some solar panels, an electric ATV, a trash pump, an electric welder, an air compressor, the conveyer belt going down to the lake, a barge, two chain saws . . ."

Rhett interrupted him. "It could be iridium."

"No. It's not iridium. That's not common in large nuggets. It's nearly always in dust form and found in deep earth extrusions," Gideon dismissed Rhett's comment and continued with the inventory. "The conveyor belt is broken and needs a lot of repair. I'm guessing it will cost about ten grand and two months' work. That's a whole mining season in this part of Alaska. The mine also has a shed full of hand tools, a first aid station, a bear gun . . ."

"I like this mine," interrupted Rhett. "Do you get many visitors?"

"That's another reason you don't want this mine," Gideon said. "We have random people coming here all the time. They interfere with our workers and get in our way. We had a guy from the federal government fly in here a few days ago. He may decide to put a non-renewal order on the mine lease, then what would your boss think?"

"Do you have tourists come in here? I saw a camping site near the glacier," asked Rhett.

"Yeah. They are a big problem. Some asshole tourists came in yesterday and did something with my small engine guy, Blaster. I'm holding the tourists until I can figure out what happened and get the authorities here."

Rhett moved in front of Gideon and faced him. "Do the tourists know about the iridium?" Rhett watched Gideon's face carefully. Rhett had to push this man, but not so hard that it would provoke a fight. He needed to get more information first.

"Maybe," said Gideon. Rhett watched Gideon's temple veins pop out and his eyes dilate. *That's a stress reaction*, thought Rhett.

"Let's go ask them," said Rhett turning toward the iridium mine shaft.

Gideon put his hand out and roughly stopped Rhett. "You aren't here to assess the value of this mine. You are on a fishing expedition to gather information about platinum or iridium, or whatever that nugget happens to be."

"Maybe," said Rhett. "So all these random visitors know about this possible iridium? If so, how did they find out?"

"How did you find out? I don't think you just saw something shiny across the room and thought: iridium. Few people on earth have seen anything like that nugget before."

Gideon took his hand off of Rhett's shoulder and wiped it on his jacket. Rhett understood the gesture as a racist signal.

"I found out because you sold my boss, Mr. Meijer, a smaller hunk of iridium that looked much like that nugget back there. He wants to know more about where it came from. He may have an offer for you. He knows you like gold."

Rhett could see the big man processing this information. His piggy black eyes told Rhett that the thought of gold had him interested.

Rhett pulled a roll of gold half-ounce Krugerrands out of his pocket. The coins were roughly the size of quarters and gleamed brightly from each end of the paper roll. After he was certain Gideon had seen the gold, Rhett put the roll of coins back into his pocket.

"We'll talk about that later. Right now, this tour is over. I'm busy. You can sleep in the bunkhouse in Blaster's bunk if he doesn't come back, but you'll need to leave in the morning." Gideon turned away and walked through a light rain toward the workshop building where several miners were welding something. "And stay out of our way!"

Rhett decided that Gideon would probably not attempt to kill him as he slept in Blaster's bunk. The idea of many rolls of gold coins would occupy his thoughts. Gideon would want to know more about the gold. He could see by faint eye twitches and changes in breathing, that the news that Rhett and his boss knew about the iridium was a powerful stress trigger and that mention of gold boosted that tension.

Rhett decided he would eat something and get some rest while he could. His military experience taught him that soldiers should eat and rest when the opportunity presented itself. Gideon would not attack him until after they had discussed the gold.

After eating some greasy peanut butter and crackers, Rhett found Blaster's bunk, covered it in paper towels, and lay down—keeping his graphite, throwing knife at hand.

45

. . . .

JENNIFER PEERED INTO the darkening dripping woods and wondered how she could have ever found this forest anything but horrible.

The Magic Ring held no wonder for her; it was just a place in the damp forest. She shivered as she realized she was cold, wet and hungry.

Angry, evil men were after her and were intent on hurting her. Wolves were lurking, probably behind every tree, to tear her apart and eat her. Likely her father was dead, and she'd never be able to recover his body. At gunpoint, they had forced Dylan into a deep pit. She had no place to go.

Remembering Dylan's safety talk, she recalled he had a satellite phone in a case in his tent back at their camp. She brightened at the idea she could use it to call for help. Maybe 911 would bring some robust rangers to save her and rescue Dylan. Jennifer didn't remember the exact path that Dylan used to lead her to the Magic Ring, but she knew their camp was downhill and not far from the glacier. It shouldn't be too hard to find.

As she left the fairy ring, she started to feel even more uncomfortable, as if there was something about the ring that offered refuge. She was abandoning the tiny bit of protection the forest offered to strike out on her own. More sobs escaped her as the trees took on a malevolent cast.

She found herself trying to hold back tears as she stumbled down the steep hillside. Distant lightning flashes over the glacier made eerie shadows and caused the glacier to shine yellow/white instead of blue/white. Everything seemed different from when she and Dylan had enjoyed the hike up the hill.

At one point she came to a stream that was too deep and dangerous for her to cross, so she had to go back up the hill and cross in a different place. She felt exhausted.

Jennifer was out of water and didn't know where to fill her bottle. She found an energy bar in her pack. When her slippery hands attempted to open the bar, she dropped it in the mud but ate it anyway—her teeth chewing through the grit. She never thought of herself as a crier, but found herself weeping, then openly gasping through uncontrollable sobs.

Soon she recognized a fallen log and saw the latrine shovel Dylan had placed behind some bushes. She was close to the camp. She could get dry clothes, rain gear, a sleeping bag and a satphone. She found herself jogging in the deepening twilight and watching for distant lightning flashes that might illuminate the open area where their tents had been set up. She stopped short.

Instead of the comforting sight of an orderly campsite, all was chaos. Someone or something had shredded the tents and flattened them. One part of her tent was torn open to the rain—falling heavily now. What was left of Dylan's tent was also filling with rainwater. The contents of their tents were strewn around the campsite, many items in muddy puddles. Her clean clothes lay scattered in the mud. For some reason, that upset her more.

In the ruins of Dylan's tent, she found a cracked headlamp that produced a weak and fading light, even though it had lay in a puddle.

Nearby she saw the case for the sat-phone. It looked like a large animal had chewed on the case. Maybe bears had attacked the campsite! Jennifer quickly looked around expecting to see horrible bears.

Evidently, animals had not targeted Dylan's clothes. She found an ugly green fleece sweatshirt and a soaking wet rain poncho in his damaged tent and decided to put them on. Large raindrops noisily pelted the hood over her head as she fumbled open the sat-phone case. The phone itself appeared undamaged.

She found the ON switch and felt relief when the screen lit up. A blinking message flashed on the screen: *authorizing.* Jennifer watched the pulsing message for several minutes. As the phone continued to flash *authorizing* at her, she began to lose hope. The bears ruined the phone! As the light in her headlamp dimmed, so did any remaining slivers of hope.

As she shivered in the poncho, a deep feeling of sadness and dread crept unbidden into her mind. Hopelessness and fear caused her to begin the sobbing again.

She heard a loud wail escape from her body. A feeling that she would die a horrible death in this awful place completely occupied her mind. Dylan was in a pit and would probably be killed. She had no way to contact help. Her shelter was destroyed. Undoubtedly the wolves would be drawn to her cries, but she couldn't stop.

A much closer flash of lighting turned the campsite into near daylight for an instant. What she saw, took her breath away.

As if summoned by the lighting and thunder, and looking like an imp from the gates of hell, a hairy man-like creature stood before her.

46

. . . .

THE RING OF THE MINING CAMP gong woke Rhett and told him the workers would soon be gathering for some reason. It was time for him to end his nap and find out what and how the tourists in Gideon's pit knew about the iridium.

Rhett had decided that if he had to kill people and the word of the iridium strike got out anyway, he was wasting his time trying to contain the news of the strike. However, if he could bury the news with just a few kills, it could be well worth it, despite his concerns about what Father Mavuso would think.

Rhett knew he must not ponder Father Mavuso. He should avoid thinking about the confessional conversation that had precipitated the destruction of the old priest.

As he lay among the paper towels in Blaster's bunk, Rhett forced himself to concentrate on the task at hand.

Father Mavuso would say that Rhett was being loyal to his white boss—which is noble, despite the race of his boss. A worker must be reliable, or he will never get ahead. Colored people will not have the support of the pure black family, and certainly not the pure white family. They must create their own connections through loyalty. Sometimes the connections are only between a colored man and his conscience.

Father Mavuso would not approve of killing innocents, even whites, just to make money. The exception would be military service when a superior officer ordered a soldier to kill. But was this just killing for money? Wasn't it a higher calling? Killing for loyalty should ennoble the killer. Rhett regretted that he had only one conversation with his beloved mentor on this topic.

Now it was too late. Father Mavuso would never again turn his wise, loving eyes toward Rhett, nor anyone else. Father's only family—his relationship with his flock, was lost.

Even Father's faith had left the old priest like water flowing from an upturned jug. Father's soul had become just a bitter, empty idea in the old man's imagination. So much was gone. Rhett felt more alone that ever.

Rhett knew that if he concentrated on his anger, his body would fill with energy and purpose. Thinking of the loss he had caused Father Mavuso could produce inaction in Rhett instead of energy.

Shaking off his sadness, Rhett focused on his job. He had to know how the tourists learned of the iridium. It meant he would need to go back to the dark pit at the bottom of the Glass Dome.

The pit gave Rhett an uneasy feeling. He could have never been a miner like his mother's people. Maybe he truly didn't belong to them. They were so different.

Rhett left the staff building, and slipped around back. He did not want any contact with the noisy, smelly miners who were gathering in the kitchen area. Grabbing a rain slicker hanging on a peg by the door, he walked through the pounding rain to the iridium mine entrance.

The noisy generator lay silent for the evening, and the camp ran on dim, battery-powered lights. He could see a yellow glow from the bleak shack that housed the Chinese miners. Unlike the staff kitchen, the Chinese had no propane to cook, but had to use a wood stove or campfire. Smoke rose from a metal pipe in their roof and added to the gloom of the evening. Far away, thunderclaps rolled up the glacier and disappeared into a purple-black mountain range.

Once in the mine tunnel, Rhett noticed all the hardhats and their headlamps were gone, probably attached to a charger somewhere. He realized he should have brought a flashlight. There was one in his pack hanging under a tree just outside the mining camp. Since the dim, widely spaced bulbs in the tunnel provided nearly sufficient light for Rhett to proceed, he decided against going back for his pack. Every 100 meters or so, Rhett found a post with switches that allowed him to turn off the set of lights he had just used and turn on the next set. This set of switches was probably a mechanism to save battery power.

As he entered the Glass Dome, he looked for lights to illuminate the pit. On a post, he saw two switches. One turned off all the lights in the tunnels, and the other controlled work lights near the current digging operation. The second set actually offered marginally more light in the Glass Dome, but he thought it was eerie how the black glass absorbed illumination but still had facets that threw off sharp points of light. The result was an otherworldly light echo of unnatural light.

Remembering his tour of this place with Kung, Rhett approached the rickety ladder that would take him from the path down to the floor of the dome.

Just as he reached the bottom of the ladder, all the lights went out. Rhett again wished he had his flashlight. The room was suddenly as black as Rhett had ever seen.

In his mind, he thought he could see just a quickly fading image of the huge domed room: the ladder, the pit, and thousands of tiny quartz crystals trapped in the glass walls, now black. He wondered if a timer had shut down all the lighting or if the batteries had given out.

He stood still, one hand on the ladder as he spoke in the darkness. "I want to talk to you tourists in the pit."

From the pit, Dylan's voice floated up. "Your accent sounds African. I'm guessing you are one of the miners."

"I'm not one of the miners," answered Rhett barely containing his rage. *He thinks that since I'm black, I'm a lowly miner. All blacks aren't miners.*

"Then bring the ladder over here. My wife and I need to get out of this place," said Dylan. He didn't need the ladder. When Rhett had turned on the tunnel lights, there had been enough illumination to allow Dylan to complete an escape plan he'd been developing by making sparks with steel and flint. His route, was clearly imprinted onto his brain and muscles. Dylan's shoes were off and tied to the back of his belt. He was ready to climb. He had to get out before the lights came back on and this mine employee sounded an alarm.

"You and your wife are not getting out of that pit until you answer some questions," said Rhett through gritted teeth. *Whites are so ethnocentric that they think blacks belong underground mucking for minerals.*

"We'll be happy to answer your questions, but why wouldn't you help us first?" said Dylan confidently reaching for his first handhold in the blackness and finding it as easily as he would in daytime. The African was obviously hostile and might not provide the ladder even after Dylan cooperated.

"Because you and your kind hurt my people?" spat out Rhett.

"Your people?" Dylan sounded confused. "Aren't you a miner? Or are you with another tourist agency? I don't hurt my clients, nor anyone else's," Dylan stretched to reach the next handhold and moved his toe to a slight bump in the wall.

Rhett decided the white tourist in the pits was playing him, treating him like a fool because of his race. Rhett felt tired and stressed. He needed information from the racist whites in the pit, not a runaround.

Rhett decided he would kill this white man and woman just because they hated blacks. His hand went to his hidden graphite knife. He did not need light to kill this horrible man.

47

· · · · · · · · · ·

"YOU LOOK LIKE YOU could use some help," Aguta said softly to Jennifer. "Bears have been here. They destroyed your camp because you wear perfume, and they are curious."

"Are you from the mine?" asked Jennifer uneasily getting her voice back. He turned on a headlamp that revealed his clothes to be a combination of furs and high-tech raingear.

"Me? No. I live here. Sometimes I work for the mine doing avalanche mitigation, but those miners are bad people. I stay away," Aguta motioned her to follow him. "My home is only a couple of miles from here. Let's get you warm and dry."

"Wait. Why should I trust you?" Jennifer's quivery voice barely rose above a whisper.

"I won't hurt you. You obviously need help. I'll help you," the man's grandfatherly voice had a tone that could calm a wild animal. It had a soothing effect on Jennifer.

Woodenly, Jennifer stood and started after the man. She decided he smelled faintly like a wet dog, but she somehow found that comforting. He stopped and handed her his headlamp. "I don't need this. There's enough light coming off the sky, but your eyes are not trained to walk on Kila Ikpic at night."

The unending uphill walk to Aguta's cabin pulled the remaining energy out of Jennifer. She found herself barely able to put one foot in front of the other. Suddenly a pile of logs loomed in front of her. Aguta pulled open a rustic door and motioned her in.

She expected a dirty, smelly chaotic cave-like place, but found it orderly, like a shipshape cabin on noble wooden sailing vessel.

It had a complex smoky smell of soup bubbling over embers, well-cured animal hides, and aromatic wood shavings. For some reason, the smells and warmth gave her profound sense of safety. She wondered if there dwelt deep in her brain, perhaps from caveman days, an association of these smells with comfort and home. Or maybe it was the just the soup steaming on the stove.

Working swiftly, Aguta had lit a lamp that gave off a faint odor of cooking bacon, and handed her a mug of soup. "Here. After you finish this, you can sleep in my bed, I'll take the floor by the fire. I sleep there anyway in winter."

In the warm yellow light and with the fragrant soup mug held under her nose, Jennifer watched Aguta as he prepared his bed by the fire. He looked short and stubby, with a generous graying mustache and thin beard. His eyes were Asian like hers but much narrower. His face was deeply lined like an old man used to outdoor life, but he moved with a vigor of a much younger man.

When she had first seen him, he looked like he was covered in hair, but it was his fur jacket and hood that had looked like hair in the dark. The jacket hung dripping on a peg near the door.

He looked at her directly and smiled. "I can see you like my soup. It's made of moose sausage, wild herbs and seasonings I get from the woods."

Jennifer noticed her soup was gone.

"Want another portion?" When he smiled, his dark eyes disappeared into the wrinkles in his face.

"No thank you. I'm so tired, I must sleep. But my friend Dylan is being held as a prisoner in a pit in the mine. They think we did something to a miner called Blaster. We need to rescue Dylan."

"Blaster's body is at the bottom of a cliff near the glacier. I saw it there this evening," said Aguta.

"You need to tell the other miners! They think we did something with Blaster. They are blaming us. I can't tell them because they want to hurt me."

"We can't do anything right now. You go to sleep, and we'll figure out something in the morning. Wrap yourself in this blanket and pass out your wet clothes. I'll put them on this rack to dry."

Jennifer found the soft blanket wonderful as she handed out her wet clothes and lay among the furs on Aguta's bed. She pushed away her worries about Dylan and quickly fell asleep amidst the gentle crackle of Aguta's cooking fire, the delicious soup smells and the feel of soft furs against her cheek.

48

. . . .

A ROCK HOLDING DYLAN's weight gave way and crashed noisily down into the pit. Dylan was able to shift his weight to a handhold, but he found himself dangling about ten feet above the sharp rocks with only his fingertips holding his weight.

Consulting the climbing map in his head, he reached out for a fissure, which was to be a secondary point.

To his surprise and relief, the fissure was a better contact point than he had first chosen. He would be able to use it as a handhold and a toehold as he moved up the wall of the pit.

"What was that?" Rhett asked in the dark at the sound of the rock falling.

"I'm trying to find a way out of here," said Dylan. "The sides of this pit are unstable in places."

"You can't climb out of there," said Rhett. "I've seen the sides of that pit under strong light. There's no way anyone could climb that."

"Maybe you are right," said Dylan as he moved upwards and placed his toe in the fissure. "What are the questions you wanted to ask us?"

"I want to know how you learned about the iridium in this place. It's not something an ordinary tourist would know anything about."

Dylan explained how Jennifer's rock-hound dad speculated about it, and how Jun had come on the trip to look for his nephew.

"Now it's my turn to ask a question," said Dylan. "What are you doing in the cave if you're aren't part of Shaman Mountain Mine? And why won't you just help us?"

"I'm here because I'm representing a buyer for this mine," said Rhett. "And I don't want to help you because of your racist comment about black Africans."

Dylan paused in his ascent and thought back to what he had said. "I guessed you were South African because of your accent. I've guided several South Africans on hunting trips. They've all been white, and assumed you are white. Most of Alaska is white. Frankly, I could care less about your skin color and would appreciate some help."

Dylan's comment gave Rhett a jolt. *Why did I assume this man was racist? The room was completely dark when I came close to the pit, so he could have not known my skin color.*

Rhett wanted to find out just how racist this tour guide was. "When you hear terms in the US press like *state's rights, law and order,* and *affirmative action* what do you think? Are these racist?"

Dylan thought back to a time where he took a wilderness first aid class in Florida. Several of the participants were black, and one fellow, a dark-skinned slender man from Boston named Jeff, had lead thoughtful discussions of those very terms over the nighttime campfires. Dylan felt he'd learned a lot from Jeff.

"I think they could be racist," said Dylan. *State's rights* could mean efforts to weaken federal protections for minorities. *Law and order* could be a dog whistle term appealing to whites who want law enforcement to crack down in minority neighborhoods. But they don't have to be racist."

Dylan was nearly at the top of the pit. If he slipped now, he would likely be severely injured on the sharp rocks jutting up below.

Dylan found a four-point contact area on the wall that allowed him to rest his cramping muscles. "Why did you automatically think that I'm against South African blacks? You don't know my racial make up. Maybe you are the racist."

Again Rhett felt a jolt of doubt surge through him. "You didn't comment on affirmative action," said Rhett listening closely to the climbing noises coming from the pit. "Why is your voice changing? Are you actually getting out of that pit?"

When Dylan didn't answer, Rhett went on. "American whites think affirmative action favors blacks, but the biggest affirmative action programs exist in places like your Harvard University. Their program is called legacy admission. Over 30% of the students are admitted under this program, and they are 99 percent white."

As he stood on a large foothold to rest, Dylan had never thought about legacy admission as an affirmative action plan.

It seemed to Rhett, that this Alaskan tour guide had few racist preconceptions; unlike other Alaskans he had met.

The conversation had unsettled Rhett. *What if I'm the only racist in this room? What would Father Mavuso say about this conversation? This white man is manipulating me. He is dangerous. I must close my mind to what he says and concentrate on my mission.*

Dylan hoisted himself up over the lip of the pit and rested silently as he consulted his mental map of the Glass Dome.

Rhett's thoughts distracted him from what was happening near the pit. The climbing sounds had stopped, and he could hear footfalls where someone was crossing the open area. "Tour guide! You are out of the pit. Is your wife out too? I can't believe it."

"She left the pit quite awhile ago. I need to get to her, and take her back to Anchorage. She's not my wife. She's a client. I need to protect her."

Suddenly the blackness brightened just the smallest amount. Somewhere, far back in the shaft, lights had been turned on and cast a weak glow into the Glass Dome. Tiny sparkles magnified the light. Voices could be heard.

Rhett took advantage of the meager light and climbed the ladder back up the to the path then pulled it up after him. He wanted Dylan down on the floor of the Glass Dome to delay the people coming down the shaft. Then he had planned to squeeze into one of the side tunnels, let the miners pass him, then leave.

He looked back to see Dylan's shadow climbing up the side of the Glass Dome without any obvious effort. He was using the inclusions in the Glass Dome like the handholds on a climbing wall. Rhett had never seen anything like it, except in a Spiderman movie.

Once at the top, Dylan disappeared down a shaft with a well-worn path. It had to be a west exit from the mine. Rhett had to ask himself if the rock-climbing tourist could see in the dark.

Rhett did not want Gideon to know he'd been questioning the tourist. He pressed himself into a dark side tunnel and listened as two miners walked past him carrying food, probably for the tourists.

What a surprise they would have!

49
....

WHEN JENNIFER AWOKE, it was to the smell of baking biscuits and a moose sausage gravy warming over the fire. It took her a few moments to orient herself.

She sat up among the furs on Aguta's bed. "I need to find Dylan. He's being held captive in that pit."

Aguta turned around, threw her clothes at her then returned to his work. "I washed your clothes while you were asleep, and I went into the mine and checked that awful pit. No one was in it." He turned to stir the moose gravy.

To Jennifer, the breakfast smelled better than any she had ever experienced. "That must mean Dylan got away! You are an amazing cook with just the wilderness to supply your larder." Jennifer, dressed and hungry, soon stood beside Aguta finger-combing her hair.

"Since I work for the mine in the winter, they pay me in money and allow me to order things to be brought in on supply runs." He took the lid off a heavy iron kettle and pulled out a perfect biscuit, placed it in a bowl, and ladled the moose gravy over it.

Sitting on a rustic chair at a homemade table, Jennifer started her breakfast. "Oh my god! This is yummy!"

"Hunger is the best sauce," said Aguta as he prepared his own bowl. "I nearly never have guests, so that's why I have only one chair." Aguta sat on the edge of his bed and started in on his breakfast.

"So you just live here on this mountain by yourself? Don't you get lonely?" Jennifer ate the salty/smoky gravy and thought it was delicious.

"I grew up just a few hundred miles from here. I served in the army, but had problems. When I live here with the wolves and the mountain, I'm happy. I'm trying to learn the magic of the wolves."

"The wolves are magic?" asked Jennifer plucking a piece of flaky biscuit from her bowl.

"Of course they are. They are my path to the knowledge of my ancestors," Aguta spoke with assurance.

"I hope you find what you are looking for. And thanks for helping me last night. I really appreciate it. I was about to have a meltdown when you came. After breakfast, I need to get back to the Magic Ring. Dylan said to meet him there," said Jennifer.

"Magic Ring?" asked Aguta.

"There's a ring of trees up the hill . . ."

"Does it have a dead wolf in it?" Aguta looked her solemnly.

"Wow. You really know this mountain," said Jennifer. "It's the smaller one up the hill. Do you know why someone would kill that beautiful wolf? Did you shoot it?"

"Me? The wolves are sacred to me. They give me power and knowledge. They help me heal from injuries I got in the army. I protect them." Aguta slid his pant leg up to show her a tattoo of a wolf on his ankle. "You could say the white wolf is my totem. I know who killed that wolf. They are planning to kill more today. After breakfast, I must check to see if they put more poison packs in a caribou they shot last night."

"But why? Why kill such a perfect creature?"

"They are bad men. I must check on that caribou carcass soon. I steal the poison from their traps," said Aguta pointing to a small burlap sack on the floor nearly overflowing with poison packs. "This is terrible poison. It makes animals bleed to death from the inside. They suffer greatly."

"Don't leave me here alone. What if those bad men come after me? I'll come with you!" said Jennifer. "Maybe there's something I can do to help you save your wolves. Can I leave a message for Dylan?"

"We will pass near that fairy ring on our way. You can leave a message."

"Yes. Let's go."

Jennifer helped Aguta clean up the breakfast dishes and start a pot of his amazing moose sausage soup to heat on the coals for later. She continued to marvel at his cabin. The cluttered cabin projected a calming sense of order. Everything seemed to have a function and a certain place. She noticed some high-tech weather instruments and a huge bazooka on the wall as well as an impressive array of hand-made furniture and tools that looked as if taken from a Native-American cultural museum.

Suddenly Jennifer found herself wanting to barricade herself in Aguta's sturdy cabin. She thought about rapists and shuddered. She wondered about her missing cousin. She worried that the miners had hurt Dylan, and that he had not escaped the pit. But when she followed Aguta out of the cabin and into the morning sunshine, her heart lifted. She felt sure she would soon see Dylan and also save wolves. Aguta would protect her from bad men.

Neither she nor Aguta knew the wolf hunters were watching their poison trap from blinds.

50

· · · · · · · · · ·

SNUFFY AND GIDEON WALKED down the mineshaft carrying some oatmeal for Dylan and Jennifer. Gideon planned on taking them out of the pit and giving them food in order to get information.

With Snuffy's height and Gideon's muscled body, they would be intimidated into telling everything they knew.

He especially wanted to know how they learned about the iridium and what happened to Blaster. Afterwards, he had to kill them. He couldn't let word of the iridium get out, and since he let Rusty and Snuffy rape the girl, that had to be covered up as well.

It was obvious that Snuffy was getting increasingly uncomfortable as they got closer to the pit. He rubbed his hat on his head and said, "I hope the girl didn't get out of the pit and run away."

"Don't worry. No one can get out of that pit. Nearly every one of the Chinese workers has tried it, and those little monkeys could do it if anyone could," said Gideon.

"Maybe that husband guy will lie and say Rusty and I never put his wife back in the pit," said Snuffy fidgeting as he walked.

"Shut up, Snuffy. You're not making any sense."

"Well, guys like that lie. You know—tourists. Tourists lie all the time. I've seem 'em lie for no reason."

"Shut the fuck up," yelled Gideon. Snuffy's chatter grated on him.

Once they reached the Glass Dome, Gideon noticed the ladder was pulled up and lay on the tunnel floor. Usually it was set up so someone could go from the shaft area down to the lower floor of the Glass Dome and then onto the area where the pit was located. "Why did you pull up the ladder? Worried that they could get out of the pit?"

Snuffy didn't answer, but looked confused. Soon they lowered the ladder the floor of the glass dome and peered into the pit. Empty.

Gideon fumed. "So you put the girl back here when you were finished with helping her wash her clothes? Did you leave the ladder in the pit?"

"No, honest. I never even came back here after we left." Snuffy was a terrible liar, but Gideon couldn't figure out what part of the story he was lying about.

"You didn't come back here? Then where did you put the girl? I know she's not in the bunkhouse. And how did the husband get out of the pit?" Gideon stared hard at Snuffy. "Where is she?"

Snuffy realized he'd better come clean, "She run off. She cuts frisbees and runs like a deer. I never seen nothing like it. I didn't even get to help her wash her clothes. Neither did Rusty."

Ignoring the frisbee comment, Gideon tried to get more information out of Snuffy, "Where did she go after she ran away? Did she come back to the mine and let her husband go?"

"I don't know where she went. She looked like she was running downhill. Maybe she's with Blaster. He might be having some fun with her."

"Snuffy, you are so fucked up," Gideon slapped him, hard. Not hard enough to cause him to miss any work, but hard enough to tell him to stop lying. With Blaster gone, Gideon needed Snuffy.

Snuffy, seemingly relieved that his punishment was over, got up cheerfully and spit blood onto the dusty floor. "I'll go get Chewy and Leo, I saw them eating cinnamon rolls an hour ago. They will find the girl and her husband. They can track anyone. Do I still get to be the first one to help her with her wash?"

Gideon felt that everything was falling apart. Blaster had the mechanical ability to keep the old generator running. No one else knew how to do it like he did. He was gone, likely dead or disabled. He never missed a meal.

Discipline was declining, and that was undoubtedly Gideon's own fault. He'd had so many distractions. It seemed like tons of strangers knew about the iridium.

Soon it would be worth no more per gram than iron. Gideon had to do something. If he killed the tourists and buyer's agent, that might delay the world finding out about the iridium.

He'd have to also kill the Chinese and probably Snuffy and his other workers. They would never be able to keep quiet about the iridium.

Maybe he'd need to go back to South Africa and kill that Mr. Meijer guy who also knew about the iridium. Everything was getting out of control.

So much to do.

51
. . . .

DYLAN LIGHTLY JOGGED through the dripping woods to the pack he had left hanging in a tree.

Under a coil of rope, he found the lunch he'd brought. He drank deeply from his water bottle and ate several energy bars and a loose apple.

He felt a jolt of panic when he realized he'd left his PTSD meds back at his camp, but told himself that missing a few doses would not incapacitate him.

His first impulse was to search the mine buildings for Jennifer, but some part of him hoped she'd gotten away. He decided he should check the Magic Ring since he had told her to go there.

Dylan's job as an outdoor guide, meant he often lead wealthy clients on hunting trips. One of his highly developed outdoor skills was tracking game. Rusty had told Dylan about the mine having expert trackers, so Dylan had to make sure he did not lead the trackers to Jennifer.

He decided to leave a clear but false trail that anyone could follow. He would lead his trackers away from the Magic Ring and into something they couldn't handle. Maybe they would get intimidated and go back to the mine, or maybe they would get hurt and give up.

Starting from the mine exit he had taken, he left a trail of broken branches, muddy footprints and energy bar wrappers for trackers to follow. His trail lead to a scree area where the mountainside was a steep, unstable jumble of pumpkin-to-car-sized rocks. Hopping from rock to rock, he climbed to the top of the scree area and fastened his rope to a tree, then returned to his false trail.

Using the rope for support, Dylan made it look like he crossed the unstable scree area by leaving a trail of muddy footprints.

It quickly became a far more difficult operation than he had planned. Once, his false trail slid down the mountain, and he had to make it again. Were it not for the rope, Dylan realized he might not have escaped injury or even death.

Once on the other side of the slope, he retrieved his rope, then continued his open trail to where a small waterfall tumbled over some mossy rocks. The slippery rocks would be dangerous if someone slid off of them. They might drop down the rocky falls about 15 feet. Anyone who fell would likely break an arm or leg or even get a serious head injury.

Again, Dylan climbed up the falls and secured his rope to a boulder. He made a trail that looked like he had easily crossed the slippery rocks below the falls. He took a baseball cap out of his pack and left it hanging on a rock in the middle of the false trail he had left.

As soon as he made it to the other side of the falls, he again retrieved his rope and made a trail that looked like he was heading up the mountain. As soon as Dylan got to another stream, he followed a more or less direct path to the Magic Ring leaving no trace of his journey as he kept his footprints in the streambed. The trackers would think he had vanished.

Dylan had decided that if Jennifer wasn't waiting for him at the Magic Ring, he would need to return to the mining camp and search all the buildings. He hoped he would not get caught.

52

· · · · · · · · · · ·

GIDEON CHECKED THE MAGAZINE on his Sig Sauer P320 for the second time. He loved this pistol for so many reasons, but top on the list was that he had fired thousands of rounds through it during his military training.

He figured he could easily subdue or kill the African with just his bare hands, but Gideon wanted the black man to see the gun as a show of force.

Gideon wasn't sure that his physical size would be enough to intimidate the confident black man. Gideon thought that Rhett would not know anything about Gideon's fighting skills, and he wanted to negotiate from a position of power.

Maybe the rich South African mine owner had an offer better than what Gideon could make off of selling all the iridium nuggets he had stockpiled. Perhaps a river of gold would flow to Gideon when the South African took over the mine. This could be better than I ever imagined, thought Gideon.

Entertaining second thoughts about confronting the black while carrying an awesome pistol, Gideon called Snuffy into the room. "Here Snuffy, put my Sig in your waist band while I negotiate."

Snuffy looked pleased. "Blaster has my gun, or whoever took it away from him. Maybe I can show off my target shooting for you."

"No. Only shoot if I tell you to," said Gideon. "I'm going to try to find out if the African can pay us more for the silver nuggets than we can get by selling them on the open market." Gideon had been telling his men that the nuggets were low-quality silver, worth a small fraction of the iridium's value.

Gideon found Rhett in the kitchen preparing a huge meal. The guy was bold. He just walked into the mine's kitchen and took what he wanted. It was as if he already owned the mine. Cookie was standing uncomfortably to the side wringing his hands in a dirty white apron.

With Snuffy behind him, Gideon entered the kitchen where Rhett was chopping an onion.

Rhett continued chopping as Gideon and Snuffy moved close to the cutting board. A glance at Gideon's relaxed facial muscles told him this was not an attack. He noticed the swagger in Snuffy's step and the gun under his belt.

He could see no obvious weapons on Gideon's body, but a kitchen was second only to a tool shed as a place where ordinary objects could be turned into weapons. Rhett already had planned a dozen offensive or defensive moves with kitchen objects: starting with the chef's knife in his hand.

"I see you are taking our food," said Snuffy, perhaps hoping to start a confrontation.

"Yes. And if I decide my boss shouldn't buy this place, you'll be well-compensated for it," said Rhett tossing the chopped onion into a cast iron frying pan with hot bacon grease and potato chunks sizzling in it. The hot grease and the metal pan were also weapons.

"We need to talk," said Gideon his thumbs in his belt.

The thumbs told Rhett that Gideon was unlikely to attack at that moment. "Sure. Are you guys hungry? I can put more potatoes into the pan," said Rhett holding a large potato up.

"Just tell me about the offer your boss has for me," said Gideon.

Rhett gestured toward Snuffy. "You want him in here?" asked Rhett. "Does he know about this?" Rhett reached across the counter and held up the tennis ball sized iridium nugget."

"Sure, I know about the silver, you dumb shit," said Snuffy.

Gideon turned toward Snuffy. "Go check the fuel in the generator."

"But why can't I stay here?" whined Snuffy.

"Just do it."

"Want me to leave your gun here?" asked Snuffy looking bewildered.

"Just go. Take the gun with you. And take Cookie. This is a private conversation," said Gideon.

Snuffy turned and left the room with a confused Cookie following. Their retreating footsteps made crunching sounds in the gravel.

"Why did you have him bring a gun in here? Worried I'll steal your potatoes?" smiled Rhett. He could see that Gideon's patience was wearing thin.

"Just tell me what your boss has to offer," said Gideon.

"I can do that. Are you sure you don't want some bacon and potatoes?" said Rhett feeding Gideon's irritable mood.

"No, damn it. Just say what you came here to say!"

"First I need to know who, besides you and these tourists, know about the iridium," said Rhett casually stirring the potato and onion mix and looking unconcerned. The kitchen was filling with the cooking odors of bacon, potatoes and onions: a smell that made most miners hungry.

"Why do you want to know?" asked Gideon looking at the browning potatoes.

"Because the amount of gold on the table varies with how many people know about the iridium," said Rhett. "Just give me an idea. How many people in this camp know about it? Who outside the camp knows about it? How did the tourists in your pit find out about it? My boss has an interest in keeping the find quiet." Rhett chopped more bacon strips into one-inch lengths and tossed them in with the potato mixture.

"None of my men know about it. I told them it was silver, and that if they kept their mouths shut about it, I could get them each about five thousand dollars. Outside of this camp, a mineralogist at University of Oregon did the testing for me, but I gave her a fake name, and said I was from New Mexico.

"And I have no idea of how those tourists found out. They got out of the pit somehow and are loose on the mountain. I have my trackers after them. They should be back here by this evening." Gideon poached a sample of Rhett's meal out of the frying pan. "Now I told you what I know. How much gold?"

"What about the Chinese? Do they know?" asked Rhett as he poured the perfectly cooked meal into a huge chef's bowl. Scooping with a cereal bowl, he pulled out a portion of the potato mixture for Gideon.

Gideon stepped forward aggressively. "How did you find out there were Chinese miners here? They don't speak English. Anyway, the Chinese don't count."

"I'd like to know if you intentionally kept information about the Chinese from me, and what else you haven't told me," said Rhett calmly. He studied Gideon and decided that he hadn't lied about anything so far with the exception of withholding information about his Asian slave laborers. *Not bad*, Rhett thought. *I'll only need to kill this terrible white man and the tourists. Maybe the idiot named Snuffy and the miner Kung.*

Rhett thought about the tourists. If he let Gideon kill them, then Father Mavuso could not be disappointed with Rhett. *I'll let Gideon take care of the tourists, then I'll dispose of Gideon, Snuffy and Kung.* Rhett felt uneasy about killing Kung, but the mission must be completed.

"I told you everything. The Chinese don't count, and I didn't know you knew about them. Now tell me about the gold." growled Gideon.

Rhett handed a bowl of crispy potato, onion and bacon to Gideon. "You are hungry. Eat this. I'll tell you about the gold.

Rhett covered the chef's bowl with a plate and started for the door.

"Where are you going with all that food?" asked Gideon.

"Oh. I'm taking this to the Chinese. Come with me and I'll tell you about the gold you'll get."

Rhett pushed through the kitchen door and out into the mine's yard. As Gideon followed him out, Rhett turned and tossed a Krugerrand at Gideon.

It was one of the several radiation-marked coins Rhett had bought back from dealers in Anchorage, and it surprised him how quickly Gideon's reactions were. He caught the coin mid-air without spilling any food. Rhett expected it to bounce off the big man's chest.

"Imagine a vault full of these Krugerrands . . ."

53

· · · · · · · · · · ·

AN EARLY FROST COVERED the ground as Slade and his team dragged the caribou carcass over a hill and into a gully where they thought the wolves might find it.

"We'll have 4-hour shifts in the blind, so the man occupying the blind doesn't get too cold or tired. Bonner, you are first. Keep your eyes on this carcass. It's our bait."

"This is a waste of time," whined Bonner. "We've only killed one of these wolves. That was with a gun, not poison; and even then, we haven't seen the body. It might have recovered from that wound. It's time to go home."

"Yeah, and I'm tired of eating MREs and caribou. How come we can't just trade some of our gamey meat for real food at that mining camp?" said Charlie picking at a scab on his arm.

"Superintendent Quigley told us to stay away from the mine. If we piss them off, our return plane can't land on their strip," said Slade. "Now these are our last poison packs," said Slade holding up a bag. "I'm tired of this hunt, too. If we strike out on this one, we're heading home as failure for an independent Alaska. Remember, our mission is to keep the federal government out of Alaska's affairs.

Once word of this invasive species of wolves get out, the feds will interfere with our right to live without government breathing down our backs and telling us what to do."

Slade hoped the pep talk would keep his men on task for this last bait trap. He had no idea why the wolves and other animals could consume the poison and not seem to die. Maybe there was a reason that every poison pack at every carcass would be eaten, or taken away, and no wolves seemed to die. He suspected Bonner might be sabotaging their traps. *But why? Was he some kind of closet liberal? Did he just want to go home early?*

Bonner settled down in the blind and yawned.

Once the carcass was placed and the poison packs shoved in among the entrails, Slade Able and Charlie trudged back toward their camp. Just out of earshot of Bonner, Slade told the others he was going on a hike up the mountain to get some exercise. His real goal was a second, secret blind he had constructed to watch Bonner. The blind was far up the canyon where the previous bait trap had been placed.

After a long hike, Slade crept into his blind and focused his binoculars on the carcass. So far, the only visible activity was the magpies quarreling and gorging themselves. But this was good. Soon the wolves would be drawn to all the fuss made by the noisy birds. He couldn't see Bonner, but he watched Bonner's blind suspecting the whiny secessionist was taking a nap.

After several hours, Slade found himself getting cold and sleepy. He forced himself to keep watch. At first, the only change he saw was that the ravens had joined the magpies in the feast. But then he saw some movement near some bushes close to the bait. He saw someone moving toward the caribou carcass. It looked like a woman—maybe Asian or Native.

Anger bubbled up in Slade, She's going to sabotage our bait!

As he watched, Slade noticed another person, much sneakier than the woman. He fit the description of the mine's winter caretaker. *So that Native asshole is putting his girlfriend up to this*!

He watched Aguta and the woman chase away the birds and paw through the carcass pulling out, what looked like, the poison packs. They placed each pack in a burlap bag. After they had assured themselves that all the poison was in the bag, Slade saw Aguta send the woman downhill with the burlap sack while he remained and peed on the carcass. So that's why the wolves avoided it! If Slade had brought his long gun, he'd have shot the saboteurs.

Slade swung his binoculars towards the hunting blind that Bonner was manning. There was no sigh of Bonner. He was probably asleep.

Anger surged in Slade. As he hiked back to the camp, he planned out just how he and his team would punish that fucking Indian and his woman.

54

....

HAVING SPENT THE NIGHT snug in a hollowed-out tree, Dylan searched for Jennifer at daybreak. His relief at finding her note calmed him.

The note told him she would be safe at Aguta's cabin.

He reread the note Jennifer left for him at the Magic Ring and found her previous night's tracks. He followed the tracks from the Magic Ring to their destroyed campsite. To Dylan, it looked like bears had ransacked their site with most of their interest focused on Jennifer's tent.

Dylan guessed that Jennifer had ignored his advice about bringing scented items—which can attract curious bears.

He searched for the sat-phone, but it was gone. Judging by the footprints around the remains of his tent, Jennifer had possibly taken it with her.

Dylan became alarmed when he saw a man's footprints near their campfire ring next to Jennifer's prints. The male's boot prints did not have the hard lug patterns common to a miner's work boots, but a softer print favored by hikers. Perhaps the man named Aguta who Jennifer mentioned in her note left these prints.

After careful observation, it appeared there was no struggle between Jennifer and helper. They appeared to walk side-by-side up Shaman Mountain.

Lowering the food cache from its treetop location, Dylan replenished his daypack and his belly with food and began to lightly jog up the track that Jennifer and the hiker had taken. Tucked into his belt, Dylan had brought his hatchet to serve as a weapon since Gideon had taken his bear spray. He wished he had brought a gun on this trip, but he hadn't planned on hunting.

After hiking and jogging, Dylan came to a hand-built log home not far from the cliff overlooking the Kila Glacier. The cabin possessed the kind of functional beauty that made Dylan long to return to a life in the woods, but it was clear that Jennifer and the helper man had come directly to this place.

Smoke curled lazily up from the chimney and a wonderful soup odor mixed with the campfire smell and clung to the clearing.

Dylan hoped Jennifer was a guest and not a prisoner. The sturdy log home could be either a welcoming refuge or a solid fortress. Dylan noticed the home had a summer and winter entrance that had once been common to Native log homes.

Taking out his hatchet and holding it behind his back, Dylan knocked on the door. Jennifer opened it, shrieked joyfully and threw her arms around Dylan's neck.

"Oh my God! Dylan! You are OK. Are you OK?" The words rushed out. "Aguta was just leaving to see if we could get the miners to let you go. I'm not ever going back to that mine," she shuttered at the thought.

In the dark cabin, Dylan could see an older Native man approaching the door with a grandfatherly smile. "So they let you go? Come in and tell us about it. Have some soup."

Dylan put away his hatchet and enjoyed his soup with gusto. He told Aguta and Jennifer about his experiences.

Aguta didn't appear to believe that he was able to climb out of the pit. "It's too deep and the sides are too smooth. You must be a highly skilled climber to escape."

"One thing I can do well is climb. But we need to get help to deal with these miners," concluded Dylan as he licked his spoon clean. "These miners are not typical Alaskans."

"Some bears chewed up our sat-phone. It lights up, but just keeps displaying the same error message," said Jennifer.

"It could be that the satellites are not in position to make a connection," said Dylan examining the phone. "This far north we'll get spotty service. We're also behind the mountain. Maybe it will work better if we take it down by the glacier."

"I don't have a sat-phone, I use the mining camp phone if I need one, and theirs is also unreliable," said Aguta.

"There's not just miners on this mountain," said Jennifer. "We know about some hunters. They might have a sat-phone, but they are here to kill the wolves. We ruined one of their bait traps this morning." Jennifer showed Dylan the burlap bag full of blue poison packs.

"That doesn't make sense," said Dylan looking at the poison packs. "This area is closed to wolf hunting until next August. And using poison is illegal."

"Wait—in Alaska people can hunt wolves?" Jennifer asked.

"I've never hunted a wolf, but they are considered 'big game' and in most areas, there's a five-wolf limit. However, taking a wolf out of season is a serious poaching crime," said Dylan looking up at the large military weapon on Aguta's wall.

Jennifer followed Dylan's eyes. "Aguta has a bazooka, but he doesn't hunt wolves. He protects them."

"It's a recoilless rifle that fires a special concussive artillery shell," said Aguta proudly taking down and handing the weapon to Dylan. "It's to limit avalanche damage on the mining property. All the miners leave in the winter, so I stay here and tame the avalanches."

"This is so light. It's like an empty mailing tube," said Dylan hefting the recoilless rifle. "When you fire a shell, does the recoil energy blast out the back?"

"Yep. Much of the blast goes out the back so it's actually a mild kick. With training, Jennifer could easily fire this. Just don't stand behind her when she does," said Aguta replacing the weapon back to its spot on the wall. "The back-blast can knock down a wall."

"What's this?" asked Jennifer taking a small item from the wall. "It looks like it could be some sort of masculine jewelry."

"That's a traditional glacier monitor. My people used these to determine when the glacier was safe to cross," said Aguta.

"How does it work? It looks like an open fish jaw on a sharp stick with some hairs stuck in it," said Dylan admiring the simple but elegant tool.

"That's exactly what it is. I use the guard hairs from seal fur for the hair because they are so reactive to subsonic vibrations. Just attach this monitor on a solidly frozen part of the glacier, and watch the hairs. If they vibrate in waves, then the glacier is unstable and probably unsafe."

Aguta's eyes shone with pride as the others examined it. "You can have it," he said to Jennifer. "I can easily make another one."

Jennifer looked pleased. "Oh thank you! It will be my best souvenir from Alaska." She put the glacier tool in the case that usually held her dark glasses.

"Let's take this phone down to the glacier and try it," said Dylan. "We need to see what we can salvage from our campsite, too."

While Jennifer got her things ready, Dylan and Aguta fell into a deep conversation about hiking and camping on the glacier. They talked gear, routes and timing.

Aguta showed Dylan some of his glacier-crossing gear. To her, it appeared that Dylan was planning on bringing more clients to the Shaman Mountain area once the he could be sure of his clients' safety.

Soon Dylan and Jennifer walked out into the daylight and looked back into Aguta's cabin.

"Be careful," said Aguta. "The mine has good trackers who can find you if you're not careful."

"I think those trackers are busy following a false trail I left up the mountain,"

He hoped he was right as he closed the door.

55

....

MINUTES LATER, AGUTA'S DOOR CRASHED inward followed nearly instantly by Slade and his armed three-man team. Slade had his deadly

Springfield .45 out of the holster and pointed at Aguta's face as he thundered, "You! You have been sabotaging my wolf hunt! You are going to pay for that."

Aguta's lined face showed no emotion. "You can't hunt wolves now anyway. They are out of season in this area. Also, you can't use poison."

"Who the hell are you? Some big government employee? How do you get off tell us what we can or can not do?" Slade swung his pistol around the cabin.

Charlie lowered his rifle. "Is that true, Slade? Wolves are out of season here? You told us you had permits for each of us to take five wolves," said Charlie looking nervous. "If I get busted with a hunting violation, I'll have to give back my moose tag. It took me three years to get it."

"This guy's no ranger. He can't do anything. All he can do is interfere with our plans," said Slade. "But this fucking Indian and his wife are the ones who have been ruining our hunts."

Slade looked down at Aguta. "You took our gear. Our poison packs. Where are they?"

Aguta, resisting an urge to look down at the burlap bag near his cooking fire, answered in a steady voice. "We threw them into a crevasse in the glacier. You'll never get them back."

"Where's that bitch wife of yours?" said Able, pointing his rifle at Aguta. "She needs to pay for damages to our hunt."

"She's at the mine using their sat-phone," said Aguta. "She'll be back soon, and so will Fish and Game."

"Fish and Game?" said Charlie. "We'll get in trouble, and I'll lose my moose tag."

"We're doing this for a greater cause than your stupid moose tag," said Slade. "I don't like killing wolves out of season anymore than you, but we have our homeland to think of."

While Slade was talking, Aguta had moved to the cooking area and stirred the soup. "You guys hungry?" he asked.

"That soup smells good," said Able. "I'm tired of eating MREs." Able turned to Aguta. "Hey, want to trade a couple of jambalaya MREs for some of that soup?"

Aguta appeared to consider the offer and decided to play to Charlie's fear of losing his moose tag. "You know—these wolves are way different from the typical Alaska wolves. The adults are smaller than the average grey wolf. These may be a rare subspecies and therefore protected by federal regulations. You wouldn't want to get in deep trouble with the feds by killing a rare wolf."

"Hey, what if he's right?" asked Bonner. "The wolves do look small. Maybe we should go easy on these wolves. We could get in big trouble."

"And probably lose my moose tag," moaned Charlie.

Slade looked at Aguta. "How did you figure that out about these wolves? Did someone tell you?"

"No one needed to. Just looking at the wolves, it's easy to see they are different. An average mature, male grey wolf is about 90 pounds. The wolves of Kila Ikpic weigh about half that. Plus their green eyes; the typical gray wolf has amber eyes. Besides all that, these wolves create paths to my spirit knowledge. They show me the way."

Slade looked at his men. "Superstitious bullshit. Now what are we going to do? If this guy knows about these rare wolves, it can screw up our plans. The feds will never let Alaska be free."

"There's a guide and his client who also know about these wolves. They're going to tell everyone that the Kila Ikpic wolves are special," said Aguta. "If you kill wolves, you guys are going to jail. Holding me under gunpoint and making threats is assault and kidnapping. Now just leave my mountain so you can avoid five years in jail."

"We can't let you tell anyone about us or the wolves," said Slade in a quiet, dangerous voice. "Not to protect ourselves, but to protect a free Alaska."

Charlie appeared on the verge of panic. "I can't go to jail. My wife's pregnant."

Slade looked at his men, Charlie and Bonner looked weak. Maybe too weak to bring about a free Alaska.

Slade pulled back the slide on his .45 and checked to verify a shell had locked into the firing position. He handed the gun to Able and spoke in a low voice. "We need to do this for Alaska. Wait until I get Charlie and Bonner out of earshot."

Slade waited until Able gave him a resolute nod, and led Bonner and Charlie outside.

56

....

GIDEON STROLLED OUT of the kitchen with his bowl of potatoes and bacon. He had to think. What if the amazing offer from the African was legitimate?

All that gold! Gideon did not trust most people, but pretty black guys with funny accents were high on that list. *But the gold*!

Since the African's proposal had been for an illegal arrangement where Gideon would pretend to oversee the zinc operation, but actually mine the iridium, there was no legal way for Gideon to force a distant mine owner to make good on his promises.

If Gideon did all the work, but received no gold, what recourse could he have? It might be possible to find the mine owner, but it would be impossible to physically force him to hand over a room full of Krugerrands. How could he trust some foreigner and his black agent?

Adding to his discomfort was the fact that the African had been able to find him. Gideon had covered his tracks well to avoid letting anyone find out about the iridium mine.

That meant that the wily black guy could bring the authorities down on him, or perhaps find him again if he ran. Gideon could end up in jail for stealing and selling iridium. He hated it when someone had a powerful lever like that over him.

On the other hand, if Gideon killed Rhett and followed his original plan of running off with as much of the iridium as possible and selling it on the open market, he was assured of millions.

It might be hard to explain to buyers where he got the huge iridium nuggets since he didn't have a mining license anywhere. There's a strong possibility that selling the nuggets all at once could generate huge legal problems that might prevent him from enjoying his wealth.

Everything was getting so complicated! Gideon toyed with the idea of just taking a sack of nuggets back to that rich guy in Africa to exchange for a sack of gold. That would be a sure thing.

He could disappear with a million in untraceable gold. The idea of having hundreds of millions kept bringing him back to the African's risky offer. That African was too clever.

Gideon didn't like the fact that his mine had already been explored and assessed. And how did the tourists escape? None of his men would have helped the wilderness guide out of the pit. It had to be the Chinese workers or Rhett.

As he ate the last potato piece in his bowl, Gideon pondered. It just seemed crazy to trust the black guy. But the gold! It was so much money; it was hard to imagine it.

As soon as the trackers returned with the tourists, Gideon decided to "arrest" them then put them into the pit. Maybe he would challenge the guide to a hand-to-hand fight and kill him with a deadly Krav Maga move.

His men would want the Chinese tourist girl to work for her keep by giving comfort to everyone, but Gideon couldn't allow it; she might tell them about the iridium.

What to do about Rhett? Gideon was not afraid of a gamble. Maybe he could hide his stash of iridium and see if the African came through with the gold. Afterwards, he could still sell his stashed iridium before the mine could produce, thereby cheating the stupid African. He couldn't lose under that scenario.

His deliberations swirling, Gideon walked toward the clattering generator building to find Snuffy.

57

. . . .

DYLAN LED JENNIFER on a circuitous journey back to their destroyed campsite, unaware of the drama occurring in Aguta's cabin.

Soft mists rose from the forest floor bringing with it a sweet, piney perfume. Jennifer found herself mimicking Dylan's gentle loping strides down the mountain.

She noticed he avoided stepping in places where he could leave a footprint. He liked to jog in streambeds, even if they went the wrong direction for a time, since no prints could be left on the rocks. They stopped often to check the sat-phone, but it displayed the same error message each time they tried it.

"Maybe it will work down at our campsite," said Dylan trying to look confident. "We're farther from the mountain peak."

"What do we do if it doesn't work down there?" asked Jennifer tucking a lose strand of hair behind her ear.

"It could mean that the phone has some damage. We could just wait for a plane to return. Shelia will probably return if she doesn't hear from us in a week or so."

Dylan looked at Jennifer and felt a sudden urge to hug her. He hated that his client had experienced such fearsome danger. The way she handled her feelings impressed him. But if he hugged her, she might feel threatened instead of comforted, so he kept his distance.

"Why couldn't you just go back to the mine and grab their sat-phone? I saw it in Gideon's room when I was taking a shower. When they are all busy, just sneak in there and grab it." Jennifer face revealed fear. Dylan wondered if she was afraid for herself or for the risk she was urging he take.

She found herself drawn to Dylan, but she was confused as to why. He was handsome and kind, but distant. Once he held her briefly as he helped her down a steep streambed. That faint citrus-coconut smell mixed with a sweet-strong masculine scent on his soft hair.

She loved his smell and wanted him to hold her. Maybe her feelings were a result of recovering from the horrible treatment of the miners. Maybe she was just horny.

Taking a break from the downhill jog, the couple took a brief rest and sat on a fallen log. As the sunlight turned the mists golden, Jennifer looked up at Dylan with a warm smile, "It's so funny that right now, I think I love Alaska. I like you, too. I like that shampoo you use and the confident way you move through this wilderness."

She impulsively hugged Dylan's arm. He couldn't tell if she was just experiencing relief over her rescue, or she was just feeling some euphoria.

Dylan smiled uncomfortably. He relished her touch, but knew he shouldn't encourage her.

"So how did you get away from the miners?" asked Dylan to change the subject from his hair.

Jennifer drew her arm back from Dylan and pulled out her water bottle. "I pretended to go along with their mad plans for me, then ran when I got a chance." She drank and passed the bottle to Dylan.

"How did you stay so poised when you thought they were going to assault you?" Dylan held the bottle without drinking.

"I really don't know. Maybe it was my love of sports and the way competition forced me to develop instinctive reactions to my opponents' moves. Perhaps it was the cold logic and mental focus of studying the law, but something kept me from freezing up when faced with danger. Maybe I just have lots of confidence in you."

"Well, we are not out of danger yet. We need to get away from the miners, wolf hunters and alert law enforcement about what's going on here." Dylan drank and passed the bottle back to Jennifer.

"And I still want to be free to find my dad's body. My family is waiting to hear so we can have some closure." Jennifer pushed the bottle back into her back and stood up.

Dylan stood and looked down at Jennifer. "For now, we need to get someplace safe and call for help. I'll figure out how to stay safe until the plane comes back."

"And while we are walking, I'm going to figure out how I want to start a lawsuit against the mine owners and wolf hunters. They will pay dearly for their crimes on Kila Ikpic. I'll need to consult an Alaska lawyer on a lawsuit."

Dylan checked the phone for signal before resuming their journey down to the campsite. Jennifer peered at the sat-phone screen and looked disappointed when it showed the usual error message. "Dylan, you know a lot about danger.

What will I do if those miners confront me again? Will I act or freeze? Sometimes I'm really scared I'll do nothing."

"No one can know how how you'll act," said Dylan. "One way to prepare for another possible confrontation with the miners, is to play scenarios in your mind and practice the reaction you want to have."

Jennifer shuddered when she realized how close she had come to a brutal attack.

Dylan spent two hours, hiking all around the perimeter of the campsite, to satisfy himself that no one had set up surveillance in the area. Like timid deer stepping out into a clearing, Dylan carefully led Jennifer to the remains of their campsite. He told her to gather up any of her personal possessions she felt were essential, but to leave any luxuries where they were. Jennifer found this nearly comical, since she had already done this before leaving on this trip. Still, she tried to think of just surviving prior to rescue, and this helped decide she didn't need to take a nightgown, personal grooming products, swimsuit and so forth.

Dylan efficiently removed items from their food cache, and packed some essentials like ice axes, crampons and camping gear.

She wished they could just enjoy a nap in the sunshine that broke through some puffy clouds. Jennifer thought it would be nice to have someone she trusted lie next to her and hold her with muscular arms. She wanted to nuzzle into the chest of a strong man she trusted.

"Help me make the S.O.S. display with these rocks," said Dylan. "Any plane flying nearby might see it."

As they worked on the heavy task, Dylan tried not to worry. He thought about the danger to Jennifer and himself from the miners. He wondered if he would face jail time for taking a client on the trip with no guiding license. His business was done for. He'd never be able to keep up the payments for the bank loan he'd taken out.

Dylan had tried the sat-phone several times near their campsite, but had no success. Jennifer could tell he was looking very serious.

"Hey, let's go to that bathing place and clean up. That shower I took at Gideon's place wasn't really a shower. There was no hot water. After we're cleaned up and have a meal, then we can try the phone again."

Jennifer hoisted her pack. "I'm going to push away my concerns about our safety, recovering dad's body and getting rescued, and just enjoy a good soak."

"Good idea! A bath and a meal will refresh us and give us clear minds to decide our next course of action." He tried not to think of his glimpse of Jennifer's naked body as they hiked toward the bathing stream. He decided he could stay away while Jennifer bathed so she would not worry someone was peeking at her.

58

....

GIDEON PULLED OPEN the door to the generator shack expecting to see Snuffy doing something to stop the odd clanking noises and excessive black smoke coming from the exhaust stacks.

Instead he saw two of his Chinese miners covered in oil and apparently working on the engine. Snuffy stood by, looking uncomfortable as he tried to hide a whisky bottle.

"What's going on here? Why aren't these men working in the mine?" asked Gideon.

"It's their lunch break," explained Snuffy quickly putting his whisky bottle behind his back. "Kung here told me it's possible to change the oil on a diesel engine while it's running. So I'm making him do it."

"Kung, what's going on?" scowled Gideon.

Kung wiped some grease from his face with an oil-soaked rag. In his strong Chinese accent, Kung spoke, "Mr. Gideon. I don't right equipment to do this. I telling Mr. Snuffy that I did this on fishing boat. But we had hoses and clamps designed for that purpose. This making a mess." Kung gestured to the other Chinese worker. "Me and Lee want lunch break. That Mr. Rhett brought some fried potatoes to our break area, but Mr. Snuffy made us leave."

"So Rhett brought you food. How did he even know you worked here? did you go to him, or did he just happen to find you?" asked Gideon his face darkening.

Kung paused, wondering if it was better to lie and risk getting caught, or tell the truth and hope Gideon didn't hit him. "He came to us Chinese with food bars. He told us he's buying the mine and asked for a tour," Kung backed away slightly, keeping his gaze on Gideon's hands.

"Where did you take him?" demanded Gideon loud enough to drown out the clattering generator.

"Glass Dome and punishment pit," said Kung, deciding to omit they also explored another place rich in iridium nuggets.

"Why didn't you tell me!" Gideon grabbed Kung's jacket and roughly pulled him outside the shed. The generator noise abated as soon as they stepped outside, but Gideon sounded louder.

"Hit him, Gideon," yelled Snuffy. "Look what he did to the generator."

"Shut the fuck up," growled Gideon. "And where did you get that whisky?"

Quickly, Snuffy attempted again to hide the bottle behind his broad back. Then he smiled guiltily and offered it to Gideon. "Here, it's good. Want some? I found it under Blaster's bed. We shared most of this bottle before he disappeared. He told me he got it from the hunters."

To Kung, it looked like Gideon's neck was starting to turn red—a sure sign of trouble. Gideon released Kung and pointed a rod-like finger at Snuffy. "What hunters? Why didn't you tell me some hunters came in?"

"You told Blaster to clear the runway. That you expecting someone to land. Someone landed. Blaster said a Cessna 180 came in and some hunters got out and went into the woods. They left this bottle." Snuffy's Adam's apple bobbed as he started to talk faster and faster. "And Blaster figured you expected the hunters, so he didn't mention it." Snuffy also didn't mention that there were three more bottles of high-end bourbon.

"How many hunters, and when did this happen?" shouted Gideon the veins in his neck popping out.

While Gideon grilled Snuffy, Kung started to inch away; the red had spread from Gideon's neck to his face.

Snuffy's voice cracked as it appeared to dawn on him, that Gideon was angrier with him, than Kung. "That 180 landed in the morning when that Solomon guy came in. I think Blaster said there were three or four hunters. He wasn't sure. They were on the north side of the landing strip."

Gideon, already overly sensitive about anyone visiting the Shaman Mountain Mine, had become enraged at the thought of all the people roaming Shaman Mountain.

"Look, there are too many people prowling around here. I want you to radio Chewy and Leo and tell them that after they track down those tourists and bring them here. And I want a report on those hunters."

"Are we putting the hunters in the pit?" asked Snuffy.

"I haven't decided," said Gideon as he watched Kung stiffly walking away. I*'m losing control of this operation. Strangers all over the mountain. My Chinese workers defy me. Some black guy talking big about buying this mine. I've got to do something.*

"Did you know Rhett knew about our Chinese workers?" asked Gideon.

"No. That fucker is sneaky. I don't trust him," said Snuffy.

"I don't trust him either. Find Rhett. Put him in the pit. I'll fix this generator myself." Gideon flipped the kill switch on the generator. The camp suddenly became eerily quiet as silence rushed in.

"What if he won't go?" asked Snuffy in a too loud voice.

"Then hurt him."

59

· · · · · · · · · ·

SLADE CLOSED THE DOOR to Aguta's cabin as he left, then opened it and stuck his head in to talk to Able. "Remember, wait until we're out of earshot. I don't want Bonner and Charlie to hear the shot. That .45 is loud. Give us ten minutes."

Able looked from the big pistol in his hand to Aguta, who seemed to be concentrating on his soup. "I get it. Don't worry."

The door closed. The fire under the soup made a crackling sound.

"The soup is nearly ready. Want some?" Aguta turned his back to Able as he stirred the soup.

The aroma of the bubbling soup would be impossible for most people to resist, but after eating so many MREs, it smelled amazing. Able walked over and stood next to Aguta. "I would love a bowl of your soup." Able needed to wait until Slade and the rest were farther away before he shot the Indian. There was no hurry.

"Then look in the storage closet in the next room for a couple of bowls and spoons," Aguta gently stirred the soup using a large metal ladle that banged noisily against the side of the pot, and he began to sing a cooking song he had heard his mother use.

Able noticed how close the storage closet was to the kitchen area. There was no way the old Indian could get away if he made a run for it.

The storage closet appeared to be full of winter supplies. Listening to Aguta sing and ladle bang against the pot, he turned searched for bowls amongst the sacks of flour and cans of food. "There's no bowls out here," shouted Able.

"Look on the shelf near the sled," called Aguta from the kitchen.

A few minutes later, Able emerged from the storage area empty-handed. "There's no bowls out there."

"OK, then just wash out one of these," said Aguta pointing to some dirty dishes.

Soon Able smiled to see Aguta ladling out a bowl of the fragrant soup. "Want some bread with it? I make my own. It's fresh from yesterday's baking."

Able picked one of the bowls and took the chair at the trestle table near the cooking fire. He warily laid his gun on the table and spooned a portion of the broth from the soup, blew on it and then tasted it. "Wow. That's good. Much sweeter than I expected."

"Try the vegetables, too. They are wild plants from the mountain," said Aguta handing Able part of a crusty loaf of brown bread.

"So do you add sugar to this? My only complaint is that it's a bit too sweet," said Able now tipping the bowl to drink the soup.

Ignoring Able's comment. "You know it's not just the wolves that are smaller here," said Aguta.

"The glacier, the mountain and the river form an area of several hundred square miles that prevents the game from traveling far."

Able speared a chunk of meat from the bowl with the back of his spoon. "Yeah, it's just too sweet, but better than most of the MREs we've been eating."

"As a result of this area's geography, the caribou are smaller, and the coyotes are bigger than most of Alaska. I wouldn't be surprised if nearly every animal in this area are genetically special and perhaps endangered." Aguta watched Able tip his bowl up to get the last drops of soup.

"Too bad you put so much sugar in this," said Able. "Or I'd have another bowl. Why aren't you eating your soup?" Able pointed to the other bowl that Aguta had put out.

"Not that hungry I guess," said Aguta looking closely at Able.

"I'm guessing that Slade and the guys are out of earshot now." Able picked up the heavy pistol and looked in wonder at his hands. "My god! My fingernails are bleeding!"

"Think about those poison packs you guys use. The manufacturer mixes sugar with the poison to mask the bitter taste. It works, too. Animals eat those packs no matter how sweet they are." Aguta picked up a hot pad and grasped the handle of the bubbling soup pot.

The whites of Able's eyes had turned bright red, and he spit blood onto the table. "Poison packs? I thought you threw them in glacier." His voice trembled as he spoke and his muscles appeared to be spasming. He dropped the gun.

"No, that was my plan, but I didn't have a chance to do it yet." Aguta walked to Able and poured the boiling soup over him. Instantly, it seemed that every place on Able's body the hot soup hit began bleeding.

Able attempted to scream, but all that came out was a red froth. Aguta matter-of-factly pulled a well-used plastic sheet from a shelf and rolled Able's spasming body onto it, ignoring the man's trembling movements as the man's organs shut down.

"Horrible way to die," said Aguta as he finished rolling the tarp around the body. "But it couldn't be helped. The wolves need me."

60

. . . .

WHEN DYLAN GUIDED a trip into a remote part of Alaska, he understood that offering his clients great food could result in positive reviews. He had a number of woodland recipes that were always big hits.

As he prepared an early evening meal for Jennifer and himself, he knew the aroma of frying sausage, onions and garlic would stimulate a robust appetite. As Jennifer sipped a cup of fragrant red wine, poured out of a bag, Dylan added fresh wild herbs to the pan and poured it over rice. It would have been a simple dinner at home, but out in the woods, it was a knockout meal.

The sleeping bags had steamed in the sunshine for several hours and were nearly dry, and the camp

Dylan had set up using the remains of their tents looked snug and inviting.

"Are you sure no one will find us here?" asked Jennifer when she could force herself to take break on eating.

Dylan gestured to the steaming bathing pool, the little waterfall coming out of the rocks and the surrounding trees that gave the impression of being in a secret place. "When I scouted this place, there were no human footprints or any other evidence that people had found this spot. I think we are safe."

Jennifer gave Dylan a mischievous look. "After dinner, I'm going to take a bath in that pool, and you are going to wash my back."

Dylan nearly choked on his food. "That would be unprofessional of me. Since you are my client out here in the woods, where you can't really leave, I have power over you. It's not fair to you."

"I'm not your client," said Jennifer putting her plate down. "I'm your partner. We decided to both come here and look for my father. Plus, I'm not paying you, just covering expenses."

Dylan felt his face redden. He knew it would be unprofessional to form a sexual relationship with this beautiful woman, but he wanted her and felt his resolve start to melt. "But we didn't decide that before we left," he said lamely. "Plus, I should stand guard while you bathe so no one disturbs you."

"Fine!" Jennifer allowed a pout into her voice. She felt that Dylan was overplaying the professional ethics, but she liked that. Even in these woods full of bad men, she found herself smiling at

Dylan. "OK. You go on guard duty. I'll take a 20 minute bath then clean up the dishes."

"After we are both refreshed, we need to figure out how to get to a sat-phone to call for help," said Dylan. "I'll think about it while on guard duty."

Jennifer noticed that Dylan turned his back as she pulled off her shirt. "You mean go back to that mine with those awful miners?"

"I think that's what I'll need to do," said Dylan as he walked away. "Unless we can find a sat-phone somewhere else."

As Dylan disappeared into the woods, Jennifer found herself wading out into the bathing pool. The clear waters had a slight mineral smell that seemed strong where the stream carrying the hot water entered the pool.

She allowed herself a soak before washing. As she lay in the almost, but not quite, too warm flowing waters, she kept thinking about Dylan. It seemed that the impulsive part of her wanted wild sex with him, and the reasonable side of her understood that a relationship between an urban girl and a wilderness man would never last. Still she wanted his arms around her.

61

....

AS RHETT WATCHED the Chinese miners gratefully finish off the potato-and-bacon fry he'd brought over, he wondered if any whites had shown kindness to his mother's people as they toiled in the mines. It was unlikely.

The stories from the mines are nearly all about the unspeakable cruelty of the whites to the blacks and the blacks to the mixed race.

Kung walked up, covered in motor oil, and looked eagerly at the large covered bowl Rhett had brought. He said he couldn't eat until he put on something clean and washed up. His coworkers had saved a portion for him. It made Rhett feel emotional to think of these hungry, overworked men saving food for one of their own. Did his black family do that, too?

A loud crunching of gravel announced the heavy footsteps of a big man walking fast. Rhett turned to see Snuffy moving his large, muscular frame on an obvious aggressive course toward Rhett while taking a swig from a nearly empty whisky bottle.

Several quick thoughts went through Rhett's mind. *This man is ready to fight. Gideon must have sent him. That means Gideon has decided to reject my offer of gold and to kill me. If I kill this man, it will cement Gideon's plans. I need to try to change Gideon's mind or get him to delay. I'll adjust my offer and see if that does it.*

From his large and small muscle movements, Rhett could see Snuffy was close to being drunk, but not close enough.

"Hey you little black turd. It's time to go to the punishment pit," shouted Snuffy as he came close to Rhett and the Chinese miners.

"And why would I go there?" asked Rhett in a calm voice shrugging off his jacket and folding it onto a log.

"I don't know why. Maybe you pissed off Gideon, but it's time," said Snuffy, now just feet away. "Or else . . ." Snuffy held up a huge fist decorated with crooked prison tattoos and made a punching motion. When his shirt lifted, Rhett noticed the Sig in his belt. The Sig changed things.

"Ok. Lead the way," said Rhett in a jaunty tone. He handed the kitchenware he was holding to one of the Chinese. "These go back to the kitchen."

"No. You walk in front. I want to keep my eye on you," said Snuffy pointing toward the opening to the mineshaft just yards away.

As they walked, Rhett maintained a distance just out reach and listened for any sign that Snuffy had drawn the Sig from his belt. "You know. I'm soon to be the new owner of this mine. That would make me your boss," said Rhett. "You should rethink this."

"Shut the fuck up," was all Snuffy could think of to say. "It's probably your fault that those tourists got away, or that Chewy got hurt looking for that tourist lady."

"Chewy got hurt?" Rhett turned to check to see if the gun was still in Snuffy's waistband.

"Yeah. I guess he fell in a creek and hurt his arm. That damn Chinese woman!"

As they entered the tunnel, Rhett decided he should act while he had plenty of room to move and lots of light. He slowed, allowing Snuffy to get close, then turned to face the huge man. "You sure you want to do this?"

Snuffy raised his fist, fast for a drunk man, and shot it toward Rhett. Rhett's mind slowed down time. He stepped back, ducked and batted the fist away. "I order you to stop this assault!" shouted Rhett.

But the heavy whisky bottle was already on a fast trajectory toward Rhett's head. Rhett stepped in close, his hand reaching up and catching the neck of the bottle.

Rhett spun on his heel, and in twisting motion, wrenched the bottle out of Snuffy's hand. It surprised Rhett that the wrenching move didn't break Snuffy's hand. The man was strong.

"Here. You can have the rest of this whisky if you stop," said Rhett stepping back and setting the bottle down between them, but he knew Snuffy would not stop. Rhett would need to disable him, and it would make it harder for Gideon to change his mind.

Snuffy charged. It was truly an intimidating sight: a 6-foot 5-inch muscular man of 280 pounds rushing with astounding force in an enclosed space. All that force could be used against an opponent if done right.

Rhett did it right. As Snuffy came close, Rhett grabbed the big man's wrist and pulled him forward. Snuffy had expected resistance, not acceleration. Rhett's ankle-breaking kick struck Snuffy as his powerful momentum drove his shoulder into the tunnel wall. A loud snap sound told Rhett that something broke in Snuffy's shoulder as the big man hit the wall then fell and rolled painfully onto his back.

As if by magic, the Sig appeared in Snuffy's hand, but Rhett had planned for that. A short, rapid kick sent the gun down the tunnel, and a second rapid-fire kick broke Snuffy's jaw. The two kicks were delivered so quickly, that only a slow motion camera could show they were actually two distinct kicks.

It astounded Rhett that Snuffy had somehow maintained consciousness despite the jaw strike. "Snuffy. I'm so sorry. I tried to dissuade you. Now I can't have you ambulatory, so I'm going to need to break your other ankle."

As if Snuffy suddenly realized he had been beaten and broken by the smaller black man, his eyes widened in fear. "No! I give up," he tried to say through a broken jaw.

Rhett stood over Snuffy and delivered an ankle shattering downward strike. To Rhett, it looked like the blow caused Snuffy to pass out. Rhett placed the whisky bottle within reach of the big man, tucked the Sig into his own belt, and started out of the tunnel.

Now to find Gideon, thought Rhett. *I'll need to see if a whole roll of half-ounce Krugerrands will change his mind.*

62
....

DYLAN LOOKED INTO THE TREES to see dozens of crows quarreling and making so much noise, he couldn't possibly hear someone approaching the bathing area.

Still, Dylan felt comforted by the presence of the crows. If an assault team was approaching, the crows would change their noise to curiosity, and Dylan would note it. Dylan wished he had a weapon beyond his hatchet and folding knife. The people threatening Jennifer and him were well armed.

Figuring that Jennifer was likely finished with her bath, Dylan started back to the bathing area. He thought about his first love, an adventurous blond who died in a climbing accident on Denali. His second love, a beautiful Hawaiian woman who seemed to outgrow her love of the woods that Dylan cherished, and ended up in Africa married to an English doctor.

Since then, Dylan had been alone. A condition that troubled him less than other people, but lately he found himself thinking of finding a soul mate to be his partner.

Jennifer was the only woman within 300 miles of him, so that made her the apparent choice for a partner. That she was a beautiful, wealthy young urban woman made her obviously out of his league, and an absurdly bad choice for a long-term relationship with a somewhat reclusive Alaskan who tended to live from paycheck to paycheck. Still, he found himself daydreaming of kissing her pretty neck.

As he approached the bathing area, he saw her sitting on a log, fully dressed, wearing one of his fleece vests, and combing her short, dark hair. How pretty she looked!

In their current situation, the bath was important to give Jennifer a feeling of control and normalcy. He needed her to be fully functioning to avoid capture by the miners until the rescue plane should arrive. Perhaps that meant, he should bathe, too. That, he told himself, would also give her comfort to have a guide who looked and smelled composed.

"How was the water?" he asked as he emerged from the dark of the woods.

"Lovely. I feel so much better. You are next. If you are modest, I'll avert my eyes," Jennifer's eyes teased him. The confident playfulness she was showing was exactly what Dylan wanted to see. As someone who had experienced profound terror himself, he knew her humor was likely a coping mechanism, but soon she would need to talk things out in order to maintain mental balance.

"You need to keep watch in case those trackers come. Go over yonder and listen to the crows. If they made a sudden change in their cries, come and get me," Dylan said as he hopped on one foot pulling off his pants. "It will only take me five minutes to wash, but you should keep watch."

Jennifer continued combing her hair as she strolled into the woods. He liked the swish of her hips.

It seemed she had just left, when Dylan, smelling of citrus and coconut and fully dressed came up beside her.

"You are really fast," she noted. "And you are starting a beard. I like it."

"I didn't have time to shave. I'm going to leave you here while I sneak into the mining camp to use their sat-phone. We need to alert the authorities, and it could be a week before Shelia flies out here to check on us," said Dylan sitting beside Jennifer and toweling his hair with a tiny microfiber cloth. It was the first time she saw his hair out of a ponytail, and he could tell she liked it.

"Can't we just walk out of here?" asked Jennifer. "Aren't you an expert in wilderness survival? You could find food and shelter until we reach civilization."

"That won't work. To get to the nearest settlement, we would either need to cross the glacier or climb the mountains, both are too dangerous and require special gear. It's out of the question. We need to either hide in the woods from the trackers and hope we don't miss Shelia's plane, or call for help," said Dylan taking a comb from Jennifer and making his ponytail.

To Jennifer, the act of Dylan taking her comb seemed profoundly intimate, as if they had been a couple for months.

Abruptly Jennifer's confidence appeared to crumble. "But to return to the mine . . ."

"You'll stay here. I'm pretty sneaky, and I bet I could get in and out without getting caught. It won't be that hard," said Dylan returning the comb, his wavy dark hair looked much darker when damp.

"But if you get caught . . ." She accepted the comb, looked at it, then held it to her chest.

"I won't. I'll be back here in a jiffy. Shelia will be here soon after with some rangers. All will be good," said Dylan standing up.

"But if you get caught . . ." said Jennifer. "I'm coming with you—back to the mine."

"Nope. You'll stay here," said Dylan firmly. "I know you are used to getting your way, but not on this matter. And that's final."

Jennifer stood, her eyes flashing.

63

....

DYLAN WASN'T SURE how she did it, but somehow they both had agreed that Dylan should take her with him to borrow the mining camp satellite phone.

As he picked his way through the woods toward the mining camp, he tried to figure out how this woman had changed his mind. *She must be an amazing lawyer*, he thought.

A light drizzle seemed to hush the forest sounds as they hiked without speaking. Dylan's plan was to pause on the edge of the camp and determine the best time to slip into Gideon's quarters to borrow his sat-phone. He hoped he could convince Jennifer to stay in the woods and not enter the camp.

FROM A ROCKY RIDGE UP the mountain, Charlie put down his binoculars. "Hey Slade. I think I see that Indian woman who stole our poison packs. She's hiking with a guy up toward the mining camp."

"We have to question her. She's in on the old Indian's plan to get federal protection for the animals in this area," said Slade taking a look. *She needs to be silenced like the old Indian*, thought Slade.

"But she's with another guy. She's not with the old Indian guy," said Charlie focusing the binoculars. "Maybe this guy is an Indian, too. He's got dark hair in a ponytail and the start of a beard. Do Indians have beards? What if he doesn't want her questioned?" Charlie watched as Dylan and

Jennifer as they climbed the hill: two dark specks trudging upwards.

"What should we do?" asked Bonner looking from Charlie to Slade.

"I'm going to make a call and check in with the boss," said Slade drawing his sat-phone from his pack. "You guys start up the hill and to the right so we meet up the with Indian woman and the other guy when they come up the slope. Stay out of sight. I'll catch up." Slade watched Bonner and Charlie trudge heavily up the hill.

"What about Able? Why does he get to eat soup while we work?" whined Charlie.

Slade picked up his walkie-talkie and called Able. After several tries he gave up and turned to the others. "You guys do what I told you to do. I'm going to check on Able then meet you up the hill. If those Indians give you any trouble, the Independent State of Alaska grants you permission to shoot to kill. Otherwise, take them prisoner until I get back with Able. Is that clear?"

Bonner and Charlie nodded, but Slade wondered if they would shoot to kill. "You want a free Alaska, right?"

The men nodded again, their eyes big. Charlie looked down at his Colt 604 rifle, "But that's murder. Nobody told me I would need to kill a girl and a man."

"It's not murder if you are following orders from a superior officer. Don't be known as the men who let freedom slip through our fingers. Follow my orders." Slade turned and walked back toward the Indian's cabin cursing. Nothing was going right.

He pulled out the sat-phone and checked for a signal. Nothing. The satellite must be below the horizon. Just to be certain, he removed the batteries and replaced them, deployed and compacted the antenna, and pushed nearly every button on the unfamiliar phone. Something he did seemed to work, because the phone showed a very weak signal.

Slade called Solomon's private number. Slade was fine killing an old Indian who would stand in the way of Alaska independence, but now kill two more people, even if they both were Indians. He needed to get orders from someone higher up.

"Solomon Quigley," came the curt answer through the scratchy connection.

"Superintendent Quigley, Slade here. I wanted to give you a report and request instructions," said Slade. He told about their difficulties in killing the wolves and, the interference of the old Indian and his wife. He explained that Able had killed the old Indian, but now another man was spotted with the Indian's wife, or whoever she was. Slade thought it likely the other man knew about the wolves.

"So what should we do?" Slade continued. "The men are tired and homesick, and we are out of poison bait and low on food." Slade wanted to hear Solomon say he'd send their plane back.

"You need to get the job done," ordered Solomon. "Kill those endangered wolves any way you can, and kill the two others who know about them. This is bigger than you or me. It's for Alaska. Wolves will eat dead Indians. Use the corpses as bait."

"What if we get caught?" asked Slade. "Some of the miners may catch on if they hear a bunch of rifle fire and all the Indians disappear."

"Whatever you do, don't bring me into it. You don't want to compromise leadership. If you get caught, say it was all your idea." Solomon's voice rose through the static.

Slade suddenly realized that Solomon was going to throw him and the men under the bus if things went south. Slade suddenly wished he were recording the conversation. He held the phone out to see if it had a recording function. It did, and the recording light was on. He must have pressed it when he was trying to get a signal. This entire call was being recorded.

"So let me get this straight," said Slade. "You want me to kill all the endangered wolves up here on Shaman Mountain and to kill two Indians. Should I kill anyone else?"

"Don't get smart with me," shouted Solomon. "Do what you need to do. This is for a free and independent Alaska." Solomon broke the connection. Slade played back the conversation and pondered emailing it to himself. *I'm not going down alone for this*, thought Slade. *But I'm not giving up on a free Alaska, either*.

64

. . . .

AGUTA STOOD BACK and examined the mess on his plastic tarp: the body, lots of blood and soup, and his handmade rag rug.

The dead man had bled out quarts of blood and the red goo mixed with the poison soup on his thick rug. The overpoweringly sweet and coppery odor caused a feeling of nausea to rumble in Aguta's gut.

Aguta decided he must get the plastic-wrapped mess outside and protect local scavengers from contact with the poisoned carcass. His bare floor actually looked pretty clean once the thick rug was rolled up with the body. He dragged the mess out the front door on the plastic tarp.

Once outside, Aguta dumped the body into a wheel barrel and walked it 200 yards to the edge of the cliff above the glacier. From the canyon, loud gunshot-sounding bangs and groans came from the active glacier as if it was ready to receive what Aguta was going to offer.

After urinating on the body, Aguta muttered, *Must keep scavengers away from this poison-filled carcass*. Aguta tipped the body to tumble down the cliff where the noisy Kila Glacier would grind it into dust. This is one man who Aguta would not help join the warriors who play in the northern lights. This bad man would stay in the dark underworld for eternity.

Aguta sighed knowing he should go down to the glacier to make certain the body had fallen under the glacier. There was always so much to do.

Several hours later, after finishing the clean up of his home, he picked up his shovel and descended the hill in his stiff-legged gait.

He wondered if he should sing the death song or the working song. Since it was an enemy's body, Aguta started singing the working song. He didn't want to do anything that would guide the bad man's spirit to the afterlife.

After digging a niche where the glacier lay on the earth, Aguta shoved the body into place and piled rocks in a way that would prevent animals from accessing the poisoned body.

It was a job well done, and Aguta felt tired but cheerful as he ascended the slope to his home. *Now maybe, those wolf hunters will leave the wolves and me alone.*

65

· · · · · · · · · ·

GIDEON STOOD OVER SNUFFY's broken body and glared at the beaten man. "So how did this happen? I gave you a simple order to put the black man in the punishment pit."

Through the broken jaw, loose teeth, severe pain and the rest of bourbon, Snuffy could only get out. "He tricked me. He has your Sig."

Gideon roared, "My Sig! You shithead! No one around here does anything I say!"

Gideon turned to two Chinese workers standing uncomfortably nearby. "Try to make him comfortable, and get Bones to come here and treat his wounds."

Gideon strode out of the tunnel entrance seething; he would kill that annoying black man himself. He'd do it with his bare hands if possible. He passed Kung, who had disassembled a pneumatic drill and was placing a new gasket on a flange.

"Where's the nigger?" demanded Gideon.

"The what?" asked Kung.

"That black shit," said Gideon, louder.

"Black shit?" Kung clearly had no idea what Gideon was asking.

"I want to know where Rhett is," said Gideon saying each word slowly.

"Oh, he's over by the generator shack. I saw him go into the woods and come back with a little backpack. I think he's still over by the shack doing exercises."

"He's a dead man." Gideon slammed his fist into his palm.

As soon as Gideon was across the yard, Kung motioned the other workers to follow him into the woods. Time to get away until things cooled down.

ONCE OUTSIDE, Gideon's eyes snapped to the generator shack. Rhett smiled and motioned him to come. Rhett pulled the Sig from his belt and tossed it into a bucket of tar-like sludge. It gradually sank and disappeared leaving a slowly bursting black bubble.

I have the little fucker now, thought Gideon pulling off his jacket and swinging his arms to warm up and striding toward Rhett.

"All right you piece of black shit," said Gideon. "Your turn to get hurt. You broke Snuffy."

"Please calm down, Mr. Gideon," said Rhett calmly. "I want to show you something." Rhett reached into his backpack and took out a roll of half-ounce Krugerrands. "If you agree to the deal I offered, this is your first payment. Imagine a chest full of Krugerrands."

In his mind, Rhett slowed down the situation. He recalled every strike in the Krav Maga fighting sequence he had watched Gideon practice. He knew that Gideon would strike first and probably not use his feet. If the big man landed a solid punch, it would cause real harm to Rhett, so he had to manage any direct hits.

In the overcast afternoon light, he could see the line between Gideon's iris and pupils. At first he saw a widening of the pupils. *He's flooded with adrenaline*, thought Rhett. "Just confirm for me, who knows about the iridium. Besides you and me, my list includes the tourists and Kung. It that it?"

"That's it," said Gideon fixing Rhett with a determined stare and doing a squatting exercise, presumably to warm up his legs. The man was strong, athletic and deadly.

"If we work together, we'll both make lots of money," said Rhett. "If you turn down the deal, you are on your own. You'll need to find a way to sell the iridium without landing in a world of legal problems."

"Why don't I just kill you and take your gold?" smiled Gideon putting his hands on his hips. Rhett could tell this was an effort to make it look like the big man wasn't preparing a strike. At this point, Rhett knew he would soon be fighting this deadly man to the death.

"If you don't take the deal, you will be the one killed," said Rhett calmly and offering the roll of gold coins.

Gideon's first strike came faster than Rhett expected. Rhett's hypervigilance and cognitive abilities had the effect of slowing down the physical universe, but apparently Gideon's moves were even faster than Rhett's powerful mind had expected.

The blond man's hand shot out from his waist toward Rhett's face. The blow was not a fist, but a flat, iron-strong hand aimed fingers-first directly at Rhett's face.

Because the hand was flat, it gave Gideon nearly six full inches of unexpected reach. The heavy gold in Rhett's left hand, slowed his reaction, so he was barely able to keep the strike from putting out his right eye. Instead, Gideon's fingertips hit Rhett's forehead knocking him back, nearly off his feet and stunning him.

It was only Rhett's instinct and muscle memory that prepared him for the second in the two rapid fire punches that Gideon had planned. Gideon's fist rose from his waist to deliver a fierce upper cut to Rhett's jaw. It was a knockout punch, but Rhett was able to deflect it so it struck his shoulder a harsh blow that spun Rhett clockwise.

Using the momentum of the turn, Rhett struck a whip-like kick to Gideon's right knee causing him to partially kneel and grunt in pain. Nearly instantly, Gideon was upright and in his Krav Maga fighting position. Blood trickled down Rhett's face from the impact of the open-handed jab.

"Hey," Gideon said ignoring the pain in his right knee. "You bleed red. I thought it would be chocolate syrup."

Ordinarily such a racist taunt would infuriate Rhett, but his mind was cold and able to discount distractions like insults and pain. Watching Gideon's eyes and his forehead veins, and recalling the moves in Gideon's Krav Maga kata, Rhett knew when the next punch was coming.

Gideon would feint with the left, then launch a thundering rib-breaking punch to the chest with a powerful right hand.

Rhett pretended to overreact to the maneuver, then met Gideon's huge right fist with his own. Normally, hitting fist to fist would be accidental since such contact could disable both fighters. But in Rhett's fist was 8 ounces of rolled gold coins. The coins slowed him down, but gave a bone-saving structure to his heavy fist.

When Gideon's own, unprotected fist collided with Rhett's, the sound was like someone cracking all the knuckles in one hand: five rapid fire snapping sounds indicated multiple broken hand and finger bones, as if Gideon had punched a concrete wall with all his force.

To Gideon, it felt like he had indeed struck a wall.

At that point, Rhett knew that Gideon's right hand was basically useless as an offensive weapon. One of Gideon's hand bones stuck out from his hand, a white and bloody compound fracture. Rhett easily parried the counter punch from Gideon's left hand.

"You little shit! You're going to die." Gideon glanced down at his misshapen hand but seemed slow to catch on to extent of the damage. It worked in Rhett's favor to let it sink in, so Gideon might begin to go into shock. Rhett backed up, letting Gideon process the injury to his hand.

Somewhere a crow's clownish cawing echoed in the nearby forest. A rushing sound swished in the treetops as a mountain breeze caused the trees to sway above them.

Rhett knew that sometimes the presence of adrenaline in the body could delay shock. Observing Gideon's pupils, heart rate and breathing, Rhett could tell the man's body was now completely flooded with the hormone.

Relying more on instinct than thought, Rhett knew he would need to make the next strike. Even with a bad right hand, Gideon was as deadly as any enemy Rhett ever faced. Something told Rhett that Gideon would be more likely to remain in a defensive mode since he was right-hand dominant and that hand was disabled.

Tossing the roll of gold coins into his left hand, Rhett feinted with his left, then his right. Faster than an eye blink, he dropped down low and shot his right leg out to strike the same knee he had kicked before, resulting in a loud crunching sound. This time Gideon went down onto his broken right knee and winced.

Rhett leaned in to deliver a killing blow to Gideon's neck, but blood trickled into Rhett's eye temporarily blinding him on that side. The big man surprised him throwing a right elbow into Rhett's chin that knocked him backward onto his side. In a normal fight, this would be where Gideon killed his opponent, but the broken knee slowed down his ability to get to the momentarily stunned black man.

Rolling onto his hands and knees, just out of Gideon's reach. Rhett wiped his eye, clearing his vision and his mind. Rhett found himself beautifully calm as if planning the next move in a chess match.

Gideon stood, his weight on his one undamaged leg effectively maintaining his fighting stance. He eyed the fist where Rhett held the gold. It would be a slow, but massive punch if Rhett could hit him with it.

Gracefully, Rhett bounced on his feet tossing feints at Gideon, which the big man ignored. Gideon's dark eyes focused on finding an opening to throw a death-dealing left-handed punch.

Then Gideon did the most unexpected move. He leaped up on his good left leg and fired off a left-legged kick toward Rhett's chest. It meant that Gideon would come down on his broken right knee, a most painful landing. Despite the unexpected high kick, Rhett avoided the impact by dropping backward onto his back, then performing a nimble kip-up move to put himself back onto his feet.

Gideon heard a loud crunch from his right knee when his right foot hit the ground, but he was able to roll onto his good leg before falling. Upright, but shaky, Gideon prepared to launch his powerful left fist at Rhett. Nanoseconds before Gideon's fist could land, Rhett's right arm came up to block the punch.

Rhett tossed the roll of gold coins from left to right hand and delivered a savage right uppercut that came from below Rhett's waist like an unstoppable bullet train to Gideon's jaw. The weight of the gold multiplied the power of the strike. It was enough to knock out a horse.

The crack of Gideon's broken jaw was so loud, crows took to the air. The blow lifted Gideon and threw him onto his back—his eyes fluttered as his body worked to regain consciousness. The paper holding the gold coins together exploded and the coins burst into the air falling on Gideon in a shower of sparkling gold.

Coldly, Rhett stood over Gideon and dropped, aiming both knees and all his weight onto Gideon's throat, collapsing his windpipe and breaking his neck with a loud snap.

Gasping for breath, Rhett grasped Gideon's wrists, dragged the dead man into the generator shack, and dropped him into a pool of muddy oil. Gideon's blond hair mixed with the muddy sludge as his lifeless black eyes stared upwards.

Now to clean up and find those tourists and Kung, thought Rhett gathering the gold coins into his little backpack.

The killing had started.

66

....

"DO YOU KNOW WHO those people are?" asked Dylan as he and Jennifer gazed up the hillside from behind some bushes. They watched Bonner and Charlie position themselves with their rifles pointed downhill as if they were waiting for game.

"Those are probably the hunters who've been trying to kill the wolves." Jennifer stepped back into the shade. "We should avoid them."

"I agree, except they might have a sat-phone we could use," said Dylan as he watched as Bonner and Charlie prepared hunting positions.

"I don't feel good about them," replied Jennifer. "Let's get out of here."

"You're probably right," Dylan agreed as he checked out the men's rifles. "Those men are using

M16s with 30-shot magazines and probably shooting military .233 bullets. Those rounds ruin meat, so they aren't hunting caribou or moose. Let's get out of here."

"Like I told you, they are wolf hunters," said Jennifer.

They skirted a quarter-mile to the south in order to approach the mining camp from the most over-grown and rocky part of the area.

Creeping up to the buildings, Dylan startled Jennifer when he harshly whispered the command: Freeze! Unquestioningly, Jennifer froze—not moving a muscle, even her eyes. From a few hundred yards away, Jennifer heard someone yell, "Gideon! Hey Gideon. Where are you?"

With her peripheral vision, she could see the back of a stocky miner wearing a cowboy hat standing amongst the trees.

After a few moments, Dylan whispered: Down!

Once they were under some dark bushes, Dylan began to speak in a quiet voice. "There are miners roaming around these woods looking for Gideon. The human eye is amazing at spotting movement, but not so good at finding still objects. That's why I had us freeze."

"I hope we don't find Gideon," said Jennifer with a little shiver.

"Let's sneak up behind the bunkhouse," whispered Dylan pointing to the nearest building. "I don't want to risk going in the front door. Once we get closer, we'll need to crawl low to avoid being seen."

Soon Dylan gave a "wait here" signal to Jennifer. She watched him disappear into the forest undergrowth near the back of the bunkhouse. She wondered how he moved without disturbing the tall grasses.

She did not want Dylan to be seen walking into the mining camp and attempting to enter the bunkhouse. He would surely be caught.

She watched Dylan try a back door. Surprisingly, it was locked. Usually the only doors locked in these mining camps are on the liquor cabinets. Dylan had assured Jennifer that no doors would ever be locked in a remote mining camp.

The windows all looked latched and probably painted shut. If Dylan broke a window to get in, it would be too noisy. Jennifer watched Dylan disappear into the bushes and signal to her.

After skirting the area by going far to the south and scrambling up some steep rocks, Dylan and Jennifer crept to the edge of the camp to observe the bunkhouse and surrounding area. Now their plan became to wait until the miners were occupied elsewhere, then somehow get into Gideon's apartment.

Just on the edge of the forest, Dylan and Jennifer prepared to wait. Faces smeared with mud and fern fronds sticking out of their hair, the couple crawled under some bushes to better see what was going on in the camp.

Jennifer felt immersed in rich earth smells as they watched two miners, a stocky fellow in a cowboy hat and a bowed skinny man, argue outside the bunkhouse.

Jennifer's lower lip quivered as she whispered, "That fat guy was going to rape me. He knocked me down with a slap. Maybe we should get out of here."

"We can do that," said Dylan, "However we risk missing Sheila's plane or getting caught. Hiding in the woods or on the glacier might be a better risk than staying here."

"I guess we need to get that phone," said Jennifer. "I saw the sat-phone by Gideon's bed. He also had swords and other weapons on his wall. We really need to burglarize his quarters."

Dylan looked into Jennifer's dark eyes. "I think the best plan is to sneak in, use the phone or take it, and get out leaving no trace. That way they don't start searching for us right away. We'll call Shelia. She can bring law enforcement and get us out of here."

Dylan and Jennifer lay still as they watched tensely as Rhett, with a bloody face pushed past the two men and enter the bunkhouse just 200 yards away. He emerged about 20 minutes later toweling off his face. A piece of white adhesive tape on the right side of his head stood out against his dark skin.

Rhett and the two miners talked. Jennifer noticed that Rhett looked and acted like he was the boss. The miners appeared deferential.

As the group walked within earshot of Dylan and Jennifer, the cowboy hat miner made a call on a radio clipped to his belt. "All SM miners, stop what you are doing and meet at the gong. This is an urgent meeting."

Afterwards the trio appeared to walk toward the metal acetylene tank hanging near the mine entrance about 300 yards away. This left the bunkhouse deserted.

"I think this might be the best time," said Dylan looking hard at Jennifer. "You stay here. I'll go in."

"No way you're leaving me out here," said Jennifer. "Besides, I know where I saw the sat-phone. I was in his room longer than you."

"OK, but stay close," said Dylan. "I don't want us to get trapped in the building by angry miners."

Just then the sound of the gong echoed up the sides of Kila Ikpic.

67
....

SLADE LEFT AGUTA's cabin confused. Where the hell is Able? Why would he wash all the dishes before he left?

As he started back to where he had left Bonner and Charlie, he decided Able must be out burying the Indian's body. *But why doesn't he answer me when I call his walkie-talkie?*

This whole operation is going south, thought Slade as he slung his assault rifle over his shoulder. He pondered calling for a plane himself, but then he'd need to pay for it.

He needed Solomon to call for the plane. Maybe he should just call Solomon and tell him the operation's a bust, or that he's worried that the men show signs they might reveal organizational secrets unless they can go home. *That last one might be true*, thought Slade.

An hour later he stopped at the edge of a clearing and looked down the hill to see Bonner and Charlie's hunter's blind. They were both sitting behind a big log and a pile of rocks sharing an

MRE and apparently arguing loudly over something. *What a bunch of knuckleheads*! Slade thought. They need a babysitter just to do a simple job.

Figuring that his men had let the Indians get past unchallenged, Slade decided to check out the mining area. Remembering Solomon's instructions not to disturb the miners, Slade walked quietly up to the far end of the landing strip where the plane had let them off.

Suddenly a loud gonging sound penetrated the woods. Slade recognized it as the signal calling the miners to dinner, but it was nowhere near dinnertime and the gong had an unfamiliar urgency to it.

Using his riflescope, he panned the visible parts of the entire mining camp. He saw a small group of men standing around a faded red acetylene tank that undoubtedly had been struck with a piece of rebar to make the gong sound.

The tank dangled from a tree limb and next to it stood a dark-skinned man with white tape on his forehead. He held a piece of metal rebar that served as the clapper for the gong. The man held the rebar like it was a symbol of power. He spoke to the men and sometimes pointed the rebar at them as if to make a point.

Scanning over to the bunkhouse, Slade watched two people, smeared with mud, stealthily move from the bushes near the bunkhouse to the door and step in. Too late he realized the woman perhaps looked Asian . . . or maybe Indian. *Hard to tell with mud on her cheeks*, Slade cursed. He had his rifle up and could have easily shot the woman, and maybe even the man. It would have made a huge racket and created problems with the miners.

Pausing to pull off his pack, Slade removed a large noise suppressor from a pouch and screwed it onto the barrel of his rifle. Solomon had supplied the rifle, suppressor, sat-phone and other tactical gear for this mission.

Slade had not taken the time to try out the rifle with the suppressor attached. He knew that suppressors would greatly reduce both the sound of the rifle as well as muzzle flash. They also diminished recoil and actually made the gun more accurate.

However, he knew that shots fired in rapid succession might create a backpressure that can wreak havoc on his rifle's function. He changed his rifle from full automatic to single shot and decided to hit both Indians with single, center mass shots if they came out the front door, and he would use a head shot if one stuck his or her head out one of the side windows.

Slade decided to move to south side of the bunkhouse to give him a shot at anyone leaving through the front or back door or south side windows of the building. He might also be able to see in through a window and get a shot off. He'd rather shoot the Indians outside so he could drag their bodies into the bushes and avoid trouble with the miners.

By their behavior, the Indians were not expected guests at the mining camp, so perhaps no one would miss them.

Hurrying through the woods, Slade found himself actively pushing back second thoughts about shooting the Indians. If his commanding officer sanctioned it, then it was a good kill.

Soldiers killed based on the order of their superior officers. Was he not a soldier fighting for a free Alaska? Besides, who would miss some dirty Indians living far away from anyone?

It might be a kindness to end their miserable lives. Especially if they threatened a free Alaska. Alaska belonged to the men who were willing to fight to make it free, not a bunch of stupid Indians.

The woman had looked like an Indian, but the man had pale skin. Maybe he was white, but if he was against a free Alaska, then he would need to suffer the consequences. *Still, hate to shoot a white guy*, thought Slade.

Behind some rocks, Slade found a perfect place to set up. He could rest in a vigilant position with his suppressed rifle muzzle resting on a rolled up sweatshirt. It would be a 200-yard shot—easy peasy.

He'd only been set up for a few minutes, when he saw the miners leave the gong area and start walking toward the bunkhouse. Leading them was the dark-skinned man.

Several thoughts ran through Slade's mind. *Maybe they would take care of the Indians. Should I shoot the Indians when there are so many people around? I need to do this quick before the Indians tell anyone about the wolves.*

Slade took a deep breath and sighted toward a window near the front door. The Indians would climb out of that window or run through the back door once the miners entered the bunkhouse.

It wouldn't be long.

68

· · · · · · · · · · ·

RHETT SPOKE IN A QUIET, calm voice to the assembled miners, the gong clapper held loosely in his hand—a rustic Alaska version of a scepter in the remote mining camp. Anyone observing Rhett would not notice his jitters as his body shed the adrenaline rush he had felt during the fight.

"This mining operation now belongs to my boss, Mr. Meijer. You are all going to receive your pay to the end of the month and a bonus. Everyone here is fired. I'm going to charter planes to take everyone to Anchorage as soon as possible. You will forfeit your bonus if you discuss this mining operation with anyone outside this camp."

A grumbling could be heard amongst the miners.

"Where's Gideon?" called out Rusty tipping his cowboy hat back. "What's he say to this?"

"He's gone," said Rhett quietly. The simple phrase seemed to stun the men. To Rhett, this gathering of miners looked pretty much like the lot he saw in the biker bar in Anchorage.

"When do we get paid? How do we know you just won't leave us stuck in Anchorage with no money? I heard you can't trust Australians," said Bones.

Rhett reached into his backpack and started tossing gold coins to the men. "I'm not from Australia, and my accent is South African. This is part of your bonus. You'll get paid like you usually do, by direct deposit or check."

"Is this real gold?" asked Bones examining his coin.

"Hey! Mine has blood on it. And it's fresh," said Rusty his voice rising.

"Hey!" yelled a wide, round faced miner wearing a too-small sock hat. "Chewy got two coins."

Chewy glared at the man. "Shut the fuck up, Gilly. I only got one."

Rhett quieted the group with a look. "I want you to go back to your bunk area and pack up to leave. You are not to take any minerals or samples of any kind. Your duffle will be searched and if you have any contraband, you will forfeit the gold coin and any pay you have coming. Is that clear?"

The miners looked at each other in a confused way and nodded.

"I need to hear you say you understand," said Rhett.

After each man in turn verbally agreed to the terms, Rhett nodded. He looked over at Chewy and Leo. The trackers had hostile looks on their faces. "You guys get an extra gold coin if you bring me the tourists."

Leo turned his rat face up toward his refrigerator-sized colleague then back to Rhett. "We tried to track that guy. It's like he vanished." Leo held up an arm in a sling. "I got hurt trying to follow him. He's like a lizard."

"You want the extra gold coin or not?" said Rhett looking around. His gaze fell on the Chinese miners. "Where's Kung?"

A round-faced Chinese man pointed toward the mine. "There," was all he said.

Rhett turned back to the trackers. "And bring me Kung, too. Don't hurt any of these people unless it's absolutely necessary."

"We get extra for Kung?" asked Leo playing with his coin.

Rhett ignored the comment and turned to Rusty. "Where the camp sat-phone? I need to arrange the flights and your pay."

"It's in Gideon's room, but you'll have hell to pay if you use it without his permission," said Rusty polishing the blood off his coin on his plaid jacket.

"It's Mr. Meijer's sat-phone now. Show me where it's at," said Rhett as he started toward the bunkhouse.

Soon Rhett found himself walking alone. The others walked behind him in a stunned group. Rhett's thoughts turned to Father Mavuso. He would not have approved of Rhett beating Snuffy or killing Gideon, even if he were just following orders.

Now he was planning to kill the tourists and Kung, he could nearly feel Father Mavuso's disapproving gaze on the back of his neck. His walking pace slowed as he pondered. *When a soldier receives an order to shoot at the enemy, that soldier is not a murderer, but a dutiful soldier nobly following orders. I've been ordered to kill by Mr. Meijer, so that's what I'll do.*

Thinking thoughts in his Zulu language, Rhett found himself talking aloud to his mentor. "Father Mavuso, please don't disapprove. This killing is not my wish, but the wishes of my boss—my commander. It is out of my hands."

Rhett could not imagine any change in Father Mavuso's disapproval.

"Father, I will complete this job, then accept no more work that involves killing. This is my last time. Please grant me grace." Rhett whispered as he slowly walked.

Unseen by the miners, tears rolled down Rhett's face. "I must finish this job, or Mr. Meijer will think I failed due to my color. Maybe he will accept me as a person if I'm successful."

In his mind, Father Mavuso turned his back. Just like the Church had rejected Father Mavuso. The old priest's excommunication had resulted from just a few words spoken by Rhett in the confessional. How could Rhett have known he'd destroy the priest by confessing?

I hate Mr. Meijer, thought Rhett fiercely. *I hate the church! I'm going to kill those white people and that Chinese miner*. Rhett put his hand on the bunkhouse door and violently jerked it. The old door did not yield. It was locked from the inside.

Rhett stepped back and prepared to deliver a wood-shattering kick.

69

....

ONCE IN THE BUNKHOUSE, Dylan locked the front door and walked into Gideon's spotless room. Jennifer showed Dylan where she had seen the sat-phone. On the shelf near his bed, there sat a large sat-phone charger, but no phone.

"I know there was one here. I saw it. It's black," whispered Jennifer.

"We just have a few minutes. Let's look around, and if we don't find it right away, then we'll need to leave and make another plan. We don't want to get caught here. We'll need to hide out. Maybe on the glacier where they won't follow us."

"The glacier! Is it safe?" asked Jennifer.

"Aguta told me about some parts that were fairly stable, but the Gila Glacier is not safe. The miners will avoid it. That's why we'll go there if we have to hide out waiting for Shelia. Plus we'll be able to see her plane when she flies over it."

Dylan started opening drawers and carefully lifting orderly folded clothes to look for the sat-phone.

Jennifer approached a closet, pulled out some tightly stuffed duffle bags and boxes and emptied them onto the floor. She kicked through the clothes and other items. "These look like someone's collection of Native clothing and tools. Why would someone collect Native clothing and tools?"

Dylan picked up a fur parka. "Because modern gear has not yet caught up with some of the ancient Native technology. Plus these handmade tools and gear are pricy and very much in demand."

Dylan decided that the stealth approach to searching the room was a waste of time, so he dumped drawers and flipped the mattress.

"Hey look, gold coins!" said Jennifer holding up a heavy roll she found in a boot. "I wonder if they're real? They seem to be the size of a nickel."

"Just look for the phone," said Dylan, his voice strained.

"These coins have Chinese writing on them," Jennifer seemed captivated by the weight and size of the coin roll.

"Jennifer, we are in a mad rush. Help me find the phone," urged Dylan.

Jennifer tossed the coins onto the upturned bed and resumed the search. She picked up a dark fur parka and patted it down.

After a few minutes, Dylan called a halt to the search. "It's not here. Let's go."

"Wait. Shouldn't we take some of these swords to keep us safe?" Jennifer gestured up to the wall where Gideon's collection of martial arts weaponry were displayed—along with some fantasy arms like Klingon blades and ornate jeweled swords and daggers straight out of a video game.

"None of those will help us since we don't have any practice using them, and we don't need the weight. I'm pretty good with a hatchet, but I already have one of those," said Dylan patting his daypack.

"OK. Any of this stuff needed on the glacier?" Jennifer picked up a different Inuit parka, one made of tan furs.

"You know, we should each take a pair of these mukluks. They appear to be made of caribou skin and wild felt. I bet you could wear your hiking boots inside one of them."

"Aguta had some of these, but the bottoms are smooth. There are no rubber nubs to grip the ice," said Jennifer looking at a mukluk.

"Rubber nubs don't grip ice, only snow. The sealskin soles will offer some traction on glacial ice.

Jennifer threw down the tan parka and noticed it made a thunk sound. Picking it up, she drew out a black sat-phone from a pouch. "Here it is! Gideon must have hidden it from the other miners."

Dylan pounced on phone. "Let me try to call for help." Once he powered the unit on, it displayed a low battery message. "Crap! The battery is almost dead! It shows no charge at all!" A look of panic crossed Dylan's face.

"Try to call anyway," said Jennifer.

Dylan watched the blinking Charge Battery message weakly pulse and waited while the phone acquired a satellite. It seemed to take forever. Then he punched in the phone number for Shelia's Flight Service. As he feared, the away message came up. "We are not available right now, but your travel needs are important to us. Please leave a message with a call back number, and we'll be back as soon as possible."

As soon as he heard the beep, he started talking. " Shelia this is Dylan. We need a pickup as soon as you can. This is an emergency. Bring armed law enforcement. There are some people who are trying to hurt us. We will hide on the glacier until we see your plane land. Please hurry!" Dylan looked down at the phone. It was completely dead. He had no idea if his message got through or not.

"I hope that message got though," said Dylan.

"Let's get out of here," said Jennifer tossing the Inuit parka onto the bed.

"Hey, that's a good parka for the glacier. You didn't bring anything like it. It has wolverine fur around the opening to the hood."

"Wolverine fur? Is that good? It smells like Aguta's cabin," said Jennifer picking up and holding the fur garment to her face. "You really think I should take it?"

"Yes. You'll be borrowing it," said Dylan grabbing the tan caribou-skin parka from a collection of native artifacts near an overturned box. "I'll take this one. It has a caribou ruff, not as good as wolverine."

"I'll shove these into this empty duffle bag," said Jennifer pushing the boots and parkas into a large canvass duffle.

"Good idea," said Dylan.

Just then the front door rattled. Several voices could be heard just outside.

70

....

RHETT PAUSED and turned to the men behind him. "OK. Who has the key to this door?" he said.

Rusty spoke up. "That lock has no key that works. If it's locked, it's a bolt on the inside. The back door is always locked because it swings open if we don't have the bolt in place. It lets in bugs."

Deciding not to risk hurting his foot with a kick, Rhett picked up a shovel leaning against the wall and shoved the blade into the door crack. With one quick thrust, the door splintered open. Rhett rushed in followed by the miners.

The open door to Gideon's quarters attracted Bone's attention. "Someone's in Gideon's room! Gideon? Can I come in? It's me, Bones."

Rhett pushed past Bones and surveyed the chaos of overturned drawers and empty boxes. It was clear that someone had tossed the place looking for something.

Bones rushed into the room. "Someone wrecked Gideon's place! There's going to be hell to pay. Maybe the robber climbed out the window." Bones waded across the room, drew open the window and pushed his head outside as if looking for an intruder. Suddenly the back of his head exploded and brain, blood and bone fragments sprayed the room.

Rhett fell to his stomach and crawled behind the upturned mattress. The others, stunned, stood as if trying to process what just happened.

"Get down! We're under fire!" yelled Rhett authoritatively.

Shocked into action, the others dove for cover.

"It's those tourists!" screamed Rusty. "We should have never trusted them. They shot Bones!"

Bones' body lay partway outside the window.

"Where can I get a rifle?" asked Rhett.

Silence greeted his question, so he raised his voice. "I want to know where a rifle is. We need to return fire."

Gilly, his small sock hat gone, whispered, "There's a gun closet with two bear guns and a deer rifle in the kitchen. The bear guns are shotguns loaded with slugs. There's an old Russian-made deer rifle, but Leo and Chewy always take it to get fresh meat when they are out tracking."

"Quick, bring to me a shotgun and extra ammo. Run!" shouted Rhett. He watched the wide man run-crawl out of the room. "Who else has a rifle?"

Rusty looked up from behind a box. "No one. They are heavy and we can only bring in 50 pounds of gear per man. Maybe Chewy shot at Bones."

"That shot wasn't from an old Russian deer rifle. Those are loud. The shot that killed bones was either from a great distance or it was suppressed," said Rhett.

Gilly returned with the shotgun and a box of shells. Rhett took the gun and quickly loaded it. A shotgun slug was a savage round for about 400 yards. After that, air resistance makes the large, heavy projectile ineffective. Using Bones' body as a shield, Rhett fired five quick rounds out the window in the general direction he figured the kill shot came from. Gun smoke and ear-splitting noise filled the room.

From somewhere in the bunkhouse, the sound of breaking glass came through the smoke.

"Ok. The shooter should have his head down for a few minutes. Everyone out of this room," yelled Rhett. He looked over at the phone charger and saw the sat-phone. He reloaded and handed the gun back to Gilly. "You and Rusty use the shotguns and guard the front door. Stay away from windows."

"First it was Blaster, now Bones. What's going on? Someone's trying to kill us all!" shouted Rusty.

"Shut up and do what I say!" Rhett's voice seemed to stun Rusty into following his orders.

Rhett picked up the phone, turned it on and noticed the battery was dead. He turned the charger upside down, took out a spare battery from the base and replaced it with the discharged one. Once the phone had connected to a satellite, he punched in the number for Mr. Meijer.

As he was waiting for the call to go through, he looked down at the blood-spattered bed and noticed the roll of gold coins. Picking them up, he observed there were 10, half-ounce Pandas—Chinese pure gold coins. The roll was worth many thousands of dollars.

Just then Mr. Meijer answered the phone. "Well Mr. Rettief Seme, what do you have to report?"

Rhett hated that he felt intimidated and a bit awed by Mr. Meijer. "Sir, now would be the time to close the deal on the mining lease. I recommend you do that as soon as possible. The man who sold you the nugget is dead and the only other people who know about the iridium is a Chinese mining engineer and a couple of tourists."

"And you plan to make sure the information does not spread off the mountain?" Rhett could tell he did not want to directly tell Rhett to kill the three other people with the knowledge.

"Yes Mr. Meijer; I'll try. But I just found a roll of gold Pandas in Gideon Schechter's things. I'm wondering if he also sold a nugget to someone else. Maybe a Chinese manufacturer."

"Tracking that down might be your next job. You need to make sure the information about the iridium deposit is contained."

Rhett wondered how many Chinese people he would end up having to kill if he accepted that assignment.

He noticed his hand holding the coins was starting to shake. He felt detached as he gazed at his hand, as if looking at someone else's fingers. *Maybe this tremor is a result of my body purging the adrenaline from the firefight. I'm not going to kill a bunch of Chinese for Mr. Meijer.*

Mr. Meijer's voice rose. "I'll find out what I can about any large iridium nuggets on the Chinese market and prepare a job dossier for you. What are your next steps there?"

"I need to get the miners off this mountain and close up the mine. I can blast the tunnel that leads to the main core of the iridium deposit, but it's possible to just find nuggets in streambeds and landslide moraines. This whole mountain needs to be controlled." Rhett's hand did not stop shaking. He'd always had perfect control over his body. He dropped the coins into his backpack.

"And the Chinese mining engineer and the tourists? You'll take care of that detail?" Mr. Meijer's voice took on a conspiratorial tone.

"Yes Mr. Meijer. They are at the top of my list. Someone out in the woods is shooting at us, so I need to put a stop to that first."

"Good job, Mr. Seme! I knew I could count on you." Rhett felt pleasure at being complemented by the rich white man and instantly wondered why. *Am I so white I need a white man's praise, or am I an inferior black who needs praise from my betters*? How Rhett wished he could talk to Father Mavuso! He'd never felt so alone.

"Yes Sir. I need to go." Rhett wondered that Mr. Meijer showed no curiosity about someone in the woods attacking the bunkhouse.

After the call terminated, Rhett called one of the many charter flight companies in Anchorage and arranged for a flight to evacuate the rest of the miners. He wondered how he would keep law enforcement from snooping around the mine. He would need to bribe the men with promises for more gold.

Now to find out who shot Bones and locate the tourists and Kung.

71

. . . .

SLADE DUCKED when loud booms from the shotgun burst from the window where he had just shot the guy who looked like he was climbing out of the window. One of the shotgun slugs impacted a tree nearby and sent a shower of fir needles to the forest floor.

Squatting behind the rocks, Slade considered his situation. He'd shot one of the Indians who was attempting to climb out the window. He was pretty sure it was the man, so the woman was still in the bunkhouse. Now the miners and the black guy were also in the bunkhouse. He needed them to turn the woman over to him.

His walkie-talkie made a squelching sound, then he heard Charlie's voice. "Slade? What's all the shooting? Are you OK?"

Slade picked up his walkie-talkie. "Just fine. Come around to the south side of the mining camp. Stay out of sight of the camp. I'm behind a big pile of rocks just south of the bunkhouse."

"Roger. Is Able with you? We can't find him." said Charlie.

"No. I hope he didn't fall down a cliff or something," answered Slade. "Come on without him." Slade put away his walkie-talkie and leaned forward to risk a glance at the bunkhouse.

Slade could see someone wearing a cowboy hat through a window. *That's one of the miners. I wonder if they caught the Indian woman*, thought Slade. He hunkered down behind the rocks and decided to wait for Bonner and Charlie before approaching the bunkhouse.

WHEN THE FRONT DOOR had rattled, Dylan and Jennifer had run to the back of the bunkhouse and burst through one of two doors in the area behind the kitchen.

They choose the wrong door. They found themselves in a storage room stacked with cleaning and cooking supplies, and a dirty toilet lacking a seat. Light came in from a large, curtainless window facing west.

About to leave, they heard the front door crash, and the sound of men running into the bunkhouse. Quickly, Dylan closed the door and propped a smelly mop against it as an improvised lock.

"We need to go out this window, or risk being seen," whispered Dylan.

"I think I'm going to wet my pants," whispered Jennifer. "What if they catch us here!"

Dylan attempted to open the window, but it was stuck. "There's no screen on this window, so that means they don't open it. Too many mosquitoes around here in early summer to just leave a window open."

"Will this help?" Jennifer handed Dylan a small screwdriver she found on a box.

Dylan tried to use the tool as a pry, but the window wouldn't budge. It was as if it had been nailed shut. "Damn! This window won't open. I can't break it because the noise would alert the men to our position." Just then Dylan heard some shouting near the front of the bunkhouse.

"Dylan, you need to break the window. Here, I'll do it," said Jennifer as she took the porcelain top off the toilet tank and approached the window.

"No, don't. There's got to be a better way," said Dylan.

Paying no attention to Dylan's warnings, Jennifer set up in front of the window like a batter at home plate. Just as she drew back the porcelain, a loud explosion, like the sound of a 12-gage shotgun fired indoors made them both jump. As four more shots rang out, Jennifer struck the window glass so hard, the toilet tank top slipped from her grip as it shattered the window and landed outside in the weeds.

Dylan used a box of paper towels to knock out the remaining shards of glass. They grabbed their duffels, exited the bunkhouse and ran into the woods in the direction of the glacier.

72

. . . .

SLADE HANDED HIS RIFLE to Bonner. "You guys cover me. I'm going to walk up to the bunkhouse unarmed. If they start shooting, direct your fire to the door and either side of the doorway."

"But why? Let's just leave," said Charlie, his lower lip quivering. "I think someone already got Able. He doesn't answer any of our calls. These people are dangerous. We heard the shots. They are armed."

"They won't shoot an unarmed white man approaching with his hands up. Only a coward would do that," said Slade. "I'm leaving my walkie-talkie in transmit mode so you can hear our conversation." Slade clipped the camo-colored device to the breast pocket of his shirt.

From about 100 yards away, Slade yelled, "You in the bunkhouse. I'm just camping in the area, near the mine, and I heard shots. Is everyone all right? Don't shoot me. I'm unarmed."

Hearing no response from the bunkhouse, Slade walked closer and repeated his little speech. This time, from the bunkhouse a man yelled in accented English. "Take off your coat and turn around slowly so we can verify you are not armed."

Slade did as he was told and showed he was not armed. He wondered why some foreigner would be in charge of the miners. "OK, now put your hands in the air and walk backwards towards me. Any rapid movements and I'll shoot."

After Slade lay his jacket slowly down in the mud, he started walking backwards toward the bunkhouse. Before he knew it, he felt a shotgun barrel against his back, and he heard the accented voice. "Careful. No rapid movements or you'll lose about a quarter of your body weight when I pull this trigger."

Once in the bunkhouse, Slade expected a pat-down search, then afterwards to be treated as an equal with the miners. Instead, he found himself tied up with fishing line so tight, it cut into his skin.

"This fishing line hurts!" Slade yelled, and to himself he mumbled that he thought the miners would be decent people.

"How many in your assault team?" A light-skinned black man spoke quietly as he sharpened a kitchen carving knife on a tennis-ball-sized pale silvery nugget.

"We're not an assault team, we're hunting here and heard some shots. Just want to help out if we can," said Slade. "And loosen this fishing line, it's cutting me."

Rhett pulled the walkie-talkie off Slade' shirt and turned it off. "I know there's more of your team, how many?"

From across the room, Rusty called out, "Kill the fucker. He shot Bones. He's going to kill us all."

Rhett quieted Rusty with a withering glance. "Listen to me. Someone just shot one of my miners with a suppressed rifle, then you show up. You smell like cordite, so I know you fired a weapon recently. Now answer my questions before I let Rusty and his shotgun have his way with you."

Slade figured his explanation should contain as much of the truth as possible. "I have two trained hunters covering this bunkhouse. We were sent here to kill wolves, and an Indian and his wife sabotaged our hunt. We think they killed one of my hunters. I saw them come in here. I guess one Indian came out and fired a shot into the bunkhouse. They were the ones who hit your miner."

Rhett watched the man's face as he spoke. He turned to Rusty. "Rusty, check the rest of the bunkhouse to make sure no one's hiding in here, then get back to me.

Rhett looked back to Slade. "There's some of the story that you are not telling me. What's this?"

Rhett held up the iridium nugget he'd been using to sharpen the kitchen carving knife.

"It's a rock?" ventured Slade. "If your man, Rusty, finds an Indian woman hiding here, I want to talk to her."

A look of confusion ran across Rhett's face, *An Indian woman?*

From the back of the bunkhouse, Rusty yelled, "Hey! Someone broke out the back bathroom window."

Nodding, Rhett cut the fishing line bonds on Slade' wrists. "OK, what's your name?"

"My name is Richard Starkhouse, but everyone calls me Slade," said the big man rubbing his wrists.

"That Indian and his wife are really two tourists that I want to speak with," said Rhett.

"They're Indians. I saw them come into this bunkhouse," said Slade licking some blood off his wrist.

"If they were here, they left through a back window," said Rusty walking into the room. He approached Slade and pointed the shotgun at his face. "Tell me you are not the guy who killed Bones."

"I didn't kill Bones, or any of you miners," said Slade. "I'm after the Indians, or tourists, who killed one of our hunters and who've been sabotaging our wolf hunt."

Rusty lowered the shotgun. "You think those tourists killed Bones? I thought they looked nasty, not like regular tourists. The girl looked Chinese."

Rhett turned to Rusty. "Call the trackers and tell them the tourists were just spotted leaving the bunkhouse. Have them report back when they find out where they are, but not to approach them."

Rhett offered his hand to Slade. "I'm not sure I believe your whole story, but I do guess you are after the tourists just like we are. Call your men in and fix them some food." Rhett gestured to the kitchen. "I'm going to look around."

Really, Rhett wanted to get out of the bunkhouse and think. He nearly killed the hunter and his two men a few minutes ago. So much killing. Seeing Bones get his head blown up brought back memories of his days in the South African Special Forces unit. How he wished he could have a few minutes with Father Mavuso!

Instead, he was going to find and kill two tourists.

73

. . . .

THE SUN HUNG LOW in the sky as Dylan and Jennifer decided on a camping spot far out on the glacier. Using the climbing and camping tools borrowed from Gideon's collection, Aguta's cabin and some from their old campsite, Dylan and Jennifer had no problems ascending the glacier.

Afterwards, they carefully traveled to an area where Aguta had assured Dylan the ice was most stable. "Whatever you do, don't go to the southwest edge of the glacier. It will kill you," Aguta had warned Dylan privately.

Dylan stood back and looked at their campsite. Set up behind a large ice wall that shielded Jennifer and Dylan from anyone visually searching for them from land, large ice chunks also protected the bright orange tent from the worst of the glacial winds.

While Jennifer unpacked, Dylan used Aguta's metal probe to check for hidden crevasses near their camp. Jennifer unloaded the gear that they had strapped to the aluminum ladder. The ladder had served as a sled to drag all the equipment Dylan had wanted to take. Dylan had also planned to use the ladder as a bridge to cross any pesky crevasses that got in their way.

Once the unpacking was done, Dylan hid the ladder in a place where they could grab it and run if they noticed any pursuit.

"Jennifer, have you seen my toiletry kit?" Dylan asked looking up from an open duffle bag.

"No, but you can use my toothbrush," smiled Jennifer.

"My meds are in it. I take pills to control my PTSD." Worry lines crossed Dylan's face. "I think I might have left it with our food cache up in a tree at our first campsite."

"You'll survive. We won't be here long," said Jennifer picking up an ice axe.

"I sure hope so," Dylan felt a familiar dread come over him. In the past, his PTSD had nearly paralyzed him.

Jennifer used the ice axe to carve out a "chair" for them in some packed snow. Dylan decided to take the other ice axe around the corner of one of the many ice walls.

When he returned, he informed her that around that corner and only 20 yards away, he had made their toilet. He made it clear that any poop needed to be "dropped" into one of the plastic bags he had brought to pack it out.

Dylan praised her organization of the tent, an amazing 5-person MSR Stormking with double walls. It had a vestibule where they could store their helmets and crampons and other gear. The tent must have cost Aguta a fortune, but it was perfect for winter or glacier camping.

Dylan figured that Aguta probably used it on winter hunting trips.

It had taken them much longer to find a flat spot than she had expected, but now the tent abutted an ice wall. "Even in this protected area, this tent will blow away if we don't anchor it," explained Dylan.

He dug in a pack and found an ice screw. Turning it into the ice using his ice axe as a handle, he was able to make six holes in the brittle ice, into which he pounded wooden tent stakes. "These are biodegradable, so we can leave these on the glacier if we want."

Jennifer stood braced on the windy glacier and looked around. Despite the emotional and physical exhaustion she felt, a profound sense of exhilaration flowed through her, as if the glacier had made her more alive and tuned to her environment.

Their campsite appeared to be surrounded by a bowl of perfect crystal mountains,. "Those mountains look so close, can we explore them tomorrow?" asked Jennifer as she watched Dylan set up a little kitchen in their tent.

"Those mountains are a two-day-hike away. The glacier creates an optical illusion that compresses distances. I hope to spot Shelia's airplane soon, so we are going to stick close to this camp. She will need to fly right over it to land on the lake," Dylan's voice came from the tent.

"I'm going to try out the toilet," Jennifer said as she walked around the wall. In a wind-sheltered area, there was a wooden tent peg holding a roll of toilet paper and some plastic bags. Dylan had done a good job providing comfort in a hostile area.

The idea of coming back to Alaska had never occurred to Jennifer. Up until this point, she couldn't have imagined she'd ever visit Alaska again. She originally came on the trip to spend time with her dad. She had returned with Dylan to find Jun's body and since then become immersed in a strange, beautiful, violent world.

Near the toilet, Jennifer looked to her right and noticed an eerie blue radiance from beneath a jumble of piano-sized ice blocks. Walking closer to the glowing ice, she saw an ice cave, presumably carved hundreds or thousands of years ago by a glacial river.

As she stepped into the cave, she saw it was about 20 feet wide and 100 feet long: a vision of aquamarine blue flowing with blue-greens and vivid blues. Her heart raced as she wondered if the cave was safe. *Would a blue wall of frigid water come rushing down at any minute*? she wondered.

She reached out to the glowing wall, which appeared to be frozen in curving movements, like a giant lava lamp. Her gloved hand traced its gem-like smoothness. Somewhere a soft gurgling sound told her of a hidden, nearby stream. Looking upward, the cave appeared as frozen river waves eerily beautiful and perfect.

Indeed, she realized, the glacier truly was a river of ice flowing down a valley from a basin of lofty frozen mountains.

Bathed in the glistening topaz light, Jennifer felt she had touched a powerful source of secret beauty. She felt herself gasp at the potent charm of the cold, blue cavern, and she knew she would henceforth always hunger to return to wild mysterious places in Alaska.

The magical, euphoric moment vanished when a gust of wind shrieked just outside the cave entrance. She should return so Dylan wouldn't worry and go out looking for her. Stepping out of the cave, a shockingly strong, cold wind seemed to draw the warmth from her body. Shivering, she returned to camp to see Dylan emerging from the tent.

"I was about to go looking for you," his voice was loud, but the wind and ice seemed to carry it away as he ducked back into the tent.

"I found beautiful ice cave over by the toilet," she said as she crawled into the tent. Dylan had set up their camp stove and was cooking something that smelled wonderful. Inside the tent, and away from the wind, she felt like she could get warm again.

"It's so windy!" her teeth chattered. "Is that soup? Can I have some?"

Dylan handed her a steaming mug. "It sure is blowing. It's a katabatic wind. They blow all the time here. As air cools, it become denser and flows down the glacier getting colder and heavier. Sometimes the winds are so fierce, they can blow a person or a campsite off the ice. Mostly they are mild. We have enough shelter from the ice walls that you don't need to worry our tent blowing away."

"Will we be able to hear Sheila's airplane when she comes for us?" asked Jennifer between sips of the hot soup.

"Maybe not, but our tent is bright orange. It's visible from the air, but hidden from land observers by the ice walls. We have a SOS signal arranged out of rocks near our first camping spot. I think she'll get curious and buzz our tent if we don't hear her." Dylan put some ice in a pot to melt for drinking water. For a moment, the wind seemed to stop and a deep rumbling could be felt as somewhere the glacier moaned and crashed.

Dylan turned off the stove. "Want a drink of water before bed?"

Jennifer shook her head thinking of how cold a trip to the toilet would be right then.

"OK. Tomorrow you and I need to practice some glacier safety techniques," Dylan proposed. "We need to both be able to arrest a slide with our ice axes, and I want to check out that cave you found to see if it's safe."

For a few moments the tent trembled as if outside a group of snow giants had grabbed it and playfully shook it.

Dylan noticed Jennifer's unease. "It will do that all night. So try to ignore it. We're safe, but a glacier is a noisy place."

Dylan unzipped his sleeping bag, which was right next to Jennifer's. He pulled off his boots and placed them near the tent flap.

"Would we be warmer if we slept naked?" asked Jennifer.

"Nope. Wear all the dry clothes you want in bed. Be sure to wear a hat. Dry clothes will keep you warmer. If you don't want to wear something, put it under your sleeping bag to provide extra insulation between you and the ice. These pads are pretty thick, but it will get cold. We can press our bags against each other to share warmth." Dylan said this without any hint of affection, as if he were explaining it to his grandmother.

Jennifer wondered, *What if we were together and both naked*?

LATE THAT NIGHT, Jennifer found she had scooted her sleeping bag close to Dylan's. She snuggled against Dylan's back and felt the warmth. Outside the wind shook the tent and somewhere a flap snapped in a random, mad pattern against the side of tent.

Outside Jennifer could sense a vast emptiness and a profound silence that seemed greater than the wind, as if the world was empty save for her and Dylan. She sat up and turned on her headlamp. A fine mist of tiny crystals, probably from the moisture of their breath, floated in the air and settled on items in the tent.

Somehow she felt safe as she turned out her light and cuddled against Dylan.

74

· · · · · · · · · · ·

CHEWY AND LEO were starting to feel like something was amiss. When they last tracked the tourist named Dylan, he had gone to great pains to either hide his tracks or lead them on false trails.

Leo had hurt his arm trying to cross a tumble of unsteady rocks that only a mountain goat could navigate. Now, Dylan and the woman were more or less going on a straight line toward Aguta's cabin. No effort had been taken to disguise their tracks.

Once the two trackers had arrived at Aguta's cabin, they found it deserted. Chewy pushed his huge shoulders through the doorway and examined the room. "Looks like a bunch of tools are missing off of this wall," he said pointing to a carefully organized partition covered in modern and hand-made native tools. Each tool or artifact had its place on a peg, but several pegs were empty.

"Look, here's a note to Aguta from someone named Dylan," said Leo holding up a paper he found on the table. "It says he and Jennifer are borrowing some equipment, and he promises to pay for the rental when they return."

Chewy squinted down at the list of borrowed tools. "They must be the tourists. What do they need winter gear for? Is he taking that woman out onto the glacier?"

Leo pulled the list from Chewy. "Shit! It's enough stuff to last a week on the ice. He's crazy. That glacier is so unstable, if they are camping out there, we'll never see them alive again."

Chewy took the list and note and shoved them into his pocket. "We need to show this to that new asshole boss. He can't send me out onto that glacier. If he wants to find those tourists, he'll need to go himself."

"Let's just see if we can track them to the glacier so we have an idea of if they actually are on the ice or if this is one of Dylan's tricks."

It turned out to be very easy to track the couple, since they appeared to hike directly down a well-traveled path to the east side of the glacier. Leo approached an area where several native symbols had been chopped into the side of the glacier and a hand-made table displayed an array of talismans made from animal fur and bones. One object appeared to have special attention in the center of the arrangement, a carved ivory amulet in the shape of a wolf: a hunter's necklace.

Chewy and Leo carefully examined the site. "I'd say they somehow climbed up the side of this glacier from this spot, but I have no idea how they did it. This wall is 10 feet straight up. There's no evidence they used an ice axe in this area," said Chewy peering closely at the steep, smooth wall of ice.

"Well, we didn't see any tracks leave this area, so we know they are on the ice. Maybe they had a ladder to get up on top." Leo pointed to some indents in the gravel that could have been made by a ladder.

Leo pulled his walkie-talkie from his jacket and reported what he and Chewy had found. "Mr. Rhett, they are up on the ice. You'll need to take crampons and an ice axe when you go out there looking for them. That ice is dangerous. If they plan to spend the night on the glacier, they could die of exposure or a fall."

Back at the mining camp, Rhett gave instructions to his trackers. "Ok. Come on back to camp and have dinner. We'll go out on the ice tomorrow and find them."

As their men cooked a common dinner, Rhett and Slade talked as they walked the perimeter of the mining camp. To Rhett, Slade had the aura of a zealot. He would do anything for his cause. This meant he could only be trusted to be loyal to Alaska independence, and not to any man.

Once Slade got on the topic of Alaska independence, Rhett decided that something besides the iridium made Slade eager to keep people away from the Shaman Mountain Mine.

Soon Rhett got Slade to admit that the eradication of the Shaman Mountain wolves were his top priority. Rhett told Slade that a new mine owner needed to keep some people silent to avoid lawsuits. The two men realized they shared a common goal: keep people away from Kila Ikpic.

"So who knows about the wolves?" asked Rhett.

"Here on the mountain? Just those tourists. I need to make sure they don't make it back to Anchorage. That old Indian, Aguta, knew about them, but my man Able took care of him."

"I'm concerned about a Chinese miner on this mountain named Kung. I don't want him to leave this area until I talk to him," said Rhett as they walked past the Chinese bunkhouse.

"OK, well how about we help each other out? If I find Kung, I'll hold him for you, and if you find those tourists, you'll hold them for me," said Slade.

"I've got a better idea. My trackers already know where the tourists have gone. We are going to get them tomorrow and bring them back here.

Tomorrow, you make the arrangements to have my miners and your hunters picked up and taken back to Anchorage. If you find Kung, hold him for me." said Rhett as they walked past the generator shack.

Slade appeared to think the matter over. "OK, but I may decide to accompany you on the hunt. I don't want those tourists to get away."

Entering the bunkhouse Slade noticed warm and spicy cooking odors. Rusty turned a steak on the grill. "We're cooking all the good stuff since we're leaving soon."

"Rusty, where's the armory? I need that hunting rifle for tomorrow," said Rhett stealing a tator-tot from a large bowl.

"We should have an old deer rifle on the rack where the shotguns were kept. But we're low on ammo for it."

Rhett returned with a dirty and battered rifle that he wondered if it even worked. "Is this the deer rifle?"

Rusty turned the steak onto a plate. "Yep. It's a Soviet era, Russian-made Mosin-Nagant Model 91-30. Gideon bought five of them for about $30. He used parts from all five to make that sniper rifle. It's got an original 3X scope."

"Does it work?" asked Rhett.

"Chewy and Leo shoot game with it for fresh meat. If you use it, you got to watch that you don't hit the scope with the bolt," said Rusty.

I'll find out how accurate the rifle is tomorrow when I locate the tourists, thought Rhett.

75

. . . .

SOMETIME IN THE NIGHT, the katabatic winds had abated to a soft breeze. Instead of the screaming winds, the clear, frozen air carried the sounds of unseen streams gurgling and glacial calving but also wolves making call and response howls that sent chills up Jennifer's back.

She hesitated before nudging Dylan. "Do you hear that? Are we safe here in this tent?"

Dylan's internal clock told him that they should still be asleep in order to be completely refreshed, but the late summer mornings came early. "We are safe. You should get some more rest. If Sheila lands here today, you'll be busy packing and hiking."

"But they sound so close, like they are right outside the tent. Are you sure we are safe?" Just then a loud throbbing crashing sound made Jennifer jump. She hadn't gotten used to the normal sounds of the Kila Ikpic glacier. Her voice revealed some real concerns she had over the wolves' proximity.

Dylan rolled over and faced Jennifer, a frosting of tiny ice crystals lay on her sleeping bag and a strand of her pretty, dark hair seemed trapped in her eyelid.

He smiled and spoke to her in his calming professional guide's voice. "They sound close because the cold air is very dense and transmits sound efficiently over ice. Two more things to think about. One, the wolves won't come on the ice. It's dangerous and there are no prey animals or carrion here. They are completely uninterested in the glacier."

"Yes, but what about us? Can't they smell our tracks and know we are here?" Jennifer pulled her hair back, and winced when a tiny fall of ice crystals fell on her face.

"Oh, they know we are here, but that's the second thing. There's nothing in a wolf's brain that identifies humans as food. They are either completely uninterested in humans or are downright afraid of people. They might be aggressive if they think a human as a possible territorial threat. In a way, you were really lucky to see that dead wolf. I've only seen wolves from hundreds of yards away or in a pen. You'll probably never see another wild wolf in your lifetime."

Jennifer sat up brushing the crystals from her sleeping bag. "But what if they think we're invading their territory?"

Dylan sat up and looked directly at Jennifer. He had a powerful urge to gently brush back her hair and put his hand on her soft cheek, but instead fell back into his professional voice.

"Here's the rules if you encounter a wolf: don't run. They may decide you are a prey animal if you run. Don't make eye contact. They will view this as a threat. Keep your eyes on their front paws. Don't turn your back. Face the animal and make yourself big. Hold your coat above your head and talk to them telling them to go away. Their brains don't process human speech, and they'll be uncertain or afraid."

"Ok. I gotta pee," said Jennifer kicking her sleeping bag off and crawling into the vestibule of the tent to put on her boots. "It's really cold outside my sleeping bag!"

"Of course, if you do everything right at a wolf confrontation, it won't matter if they feel their pups or a kill is threatened," said Dylan turning toward the tent. "I'll heat up some water for breakfast and coffee for when you get back."

Sometime later they met in front of the tent to see the sun had peeped out from behind a cloud. Instantly, the glacier became a sparkling wonderland.

Slowly blowing, hypnotic fractal patterns of fine ice particles flowed over the ice. Jennifer, seemingly stunned by the view of the distant, dark, sharp mountains with soft snowfields rising above the sparkling river of air-suspended crystals. Shining through the crystals, an iridescent topaz-colored ice floor appeared and disappeared.

Her gloved hand went to her mouth. "Oh Dylan! I've never seen anything like this! It's so beautiful!" She looked at him directly. "And it's all ours, isn't it?"

"I would guess we are the only living creatures on this glacier," Dylan smiled. "Check out this view." He took her hand and led her up a pile of ice to better see the distant bowl of mountains.

As they climbed, he thought back to the first time he'd spent a night on a glacier. On that occasion, unbearable cold had kept him awake all night and spoiled much of the beauty. This was different.

"Dylan, are you married, or do you have a girlfriend?" blurted Jennifer ignoring the view.

Dylan self-consciously dropped her hand. He became suddenly uncomfortable by Jennifer's direct, personal questions. "I'm not in a relationship."

"Then we should have sex. I want you to seduce me after I show you the cave." Jennifer spoke matter-of-factly.

Dylan suddenly remembered something that happened when he was in high school. The young middle-school daughter of one of his mom's friends threw herself at him, not knowing anything about sex, but convinced she was in love.

He had gently discouraged her advances, but his young body and high levels of testosterone kept telling him to go ahead and kiss the pretty, young girl.

When he thought back to what could have happened if he had just gone along with her advances, he shuttered—a feeling of relief that he had chosen the right action. He imagined he had avoided years of regret over taking advantage of the vulnerable girl.

Now it was happening again. Jennifer, a beautiful young, adult woman viewed him as a sex partner, but she was also so vulnerable. Escaping a brutal assault from one of the miners, nearly getting killed and now hiding out in a remote and dangerous place with a man she viewed as safe and competent. Her emotions pulsed in a volcanic state and hardly containable.

"Jennifer, you are a beautiful and desirable woman . . ." Dylan began.

"Don't say 'but'. I want you to make love to me and hold me." Jennifer fumbled in her pocket for her goggles. Dylan could see she was about to cry.

"When we get back to Anchorage, where you are able to go where you want and do what you want, you can ask me again. Until then, it's not right. I'm your guide." Dylan watched her turn away from him.

"You are so prudish! We could be dead tomorrow. We need to seize life and live it while we have it."

Dylan changed the subject. "Something else to think about when we get back. You've had a traumatic experience when those miners threatened you. You should have your doctor or counselor evaluate you for PTSD."

"Why" Am I acting crazy just because I'm horny?" said Jennifer, the inside of her goggles moist.

"Not at all. As far as I know, increased libido is not a common reaction to a traumatic event. I would like you to talk to an expert after this trip."

Just then a bright flash from near Aguta's cabin on the rock face overlooking the glacier got Dylan's attention. He pulled Jennifer down behind a nearby ice wall.

"What is it?" she asked.

"It could be a rifle scope reflection," said Dylan. "We need to stay out of sight of those cliffs."

Just then a particularly loud glacial boom echoed off the cliffs.

76

. . . .

RHETT STOOD IN THE SUN looking down on the glacier through Leo's binoculars. A loud boom like a rifle shot echoed across the distance. Rhett was able to differentiate between the concussions of glacial ice cracking and a rifle shot.

"Did you see them? They just ducked down, but they are about a mile out. Too far to follow. The glacier's too dangerous," said Chewy peering through his binoculars.

"What do you mean, too far?" asked Rhett turning toward Chewy. "If those tourists can walk out on the ice, so can we."

"That glacier will kill them," said Leo putting his binoculars into his pack. "It's very active and it flows over uneven rock formations. The uneven surface of the underlying rock slows and speeds up different parts of the ice flow so crevasses constantly appear and close up. This time of the year, glacial rivers are most dynamic. Anyone would be crazy to try and camp on it."

"We don't need to camp," said Rhett. "Let's get some gear and one of Slade's rifles and get going. I want to be on that ice by noon," Rhett turned to walk back to the mining camp to get equipment while Chewy and Leo exchanged significant glances.

"Slade won't loan out his rifles. He told me that," said Leo. "We'll need to just scrap this glacier walk."

"Then get that Russian sniper rifle," said Rhett. "I don't want any more excuses."

LATER RHETT LOOKED down at what Leo and Chewy brought. He did not bother to hide his frustration. "You mean to say that in the whole mining camp, you could find only two ice axes and two sets of crampons?"

He and the trackers stood at the edge of the glacier near Aguta's spirit alter.

"That's all we had. Most of this stuff belonged to Gideon. It won't fit on my boots," said Chewy looking down at his huge feet.

"I can't come along, the crampons will fit my boots, but I still have a bad arm," said Leo rotating his shoulder and making an exaggerated painful expression. "I can't hold the ice axe."

"Leo, you'll come with me and hold the axe with your other hand," said Rhett looking up at the ice wall, unsure of how to climb it. "How did they get up this wall?"

"They had a ladder and took it with them. This is about 15 feet of ice straight up. Very hard to climb," said Chewy.

"I guess we'll just need to wait for them to come back," said Leo hopefully as he rubbed his arm.

"No. We'll just hike in this chute between the glacier and mountainside until we can find a place that's easier to climb," said Rhett putting his arm through the shoulder strap of the rifle and crunching through the gravel as he walked parallel to the glacier.

About a half-mile later, they came across a tree that had fallen across the gap between the side of the mountain and the glacier. Rhett scurried up the hillside with the tree and calmly walked across the gap, the tree bouncing precariously.

"That skinny tree won't hold my weight," said Chewy looking up at Rhett standing on the ice.

"I have problems with heights," said Leo. "I'll stay here with Chewy."

Rhett looked down at the trackers. "Chewy. You go back to camp and tell Slade where we are. I expect Leo and I will be back before dinner. Leo, you need to cross over here so we can complete our mission." Rhett held up the rifle. "All I need to do is get close enough to get a couple of shots off."

The order was given with such confidence and Rhett's willingness to kill was so clear, that Leo obeyed. He did not walk across the bouncy tree. He sat down and scooted. Whenever he came to a branch, he had to squirm his way around it while the tree creaked and swayed. Rhett waited patiently. He knew Leo was shirking when he complained about his arm, but it was easy for Rhett to see that the thought of a fall terrified Leo.

Once on the ice, Leo pulled a rope from his pack. "We should rope up in case one of us falls into a crevasse."

Rhett shrugged and tied the rope around his waist like a belt. Both men carried their ice axes as if ready to arrest a slide.

Leo constructed a complex harness around his chest, waist and groin. When he was ready, he looked up at Rhett. "I suggest we go back to where the tourists mounted the ice and follow their trail. It shouldn't be too hard if they are dragging a ladder."

Soon after they located the tracks, Leo cautiously began to follow them.

"Can't we go faster?" asked Rhett. "If the others walked here, then surely you are not worried about hidden crevasses."

"Like I told you, sometimes this glacier changes rapidly," Leo said, then hesitated as if trying to get his courage up. "So Mr. Rhett, what happened to Gideon? Did you shoot him?"

"No. He wanted to fight to the death hand-to-hand. He lost," said Rhett as he scanned the ice with his binoculars from the top of an ice wall.

Leo shook his head. It was impossible. Gideon outweighed Rhett by 50 pounds and maintained a top fighting condition. Even Snuffy and Chewy were afraid of him.

"Look!" called Rhett peering through his binoculars. "There's something orange over there." Rhett pointed west. Leo could see the tip of an orange tent just above an ice wall.

"They're only about 3,000 yards away. Let's go," said Rhett.

Leo led as they came to an area that looked like it could be a snow-covered crevasse. Clearly, Dylan and Jennifer's footprints walked straight across it, but a gaping eight-foot crack leading down into a blue-blackness showed on either side of the footprints.

"I don't like this," said Leo. "It's a snow bridge. They are dangerous."

"Why don't we just jump over it," asked Rhett. "We can get a run and jump the 8 feet."

"I can't run in crampons. You jump over it," said Leo.

Rhett did just that. He walked back a few paces, took three running steps and landed on the other side of the snow bridge.

"OK, brace yourself," said Leo uneasily. "I'm going to walk over it, and you will need to pull me out of the crevasse in case the snow bridge collapses."

Leo started across the snow bridge when suddenly it gave way. Leo and snow disappeared with a terrified scream. Unlike Dylan's technique of keeping nearly no slack in the rope between he and Jennifer, Leo and Rhett allowed several yards of slack.

A falling object accelerates at 32 feet per second and Leo's 145 pounds pulled on Rhett's waist as if it weighed 350 pounds. Unthinkingly, Rhett slammed his ice axe into a wall as his feet were pulled out from under him. Rhett lay on the ice at the brink of the crevasse with only his ice axe keeping both men from falling to their icy deaths.

Somewhere a groaning sound emanated from the glacier, then Leo found his voice. "Pull me up! I think I broke my arm."

Rhett saw Leo's ice axe slammed into the smooth edge of the crevasse just inches away. Leo had almost made it. Rhett looked up at his own ice axe and saw it was only buried about a quarter-inch into a mound of ice as round and smooth as a marble. It wouldn't hold much longer.

"Can you climb up the wall using your crampons and the rope?" called Rhett straining at Leo's weight. Rhett felt that at any moment, his fragile quarter-inch anchor would give way.

"No. I lost one of my crampons. You'll need to pull me up," Leo's panicked voice sounded nearly hysterical.

Rhett reached behind his collar and drew out his ceramic throwing knife from its sheath. Quickly, he laid the razor-sharp blade on the rope. The rope frayed instantly and parted. The only sound Leo made was a gasp as he disappeared into the blackness. Rhett did not hear him hit bottom, but the glacier seemed to groan again.

Picking up Leo's ice axe, Rhett continued following the trail left by the tourists for another half-mile, then decided to climb a tall ice wall to get another look at the orange tent.

Rhett had now killed so many. He felt as if he was on an ice chute to hell, unable to stop: unable to stop killing or arrest his inevitable slide to the bottom.

As he hiked, he wondered what Father Mavuso would say about Leo's death. *He was a fool. He deserved to die,* Rhett told himself, unwilling to examine his actions. *It was his life or mine. Surely taking a life under those circumstances is justified.*

Now Rhett was going to take the lives of two others: innocents who just happened to learn about the iridium. *Do they deserve to die?* Rhett felt his stomach cramp. *Maybe I don't have to kill anymore. Would restore what I took from Father Mavuso if I kill these people? Will my life be better? Father Mavuso would never approve of killing innocents. Even white people. Even if ordered to do so by a superior officer. Poor Father Mavuso.*

Rhett attempted to push these thoughts aside as he squirmed onto the top of a tall ice wall. He observed what he was doing as if looking down from above.

Inertia seemed to be taking him to a place where he would complete this mission for Mr. Meijer. Rhett watched his own movements, wondering why he seemed unable to stop or turn back. *Why can't I stop*?

Once in a prone firing position atop the high ice wall and looking down, he could see the orange tent and most of the back of Dylan's head as appeared to talk to Jennifer. Rhett steadied the old sniper rifle and chambered a round. He noticed the rifle bolt hit the scope as he slid the round into the chamber. *Bad design*, thought Rhett. Sighting on Dylan, Rhett slowly let his breath out and squeezed the trigger.

77

....

CHEWY FOLLOWED his own huge footprints back up the mountain. Walking on the trail to the mining camp, he noticed fresh tracks, lots of them, heading toward Aguta's cabin. Curious, he followed the tracks to the little dwelling.

Standing outside was Slade, Bonner and Charlie: the hunters. Holding Aguta by the scruff of his neck, Slade yelled at him. "Where's Able? You have ten seconds to tell me."

"He's gone. He went down to the glacier," said Aguta, his normally impassive face revealing fear.

Slade looked up at Chewy. "OK you were just at the glacier, did you see Able?"

"Who?" asked Chewy. "No. I was just down there a couple of hours ago. Mr. Rhett told me to tell you that he and Leo were going after the tourists on the glacier."

"On the glacier? Are you sure? The tourists and the African together on the glacier?" Slade dropped Aguta. "Where on the glacier?"

"I don't know. They were going to follow the tracks of the tourists," said Chewy.

"OK," said Slade wiping his hand on his pants as if soiled by touching Aguta. "Go back to mining camp. Pack up. A plane is coming in tonight to pick everybody up."

Chewy shrugged and trudged off in the direction of the camp wondering if he and Leo would get their extra pay.

Slade turned to Bonner and Charlie. "Those tourists know about the wolves. So does that black guy. I had to tell him so he'd trust me."

The two men looked at him blankly.

"If we take care of all three, that solves our problem. No one will find out about the wolves. We will have accomplished our mission—except the part where we were to kill all the wolves."

Charlie spoke up. "Wait. I thought that was our mission—the wolves. Now our mission is to kill those guys? That wasn't part of the mission I signed up for. I'm a wolf hunter, period."

Bonner looked stunned. "Slade, we left our rifles back at the bunkhouse with our other gear. You said we were leaving. We're all packed up and ready to go home. How are we supposed to kill those three people?"

Slade looked down on Aguta. "Do you have a hunting rifle?"

"He's got a bazooka," said Bonner. "I saw it on his wall."

"How far will your bazooka shell travel? Will it reach the glacier?" asked Slade.

Aguta stood and brushed off his pants. "It's not technically a bazooka. It's a recoilless rifle. The range is about 1,000 yards, but since the glacier is far down the mountain, it will go much farther. However you would be crazy to fire a concussion shell at the glacier."

"And why is that?" asked Slade stepping threateningly close to Aguta.

"Because the glacier will change. Thousands of tons of ice press down from the mountains and only friction holds the flow in check. The forces are delicately balanced. You don't want to disturb the glacier. Let it complete its journey naturally," said Aguta looking up at Slade.

"Well far be it from us to hurt the feelings of the glacier." Slade turned to Bonner. "Go with this guy and have him bring out his recoilless rifle. We are going to see how far over the glacier it will go."

Once in the cabin, Aguta lifted the 84 mm Carl-Gustaf recoilless rifle off its pegs.

To Bonner, the weapon looked like a four-foot long empty tube with handles and sighting gear attached.

Aguta opened a sturdy metal box and removed a heavy artillery shell about 20 inches long and 3.3 inches thick. He gently placed the shell in a waist holster and bucked it around his waist. He plopped a helmet on his head and reached for a pair of goggles from a peg and placed them on his helmet.

"What's that shell? Anti tank?" asked Bonner.

"Nope it's a HE 441D high explosive shell set for air burst detonation. In combat situations, it creates a powerful blast wave that kills enemy troops hiding in trenches, trucks or wooden buildings. The blast wave also triggers minor avalanches so the larger, destructive ones never develop. You are crazy to send this over the glacier. It will kill anyone nearby and seriously damage the glacier. You don't want to do this."

"You know why we're doing this?" Bonner said. "We want a free Alaska. Once the feds find out about the rare wolves around here, they'll make it a national monument. It will delay a free Alaska for decades."

"That's why you were trying to kill my wolves? To avoid federal protection?" Aguta shook his head. *These men are crazy*, Aguta thought. *Slade is going to kill me right after I fire the shell over the glacier.*

Once outside, Bonner and Aguta approached Charlie and Slade as they launched their drone. Looking down at a small, cell-phone-sized screen, the men sent the drone out over the glacier. Aguta thought it went remarkably fast.

Slade pointed to the screen. "There they are. That's their orange tent with them standing by it, and over there is that African guy." Slade motioned Aguta over to look as the screen.

To see out over the glacier through the drone's powerful lens, sent strong emotions through Aguta. It was as if he were seeing a new private world: a world that heretofore had been secret and concealed. Tears sprung to his eyes. This is a violation of nature, thought Aguta.

Slade punched Aguta's shoulder. "Hey! I asked you a question. Can you send your shell over this area low enough to take out those three people?"

Aguta buckled his helmet under his chin and pulled the goggles over his eyes. "Yes. Everyone stand back about 10 feet. You don't want to be in front of this weapon when it fires."

Slade pushed the Come Home button on the drone control that brought it back to where it took off. Then the hunters spread out behind Aguta as he slipped the shell into the recoilless rifle.

Charlie looked uneasy anticipating the discharge of the powerful weapon, but Slade looked flushed with excitement. He wanted to see the glacier change and bring forth a new Alaska.

Hefting the weapon on his shoulder, Aguta looked through the sighting scope. Then he relaxed and looked back to Slade, who was standing behind and to the right. "Cover your ears," was all he said, and then uneasily placed his finger on the trigger.

78

....

THE SOVIET-MADE rifle bucked in Rhett's arms. The bullet struck just inches from Dylan's head and sent ice shards sparkling into the air. When the loud report of the rifle followed moments later, Jennifer screamed. Dylan pulled her down.

The scope, tapped many times by the rifle's bolt, needed adjustment. Rhett noted where the round struck in relation to where the scope predicted and mentally adjusted his aim. The bolt again hit the scope as he ejected the spent cartridge and chambered the fresh one. *The next shot will tell me if this is truly a solid rifle with a poorly adjusted scope, or just a bad rifle.* Thinking back to the shot, Rhett knew he'd need to either spend about twenty minutes and ten or so shots to properly line up the scope, or to just aim a bit down and to the right depending on the weather and the target's position.

As he was getting ready to find another location to shoot at Dylan, he heard a buzzing overhead. Looking up, he saw a drone hovering above his position. It looked to be a foldable quadcopter. It had to belong to the hunters.

Looking up at the cliff, he could make out several people standing at the edge. Using his binoculars, he could see one was a drone pilot and one held, what looked like, a recoilless rifle tube.

Having seen the power of artillery shells shot from a recoilless rifle, Rhett was knowledgeable about their destructive capabilities. Rhett spun around so he could aim up the mountain. There was no way to get an accurate shot with a bad scope and the distance to the target, but he could fire a few shots to make the group back up. Maybe he could put some more distance between them before they regrouped and tried to fire an artillery shell at him.

Through the scope, he watched a person set up to fire the recoilless rifle. As quickly as possible, Rhett fired three careful shots toward the group of men atop the cliff using what he knew about the scope's alignment with the rifle barrel.

Without waiting to see if he hit anyone, he slid down his ice wall perch, put his arm through the shoulder strap of the gun, and started across the ice, an ice axe in each hand.

"WE NEED TO MOVE," whispered Dylan harshly. "Someone on the glacier is shooting at us." Just then, three more shots echoed across the glacier.

"We don't have time to pack," said Jennifer. "What should we do?"

"Grab your ice axe, we'll abandon the campsite and just take the ladder, what we can quickly grab, and find a place to hide." In moments, Dylan threw nearly their entire campsite into Jennifer's pretty ice cave.

"Let's hope the shooter doesn't look in there," said Dylan rushing over to the ladder. "It's doubtful that whoever is after us has anything like the camping gear we were using. We don't want our pursuers to have the ability to get comfortable."

"Where do we go?" asked Jennifer bending low behind the place where their tent stood.

"Aguta told me the southwest side of the glacier was the most dangerous area, we have a ladder, rope, crampons and ice axes. We should be able to hide out someplace where they can't or won't go."

Just then the glacier groaned, as if disturbed by the rifle shots. From far down the glacier, on the southwest side, loud ice explosions boomed and echoed off the mountain.

Dylan tied the ladder to his belt, and he and Jennifer started toward the southwest side of the glacier. "We'll stop and rope up once we are away from this spot," said Dylan leading with his crevasse pole.

Just then Dylan thought about his PTSD meds left in hanging in a tree with the extra food at their first campsite. Instead of the calming focus he typically possessed with clients, he detected a jittery, anxiety nibbling at his mind.

RHETT STOOD LOOKING down at the place where the tourists had camped. It was obvious they left in a hurry. *How could they have packed their tent, cooking equipment and so forth so fast?*

Taking his time, Rhett explored the area. Just inside an ice cave, he found most of their camping gear. After helping himself to a couple of Kind bars, Rhett resumed the slow chase. All he had to do was to get within rifle shot of the pair. He checked the magazine of the Soviet-made rifle, just two shots left. *It will be enough*, he thought as the boom of the recoilless rifle echoed across the glacier.

79

....

AGUTA KNELT on the edge of the cliff and sighted the 84mm recoilless rifle as it rested on his right shoulder.

He knew exactly where to place the shell to kill the people out on the glacier. The concussive blast from the shell was designed to kill or disable soldiers hiding in trenches or behind walls.

He paused and looked to his right at Slade standing 10 feet behind and to his right. "We don't need to do this," Aguta spoke quietly.

Slade stomped over to Aguta and pulled the weapon from his hands. "OK, how does this thing work?"

"I've had over 96 hours of training on it," said Aguta. "I can't teach you how to effectively use this in just a moment."

"Well give me the one-minute version," demanded Slade.

Aguta began speaking in a quiet, authoritative voice about the theory of artillery and its use on the battlefield. From there he spoke about trajectory, muzzle velocity, propelling charges and terrain considerations in order to acquire the target correctly and achieve battlefield priorities.

Bonner, standing near the cliff's edge for a good view, thought that Slade was letting the old man go on too long. "Slade, you're just letting him stall you. Make him fire the weapon."

"OK, first I want to know how the firing procedure works. I may want to take this with me when we leave here."

Aguta started explaining how to fire the weapon. "First, cock the weapon by pushing the cocking lever forward like this." He pushed the lever forward toward the pistol grip.

"Now, move the safety catch toward safe," Aguta showed how this was done. "Now this is important; you need to push the venturi lock knob forward and raise the venturi level thus. This opens the breech and allows you to load the weapon."

Slade reached out to touch the breech, but Aguta stopped him. "Don't touch! Always assume the breech is hot. Do we have time to discuss safety issues?"

"No," said Slade. "Just give me the basics."

After several minutes of instructions, Slade gave up. "You fire it. I don't have time for all this."

Aguta began the process of re-checking all the settings on the weapon.

"Fire it you dumb Indian!" yelled Slade. "We don't have all day."

Just then Bonner's body jerked forward followed by the harsh sound of three Russian-made Mosin-Nagant Model 91-30 rifle shots.

Slade froze as he watched Bonner fall writhing onto his back, a red stain spreading on his chest. Aguta, a combat-experienced veteran knew that this was a time to act, not freeze. Looking over his right shoulder, Aguta turned his body so the exhaust port on his recoilless rifle was aimed at Slade and pulled the trigger.

When firing the 84 mm Carl-Gustaf recoilless rifle, there's a quarter-second delay from when the trigger is pulled to when the artillery shell's propellant ignites. Looking over his shoulder at Slade, Aguta saw the hunter's eyes widen.

The shell launched with a powerful concussive boom. The blast temporarily turned the ground around Aguta's feet to liquid as earth and forest debris lifted several inches off the ground.

The back discharge hit Slade in the face blasting off his skin, nose, eyes and several inches of bone. His body, with its flaming head, was knocked backward about 8 feet.

Aguta moved away from the cliff and turned to Charlie, who'd wet his pants. "He should have asked for the safety instructions. Now go away. Don't come back."

Charlie, unable to move, stood there trying to process what had just happened. His eyes traveled from Bonner's bleeding chest wound to Slade's smoking black head.

Aguta turned his weapon toward Charlie, there was no shell in it, but it had the effect of thawing Charlie's legs. Clumsily, Charlie ran, but in the wrong direction. Instead of running back toward the mining camp, he started running downhill.

Turning away from the glacier, Aguta knew the shell–presently arcing over the glacier, would explode in a few moments. In order to use the back blast against Slade, Aguta had more or less aimed the shell downrange toward the glacier's terminus, which would result in far less blast damage to the great ice river and anyone on it.

The glacier's reaction to the concussive shell burst would probably still kill the people trapped on the ice. Aguta did not want to watch.

Instead, he bowed his head and waited for the explosion. When it came, it seemed louder than ever. For the last six years, he'd been using the same shells on the mountain near the mining camp. There, the soft snow and snow-laden trees had absorbed much of the blast and noise. But in the glacial canyon, everything was rock and ice.

The explosion roared and echoed, seemingly gaining strength like a powerful locomotive rushing louder and louder with a terrible sound before traveling up the glacier toward the faraway mountains. Weaker echoes came back like the sound of a military jet fighter and tore at Aguta's heart.

Aguta forced himself to look down at the glacier. It looked perfect for a moment, then started to change. The glacier started moving like an ice monster waking up in slow motion.

Painfully turning away from the writhing, cracking, crashing glacier, Aguta started what he called, his woman's work of burying the bodies. After rolling Bonner's body down the hill toward the cacophonously noisy glacier, he started to drag Slade's body to the cliff edge. The front straps on the big man's backpack were burned away, but the pack had been protected from the blast by Slade's body. From out of one of the pack's pockets fell Slade's sat-phone, in pristine condition.

Aguta picked it up, *If Dylan survives his time on the Kila Glacier, he'll want this*.

80

....

ICE AXE IN EACH HAND and the rifle slung on his shoulder, Rhett began a light high-stepping jog in his crampon-laden feet, as he followed the tracks made when Dylan and Jennifer had dragged the ladder across the ice.

He had barely gone 100 yards when a massive concussive explosion boomed far to the south side of the glacier near its terminus. The concussion wave knocked Rhett down to the ice and seemed to vibrate through his whole body. Rhett briefly wondered if it loosened a filling he had in a back tooth.

Thousands of years of immense gravitational stresses and hydraulic pressures were suddenly released by the concussion wave causing radical changes in the ancient river of ice.

Somewhere a roaring, like the sound of a huge river rushing over rocks, mixed with the crazy groaning and shotgun-sounding bangs as highly compressed ice bent and broke. Nearby a geyser of icy blue water burst into the air and rained down with an intensity that made Rhett wonder if he was under a waterfall. He clung to the handle of his ice axes as the icy water pounded him.

Beneath him, the ice bucked and fell away merely to rise up moments later. Only his lighting fast reactions and his brain's ability to slow down movement saved Rhett from falling into a crevasse that opened like a yawning blue mouth, then snapped shut.

The opening swallowed his rifle, but his ice axes and crampons kept him from disappearing into a hellish, blue crack big enough to swallow a house. The glacier moved as if alive, and several times Rhett had to leap from one icy perch to another. At one point, an ice wall he had perched on, began to slowly rise as if being squeezed up from below. Nearby a taller ice wall tumbled down into a jumble of car-sized ice chunks. From somewhere, like the breath of an ice god, a cold wind blew down the mountain with a hurricane-like ferocity.

Rhett sheltered behind a huge shard of ice while the wind carried baseball-sized ice balls that smashed into stationary ice sending razor-sharp fragments to ricochet dangerously. While planning a decent from the top of his ice wall, Rhett watched a ten-foot wave of water wash over the glacier below, sweeping away thousand-pound ice chunks as if made of styrofoam. Rethinking his plan to descend, instead, Rhett planned a leap to a nearby ice wall as his perch started to crumble. The chaos lasted for about a half hour, before the glacier's movements began to slow down.

Less than 300 yards away, Rhett caught a glimpse of Dylan and Jennifer clinging to the bottom of a tall ice wall like two drowned rats. By their movements, Rhett could tell they were preparing to climb the ice wall. Rhett gritted his teeth. He would complete this mission. He would kill the tourists before they could tell the secret of the mine to the outside world.

Rhett called over to the pair. "Hey!" But his voice was lost in the glacier sounds.

DYLAN CONTINUED PREPARATION to get he and Jennifer over the ice wall. A wall so steep, only a trained expert like Dylan could climb it. Rhett would be unable to pursue them and be forced to return to the mining camp. This would allow Dylan and Jennifer to escape the glacier as well and hide out on the mountain until Sheila returned.

Dylan turned away from the rope harness he had tightened on Jennifer. He saw Rhett making his way toward them.

"Hey! Are you guys OK?" Rhett's voice reached across the ice.

"Yes. Where's your rifle?" asked Dylan.

"It's gone, but I don't need it," yelled Rhett.

"Why do you want to kill us?" called back Dylan. To Jennifer he whispered, "I'm going to ascend this wall and make some anchors to help you climb up. I'll be in your eyesight the whole time. I'll come back for you."

Jennifer nodded. She wondered if Dylan would fall and kill himself, or if Rhett was lying about losing his rifle.

"You know too much," called Rhett. "My boss can't have the world knowing about the iridium on this mountain."

Using Jennifer's ice axe in one hand, and his own in his other, Dylan started climbing the ice step-by-step. He called out over his shoulder. "You don't need to do what your boss says, because we don't want this mountain mined either. It's full of rare animals that need protection."

"Are you telling me you won't tell anyone about the iridium on this mountain?" asked Rhett as he looked for a path down to the base so he could be directly under Dylan.

Dylan had stopped near a jutting fin of clear, strong ice about the size of a shoebox. From a holster on his belt, he took out his ice screw. As he began turning the screw into the fin, he turned to answer Rhett. "That's right. Also, you know it's wrong for you to kill us. Why do you do something that you know is immoral?"

Working quickly, Dylan unscrewed the ice screw from the wall leaving an 8-inch deep shaft that was about an inch in diameter, and began screwing it the other side of the fin. Soon the two eight-inch shafts would meet at a 60-degree angle, and he could thread a rope through the shafts that would form an anchor point on the wall for Jennifer's climb.

"You don't understand," called Rhett as he began his careful decent. "I'm a man of duty.

That's who I am. If not a man of my word, what do I have?"

"But your word to someone who wants you to commit crimes isn't bonding. What kind of person are you? A slave or a master?" yelled Dylan.

When Rhett didn't answer, Dylan turned around to see Rhett was out of sight. Dylan wondered if Rhett had even heard him.

Rhett had heard. As he climbed down, he kept asking himself, *Who am I?*

The question echoed uncomfortably in Rhett's mind as he began the perilous short journey to the wall where he had last seen his prey.

Rhett pushed away his questions. First he would kill Jennifer, who he last saw at the base of the wall.

81

. . . .

AFTER MAKING SEVERAL more of the ice anchors, Dylan arranged the ropes in such a way as to allow him to repel quickly down the ice wall. Jennifer looked so relieved to see him, that Dylan took the time to give her a quick hug as he gave her instructions.

"I'm going to hold the rope from down here," he whispered confidently. "You are going to climb up to the first anchor point and rest on a ledge, then lower the ice axes to me."

"I don't know how to climb ice," Jennifer's chin quivered. "You looked like a human fly."

"There's really nothing to it," Dylan spoke calmly. "You keep your feet shoulder-width apart and parallel. You don't want to have one foot higher than the other while swinging the axe.

Then lean back, the rope will hold you, and swing your axe so it hits the ice above your head. It should land with a solid sound. You know your axe is set by the sound it makes when hitting the ice." Dylan demonstrated, then handed the axe to Jennifer.

Jennifer stood before the tall ice wall in her crampons, and with an axe in both hands. She leaned back and swung her first axe, it made a satisfying sound as it bit. She turned and smiled at Dylan. "Like that?"

"Perfect," Dylan smiled back. "Then land the other axe a bit higher."

After both axes were set above her head, Dylan said, "Then bring your hips out and look down at your feet. Holding onto your axes, you watch your feet as the crampons dig into the wall. You climb up so your feet are in the same configuration as they are now with the lowest axe handle about shoulder height."

Moments later, Jennifer found herself about 10 feet up the wall with very little effort. "Now I know why some of my friends love rock climbing," she smiled tightly. In just a few minutes later, she had reached the first anchor point.

Dylan looked over to see Rhett about 50 yards away, working his way around a narrow crevasse using his two ice axes. "OK, lower the axes," Dylan tried to keep the urgency out of his voice.

One axe fell as Jennifer attempted to use the rope to lower them. Dylan dodged, grabbed it and started climbing. "Pull the rope up. Rhett is getting close!"

By the time Rhett had reached the base of the wall, Jennifer was about 30 feet up and resting at the second anchor point. Dylan climbed and would soon be next to her.

As Dylan climbed, he looked down at Rhett. "You can go back now. You don't need to complete this mission since it's not necessary. We want to keep people from this area," said Dylan as he reached the rest point at the second anchor point. He handed the axes to Jennifer so she could continue the climb.

Rhett had calmly observed Dylan's climbing technique, and realized he'd been doing something wrong when he'd been climbing earlier. He had been using his strength and wearing himself out. If he had climbed like Dylan, his arms would not be cramping up.

Rhett looked up and watched Jennifer easily ascend to the third anchor point. "You don't understand. I really have nothing and no one. I'm empty except my devotion to duty. It's not that I work for a rich white man, it's that I'm nothing without completing my missions."

"You shouldn't free climb this ice wall," said Dylan as he took the ice axes that Jennifer lowered to him.

"There's some rotten ice that will not hold your axe if you don't know where to put it. You'll fall."

Dylan had also noticed that under the ice, in thin areas, liquid water flowed, probably under pressure. If Rhett pierced the thin skin of ice, he could release a blast of water that could hit with the power of a fire hose."

"I'll soon have your rope for my trip down," said Rhett. "And I'll follow your route up. How do you want to die? Ice axe to the neck or with a fall? You get to pick."

Dylan untied the rope from his makeshift harness and told Jennifer to climb the last bit by herself and then to clip her carabineer into the ice screw he had installed at the top of the wall.

Dylan edged away from the rest stop and ventured to the left into the rotten ice area. If anyone could manage to find good places for his axe, Dylan decided, it would be him.

If Rhett followed him, the African would die when the crumbly ice would not hold. If the African passed Dylan on the right, and headed for Jennifer, Dylan could follow and put an axe blade into the man's heel and pull him off the wall. It was a terrible plan, but it was all Dylan could think of.

Soon, Rhett was even with Dylan on the wall but about 20 feet away. Rhett began to work his way toward Dylan until they were only 10 feet apart.

Rhett looked at Dylan with a steady gaze. "You must die now." With his right hand holding his axe and his crampons firmly set on the ice wall, Rhett reached around his back with his left hand and drew his carbon fiber throwing knife from its shoulder-blade scabbard.

Lightly holding the black knife by its handle, Rhett gave a final look at Dylan. "You are an amazing climber. You also speak with a powerful logic. But I need more than logic. I need completion."

The glacier groaned, and somewhere ice explosions indicated that brittle ice under pressure was breaking. Dylan shifted his weight to his left hand as the wall shuttered. Atop the wall came a surprised yell from Jennifer. "This wall is moving!"

The ice axe in Rhett's right hand shifted. Putting the knife blade between his teeth, he swung the axe sharply into the wall for a better hold. A blast of water blew the ice axe out onto the glacier and hit Rhett's left arm. Rhett swung around his right hand still holding the other axe—now his only support.

From above, Jennifer tipped a heavy ice chunk over the wall at where she thought Rhett was holding on. The ice missed Rhett, but knocked his other axe off the wall. Like lighting, Rhett stabbed his knife into the wall and clung there his chest heaving.

"I'm dropping another piece of this ice if you don't agree to abandon your mission," said Jennifer her voice shaking with emotion.

Both Dylan and Rhett realized that anyone without an ice axe would be unable to descend. Rhett needed to have Dylan assist in recovering the dropped ice axes. Otherwise, Rhett would cling to his knife until exhaustion forced his muscles to release the knife.

Balancing on the toes of his crampons, Rhett drew the knife out of the wall, as his arm cocked to aim a lethal throw at Dylan, the glacier shuddered again shaking the wall. The knife sparkled as it left Rhett's hand and spun through the arctic air. It glanced off the ice wall in front of Dylan sending a shower of sharp translucent ice chips to rapture into the cold, clear air near Dylan's face. Rhett started sliding as his crampons lost their grip.

82

· · · · · · · · · ·

CAT-LIKE, Rhett's body twisted in space as he made an amazing grab for an ice ledge. His momentum made it impossible to hold for more than a moment. Rhett landed face-up on the glacier with a sickening thud; his left boot torn off his foot.

Dylan looked down to see Rhett's eyes open and unblinking and his left leg at an odd angle. It was clear to Dylan that Rhett was no longer a threat.

The glacier moaned and vibrated deep within as it continued to settle.

"Jennifer, wait for me. We're going back," called Dylan. He craned his neck up to see Jennifer peering over the edge of the ice. She held a basketball-sized chunk of ice in her hand.

"You can put that ice down. We're safe," said Dylan. Then he thought, *If we can get off this glacier*.

Twenty minutes later, Dylan and Jennifer leaned over Rhett and determined that he was still breathing. A funny bump at the base of his skull indicated he'd fractured his neck, and that he was probably paralyzed.

Looking down at Rhett, Dylan shook his head. "We are going to need to make him comfortable and get help." In order to get his guiding license, Dylan had taken rigorous first aid training and seemed to know what to do.

Their first aid kit was back at their previous night's campsite, so Jennifer searched Rhett's backpack for supplies. She found a half-kilo of gold coins. Showing Dylan she said, "This guy is going to reimburse us for our troubles and pay Aguta for his lost gear."

"We can't just take his money," said Dylan as he worked to aid Rhett.

"Oh yeah. He owes us. This is our money now," Jennifer pushed the coins into her pack.

After several trips back to their campsite, they had enough gear to keep Rhett warm and his elevate his body off the ice.

"The ladder is gone," said Dylan as he worked to stabilize Rhett body. "It's going to be harder to get back to land."

"You can find a way for us," Jennifer said as she hung their orange tent nearby so a rescue party could find the injured man. But Dylan did not expect the African to survive much longer. It might take a rescue party several days to organize and make the trip across the dangerous ice.

Twice on their journey off the glacier, they were thrown to their knees by glacial movement.

Dylan missed the ladder as he and Jennifer found a new route back to the glacier's edge.

When they finally reached land, they both experienced a feeling that the earth was moving, much like a mariner experiences when reaching dry land.

ONCE AT AGUTA's cabin, Dylan explained the situation and offered enough of Rhett's gold to more than cover the loss of his gear.

"He won't last long on the glacier," said Aguta. "I have a sled I can use to bring him back, if he's still alive. I'll take care of him." Aguta handed

Slade's sat-phone to Jennifer. "Listen to the audio files saved on this phone. You're a lawyer, right?"

Jennifer nodded.

"Then this will give you a way to protect the wolves of Kila Ikpic. Those wolf hunters knew that these wolves are special. The hunters were trying to kill them all." Aguta handed the phone to Jennifer.

"Wait, is that phone working? Let's call Sheila for a ride out of here," said Dylan restraining himself from taking the phone from Jennifer and examining it.

"I already called for state police to come out here. They arrived an hour ago," said Aguta. "What a mess. Police everywhere and everyone else has left: the miners, the Chinese workers, the last hunter—everyone but me. They want me to go to Anchorage to make a statement, but I'm not going."

"What do they want with you? You didn't do anything wrong," said Dylan as he stared intently at the sat-phone.

"They can't find the bodies of many of the missing," said Aguta. "They think I know something about it."

"Where do you think the bodies are? My dad's body is probably with all the others," said Jennifer as she handed the phone to Dylan.

Aguta's gaze traveled out to the glacier. "Probably buried out on the ice. It's a sacred and holy place where bodies should be buried." Aguta turned. "The sun is getting low. I need to go deal with the African."

Dylan watched the phone acquire a satellite. He looked up at Jennifer. "We'll have you back to Anchorage soon."

83

. . . .

RHETT COULD NOT TELL if darkness was falling, or his vision was fading. He felt no pain, but was acutely aware of being heavy. So very heavy. Like sinking into the earth. A sleeping bag lay over his face, so he could not be sure what was happening outside.

Before him a figure appeared: Father Mavuso, his dark robe emphasizing his white beard and hair. The kind man was smiling and holding out his slender dark hands. "Rhett, come home. You belong here with me and your people."

"But I have no people! And you have no people," Rhett shouted. But his voice was silent. "Father, have you forgiven me for ruining you? If I hadn't told you about my plans to get an abortion for my girlfriend, you would not have broken the seal of confession. How would I know that telling authorities that something you heard in confession would result in your excommunication and your loss of faith. You lost your congregation—your only family. And I lost you—my only family."

"That is in the past. You have me now, and I have you. You belong with me and your mother's people," said the priest, no longer bitter. He sounded so clear and so close.

Rhett felt heavier physically, but lighter emotionally. He was aware that his breathing had become shallow and his heart rate had slowed to half its normal rate. "Did you say I belong?" Rhett wanted to believe Father Mavuso, but Rhett had never belonged anywhere. He was no one.

From somewhere Rhett heard footsteps. It was the sound of crunching snow and ice underfoot. Suddenly the darkness lifted outside his closed eyelids. *Perhaps someone removed the sleeping bag from my face.*

Rough hands unzipped his jacket and a man's head pressed against Rhett's chest. Rhett could not feel him, but somehow he was aware of the man. *Is someone listening for my heart? It's inaudible, I'm sure.*

A finger searched his neck for a pulse. *They won't find my heart beat there; it's too slow and quiet.*

A vague feeling of being moved and pulled came over Rhett. *Someone is removing my clothes. How cold I must be!*

As he prepared Rhett's broken body for the ritual, Aguta spoke. "Time to enter the eternal home of all warriors. Once there, you will be with friends who will show you how to dance in the aurora at night. There you will belong with the other warriors who've gone before you."

I can be with other warriors? thought Rhett hopefully. *I will have friends. I will belong.*

Above him Rhett heard sounds: a man sang an ancient song in a high reedy voice, the rasping sound of a walrus-tusk knife being sharpened on a heavy silvery stone, the moaning of the glacier, and the wails of the katabatic winds rushing down the glacier.

Slowly the sounds began to fade. Rhett thought to himself, *I will belong. I will dwell among the other warriors and my Father Mavuso. I will no longer be alone.*

At some point, the song stopped and a new song started. It was a warrior song, and a sharp, painless blow to Rhett's right leg punctuated it. The song stopped abruptly when the singer noticed slow bleeding from the wound. Aguta had never seen a dead person bleed before.

Surely the African was dead. No heartbeat, an obviously frozen foot, no reaction to pain—the man was dead. Aguta had to send the African to the Northern Lights where he could play with the other warriors. It was Aguta's duty to make the battle injuries on the African's body since there were no women to do it.

Rhett remembered something Father Mavuso told him. "Rettief Seme. You worry too much about what you don't have. Why don't you think about what you do have?"

The next blow of the ivory knife fell on Rhett's arm. It too, bled. Confused, Aguta uneasily continued with the ceremony and warrior song.

Rhett's mind traveled to a time where he and some mixed race friends in Soweto had started a business where they would steal batteries from toys in a store, replacing the stolen batteries with dead ones.

With the help of a battery tester, they could prove to street customers that their batteries were good and get enough money to buy sweets.

During an uprising, a crowd of black children had trampled their battery stand and destroyed their tester.

The business was ruined and the mixed race gang broke up. These were the last friends Rhett could remember. *I will soon make friends and dance in the aurora with my brother warriors.*

Aguta paused the song and held the ivory knife up to the sky and sang, as he prepared the last blow.

Rhett tried to remember his mother as he struggled to remain conscious. She was just a hazy memory of a beautiful woman who loved Rhett very much.

At least, he hoped *that's whom I was remembering*. The woman left at some point and the streets of Soweto became his inattentive guardian.

The last blow was to Rhett's neck. After a single weak spurt of blood, no more came. Once the body was decapitated, the ritual cutting was over.

Aguta stood and looked down at Rhett's body. It would fool the gods into thinking the man had died nobly in battle. He dragged the body to a deep crevasse and heard it fall hundreds of feet down into a cold, blue nest. The glacier seemed to tremble.

Cleaning the knife on the glacier, Aguta sang a woman's work song and looked upward.

A feather of red aurora arched across the blackening sky. Aguta smiled. Rhett was with the other warriors where he belonged. He would play with them for eternity.

84

....

SHELIA POWERED up the noisy Beaver, and it lifted up over the glacier and into the dense, cold air flowing down the glacier. The powerful engine clawing into the cold air allowed the plane to quickly gain altitude.

When they boarded the plane, there were only two seats open, one in the front and one in the back. Dylan wanted to sit with Jennifer and to feel her leg next to his. He wanted her to look at him and smile. That mischievous smile!

Sitting in the back, Dylan watched Jennifer in the front seat as she compulsively tapped on her phone using Slade's sat-phone to connect her cell phone to the internet.

At one point, she turned around and called to Dylan. "I talked to my family. Mom told me my cousin Kung is working in Canada. The Chinese mining engineer at Shaman Mountain is no relation." The last Chinese worker had been evacuated earlier that day, and Jennifer hadn't had a chance to talk with Kung.

Dylan nodded and smiled. He was happy she found her cousin, but wanted to hear that she was going to stay with Dylan for a few days. He yearned to hold her, but felt he unable to say anything.

An Alaska State Trooper sitting next to Dylan, attempted to make conversation in the noisy plane. "So you camped out on Shaman Mountain. See any ghosts?"

"No, but saw plenty of scary stuff. Got shot at, chased across a glacier, witnessed the Chinese workers forced into slave labor, and thought Jennifer and I would die when an artillery round exploded over the glacier." *And I am wondering if I'm in love with Jennifer or just feeling an attachment due to shared stress. Or are these feelings due to PSTD?*

"That sounds plenty scary. We are very concerned about the human trafficking," said the trooper. "We're going to need you to come in tomorrow to give a statement."

"Sure," said Dylan looking up and gazing at Jennifer's smooth neck and cheek as she typed on her phone.

When the plane touched down in Anchorage, a small group of Jennifer's family greeted it. They whisked her away before Dylan could say anything.

When he entered his apartment, it felt so quiet and lonely that he found himself moving a cereal box to the wrong cupboard to imagine Jennifer was there with him.

85

....

OVER THE NEXT WEEKS, after giving a statement to the police, Dylan looked at his share of the gold coins that Jennifer had found in Rhett's backpack downtown.

Deciding that it was fair to take Rhett's money for all the trouble the African had caused, Dylan found himself at Greg's Coin, Gun and Small Engine Repair Shop, and left with enough cash to nearly make up for his lost summer earnings.

He wondered if it might be enough for him to restart his business the following summer. Earlier, he'd gotten an email stating that his guiding licenses were being restored.

Jennifer had seen to that. She had used the recordings on Slade's sat-phone to show that the complaint against Dylan had been fabricated by Solomon Quigley to keep him away from Kila Ikpic.

After learning of the unique animals in the area, the feds decided that Shaman Mountain would soon be a new federal wildlife preserve.

The DNA captured by Slade added proof that some animals in the area were rare and endangered, including the Kila Ikpic white wolves.

Since Ursula's lease on the mine was going to expire, the State of Alaska decided to allow for bids on a lease to mine iridium in an eco-friendly manner. The lease auction was open only to U.S.A based firms, and would bring in millions in royalties to the State of Alaska. The mine would cause the economic destruction of Mr. Meijer and his South African iridium mines.

Dylan started the process of rebuilding his business, but it was slow. He thought about Jennifer. She'd sent him some more emails about the legal fallout from the Kila Ikpic trip.

In several emails she sent, he observed the joy she expressed when talking to the federal prosecutors who had brought serious charges against Superintendent Solomon Quigley. The Alaska Opportunity Party and thrown him out, and he was facing embezzlement charges for using their political action money to kill native species.

She told Dylan that Ursula Schiffmeister gave up her fight to avoid human trafficking charges and had to pay restitution to Kung and the other Chinese miners and was facing serious prison time.

Then he got an email with a plane ticket to Seattle. She wanted to show him her wilderness—a place where she was the expert. ". . . and I will not be your client." was how the messaged ended, along with a winking face emoji.

Epilogue

....

AGUTA PADDLED his kayak across the milky-green glacial lake near the terminus of Kila Glacier and noted how far it had retreated in just the last season. He estimated that within the next five years, some of the bodies might be revealed by the retreating ice.

Would the gods be displeased? wondered Aguta. He rubbed his leg where the wolf tattoo itched and looked across the water to a newly constructed campsite.

Earlier, some people from the federal government had made a camp down by the glacier lake. They said they were there to survey the wolves to insure their protection. So many deaths on Kila Ikpic! It was a wonder more people came.

Aguta decided to trust the people and guided them on their survey. Aguta had named all the wolves, but the government people wanted to call each wolf by a letter followed by four numbers. Aguta would only refer to each wolf by its native name.

From across the lake, the glacier moaned and boomed in the quiet forest amongst the lonely cries of the Kila Ikpic wolves and quarreling birds.

THE END

Also by Tyler Blackthorne

Denali

What happens when Dylan Baker's best friend comes to his door and tries to kill him? Then a group of hired mercenaries chase Dylan into the woods—his woods. They never should have messed with Dylan Baker.

Arctic Forces

Dylan Baker has established a peaceful life near a small Alaska town, when a mysterious young woman, who claims to be his daughter, appears at his door and draws Dylan and the governor of Alaska into plan that could end climate change. Signs of fraud and deception emerge as an election draws near, and Dylan must rely on his outdoor skills to save himself and others.

Acknowledgements

I want to thank my family and friends who supported me in this solo writing effort. The highly skilled authors in my writing group get credit for making me look again at certain aspects of style. A special thanks to my best editor, Sharon Hansen.

About the author

Novelist Bruce Hansen is also author of *Motorcycle Journeys Through the Pacific Northwest* (Whitehorse Press), *Literature Based Writing* (Mt. Hood Press) and scores of magazine travel articles. He is also a fine art photographer whose photos can be viewed/purchased at www.brucehansenphoto.com. He lives with his wife in Portland, Oregon.

www.ingramcontent.com/pod-product-compliance
Lightning Source LLC
Chambersburg PA
CBHW050553260626
47157CB00002B/542